B.J. DANIELS

NEW YORK TIMES BESTSELLING AUTHOR

HEART OF GOLD

HQN

HQN

Recycling programs
for this product may
not exist in your area.

ISBN-13: 978-1-335-00983-8

Heart of Gold

HQN
22 Adelaide St. West, 40th Floor
Toronto, Ontario M5H 4E3, Canada
www.Harlequin.com

Printed in U.S.A.

This book is dedicated to Dawn Stenvik,
who taught me a lot about quilting and patience
(she has it; I don't). She also taught me how to
make her favorite apron pattern. It was a
fun day and fun getting to know her better.

HEART OF GOLD

CHAPTER ONE

"JINGLE BELLS" PLAYED loudly from a nearby store and a man jangled a bell looking for donations to his bucket as Charlie let her apartment door close behind her. Snow crystals drifted on the slight breeze making downtown Bozeman, Montana, sparkle. Pine scented the air as shoppers rushed past, loaded down with bags and packages after snagging early morning deals.

Charlie had just stepped onto the sidewalk when she saw a woman standing across the street under one of the city's Christmas decorations. Shock froze her to the pavement, and she stared in disbelief. The woman, looking right at her, smiled that all too familiar smile—the one that had haunted Charlie's nightmares for years. Even as she told herself it wasn't possible, she felt the bright winter day begin to dim and go black.

Charlie woke lying on the icy sidewalk surrounded by people. She'd never fainted before in her life. But then she'd never seen a dead woman standing across the street from her apartment either.

As she lay there dazed, she realized that she probably wouldn't have even noticed the woman if it hadn't been for her horoscope that morning. It had warned that something bad was going to happen. Not in those exact words. But when she read it, she'd had a premonition she couldn't shake.

Not that she would admit checking her horoscope each morning. It wasn't that she believed it exactly. She just hated the thought of walking into a new day not knowing what to expect.

Earlier this morning she'd actually considered calling her boss and begging off work. She knew it was silly. But she hadn't been able to throw off the strange sense of dread she'd had after reading the prediction.

Unfortunately, she had a design project that was coming due before Christmas. She couldn't afford to miss work. So she'd dressed and left her apartment—against her instincts. If she hadn't been anxiously looking around, worried, she might not have seen the long-dead Lindy Parker standing across the street looking at her. And she wouldn't have dropped in a dead faint.

Becoming aware of the cold, icy sidewalk beneath her, she struggled up with some help from the onlookers. For a while, all sound had been muted. Now she heard the clanging bell again, and the Christmas music from a nearby store. She could also feel a pain in her knees; she must have scraped them when she fell.

"Let me help you," an older man said, taking her arm so she could stand on her wobbly legs.

Her gaze shot to the spot where she'd seen Lindy. There was no one there. If there ever had been.

Charlie felt her face flush with embarrassment. Her foolish feeling was accompanied by nausea. She knew rationally that she couldn't have seen Lindy. Yet she couldn't stop quaking. She'd seen *someone*. Someone who looked enough like the dead woman to give her more than a start.

It didn't help that her rational mind argued against the chance that Lindy's doppelgänger just happened to be standing across the street from her apartment smiling that evil smile of hers.

"Are you sure you're all right?" the elderly man asked. "You're awfully pale."

She couldn't speak around the giant lump that had formed in her throat. Hadn't she been expecting something bad to happen even before she read this morning's horoscope? Her life had been going so well lately that she'd had to pinch herself to believe it.

Of course, being the negative Nancy she was, she'd been waiting for the other shoe to drop. Happy was a feeling she wasn't familiar with. Good things just didn't happen to her. So why would she trust it? Her friends told her she was silly for thinking the worst. "Just enjoy life," they'd said. "You deserve this."

Did she though? They didn't know about her darkest secret. They didn't know about Lindy.

Once on her feet, the crowd around her dispersed, including the elderly man. Seeing the time, Charlie pulled out her cell phone and dialed the emergency-only number she'd kept while hoping she would never have to use it.

When voice mail picked up, she said, "I just saw a dead woman standing across the street from my apartment. I'm not drunk or crazy, but I'm scared because…it was her. It was Lindy Parker." Her voice broke, her eyes filling with hot tears.

Fingers trembling, she disconnected, took a couple of breaths and tried to regain control of herself. This wasn't like her. She was no longer a victim. She was strong, determined, capable. But even as she thought it, she recalled the feel of Lindy's ice-blue eyes meeting hers. Lindy had always been able to make her doubt herself. Even dead. She shivered.

Still shaking, she called her boss. She was planning to tell him she was sick and wouldn't be in to the design company where she worked. But by the time Greg Shafer came on the line, she'd calmed down and changed her mind. She couldn't think of anything worse than spending the day locked in her apartment alone, staring out the window at the opposite street corner, expecting the woman to reappear.

"Charlie?" Greg asked. "Is something wrong?"

"I had an accident," she told him, buoyed by the concern in his voice and knowing that the one place she would be safe was work.

"Are you all right?"

"I'm fine." A lie. "I'm just running a little late."

AMANDA BARNES GROANED to herself as she watched Greg hang up his phone. "Let me guess, that was Charlie and she's going to be late. *Again.*" She couldn't help giving him an impatient look. He cut Charlie way too much slack. It made him look weak as a boss—even worse as a fiancé. "What was her excuse this time? Christmas shopping?"

"I don't want to argue, Mandy," he said with a sigh. "Charlie said she had an accident. She's on her way."

She hated when he called her Mandy with that tone of voice. It made her teeth ache. She flipped her blond hair back and stretched out her long legs, her best assets. Both had reeled Greg in, she thought with a smile. She was also a damn good office manager. Altogether they'd resulted in a huge diamond on her finger.

"Charlie is my most creative designer," Greg was saying.

Amanda rolled her eyes. It wasn't like she hadn't heard this before. "She's a flake and you know it."

"Can I assume you got up on the wrong side of the bed this morning?"

"You would know since it was your bed," she said, lowering her voice as she felt her expression soften. She glanced at the ring he'd put on her finger recently. He'd told her that he'd been planning to wait until Christmas, but he'd disappointed her on her birthday in October when he'd given her a small box with silver earrings inside. Obviously, he'd known then that he'd better take the next step and soon or risk losing her. A few weeks ago, he'd popped the question and of course she'd said yes.

"Cut Charlie some slack," he said now. "She's just not a morning person. She's an artist. Her creativity kicks in later in the day. I'm sure she—"

Just then the young woman in question arrived. Through the glass wall of his office, they watched Charlie burst through the outer office door in a flurry of flapping winter coat and scarf. She always swept in, often in a rush, always exuberant and usually running late. This morning appeared no different—except for the fact that she was later than normal.

As Charlie shrugged out of her coat and scarf, Amanda saw that she wore a bright-colored sweater that hit her small frame mid-thigh with dark leggings. Her long curly dark chestnut hair was pulled back in a high ponytail. A few errant locks had come loose and now framed her face, making her look much younger than her twenty-nine years.

Amanda didn't have to look at Greg to know that he was smiling. Had either of them ever been that young, and so wonderfully naive and full of life? Charlie radiated an innocence and a kind of energy that she knew enchanted him. He'd told her that Charlie reminded him of summer days growing up.

This morning Charlie's big brown eyes were wide and her complexion so pale that her freckles only looked more adorable. Amanda feared that the young woman brightened her fiancé's days a little too much and that alone was troubling.

"She's limping," Greg said, frowning.

So she hadn't been exaggerating about having an accident, Amanda thought as Charlie stopped in Greg's office. There was a tear in the young woman's leggings at one knee and the skin underneath was scraped. Nor was she her usual cheerful, apologetic self.

"Are you all right?" Greg asked, clearly genuinely concerned.

"I took a tumble, that's all." Charlie's gaze breezed past him to Amanda and back. "I'm so sorry. My horoscope warned me not to leave the apartment. I guess I should have listened."

Her horoscope? Amanda turned away so Charlie didn't see her eye roll.

"I'm just glad you're all right," Greg said. "Do you need to see a doctor?"

"No, I'll be fine."

Turning back, Amanda watched Charlie head for her cubicle, her limp more pronounced.

"I hope she's all right," Greg said.

"It's just a skinned knee. I'm sure she'll survive." Amanda sighed. "It is always something with that woman." She started toward the door. "You really need to get tougher with her."

Greg said nothing. Then he asked, "Are we interviewing more candidates for office manager today? I'd really like someone to fill your position right after the first of the year."

She'd been so excited when he'd told her that after they were married, he would invest in any enterprise she wanted.

He didn't think it would be a good idea for the two of them to be working together at his company once they tied the knot right after Christmas. She'd been so excited by the prospect of being able to start her own business that she hadn't minded leaving his design company in the least.

Now though she wondered if he just wanted her out of this office so she couldn't see what was going on with the *staff*.

CHARLIE TRIED TO concentrate on her work. She had to have at least six designs to show the client by the end of the week. While she already had more than that, she wasn't happy with a few of them. She wanted them to be perfect.

But as hard as she tried to keep her mind on her designs, she kept thinking about what she'd seen. Or hadn't seen. She knew she couldn't have seen Lindy. Lindy had been dead for years. So why would she think she saw the woman standing across the street? Why now?

Her cell phone rang. Seeing it was her boyfriend, she quickly picked up. She did love the sound of the word *boyfriend*. "Hi," she said.

"Hey." Daniel's voice made her smile. "I know you're at work. Just had to call. I missed you last night." They still had their own apartments. Often they slept over at one or the other. That was why Daniel kept pushing for them to move in together.

It would be cheaper, and they would see more of each other, he'd argued, but Charlie couldn't help dragging her feet. She liked having her own place. If she was being honest, she also didn't trust that this relationship would last. From life experience, she knew she couldn't count on anything. She feared that living together would make the breakup worse. Not that she told Daniel this, but she did question after a couple of months where he thought this was going.

He was the one who'd brought up moving in after their first month of dating. "We're happy now, that's all that matters, right? I mean, we don't have to spell out what this is, do we? Just let this play out and see where it goes."

That was Daniel's laid-back approach to everything. He worked at a local video gaming company where he could wear shorts all year and skateboard around inside the building. She doubted he was putting money into his 401 plan— if the company even had one.

Besides it wasn't like she was ready for anything serious. She enjoyed having a boyfriend maybe a little more than she enjoyed Daniel some days. She feared there might be something wrong with her.

From as far back as she could remember, she'd had this feeling of doom as if a black cloud followed her around and one day lightning would strike her dead. She had good reason to expect the worst given her life so far. Maybe that was why she read her horoscope every morning. Was today the day?

After who she'd seen standing across the street this morning, she feared it was.

"I missed you, too," Charlie said into the phone, deciding not to say anything to Daniel about what had happened this morning. She'd never told anyone about Lindy, and she decided to keep it that way, even though there were times she yearned to share her worst secret.

"See you tonight?" he asked. "Anywhere special you want to go for dinner?"

"Surprise me."

He laughed. "You do realize that you're giving me the thumbs-up to select the nearest drive-through…"

"Daniel?" asked the designer in the cubicle next to her when the call was over. Tara was a petite blonde in her midthirties, married and very pregnant with her third child. "I love living vicariously through you," her friend said as she patted her huge belly. "It beats waiting for this baby to make an entrance."

Charlie smiled at her. "It will all be over soon."

Tara laughed. "Spoken like a single woman without children. Delivery is the easy part."

"Daniel just wanted to know where I might like to go for dinner," she said. She'd dated in college and some after, but most hadn't lasted long. When Daniel came along, it had been a while since she'd had a boyfriend. Often, that made him seem too good to be true.

"Oh, I wouldn't dream of doing that with Bud," Tara cried. "Who knows where he would take me. He's tried surprising me with a home-cooked meal. The man can't boil water. He set the kitchen on fire."

Charlie laughed. "I'm sure it wasn't that bad."

"That's what the firemen said."

"Daniel doesn't apparently cook either or know the way to a grocery store. So don't be too jealous."

They went back to work when Amanda walked past, giving them both The Look. Once she was gone, they shared a conspiratorial headshake.

"I used to think that she just needed to get laid," Tara whispered. "But apparently not even that can change her disposition. Did you see the ring?" She laughed. "How could you not see it? She waves it in everyone's face. That diamond set Greg back plenty."

Charlie wondered if everyone in the building saw how much Amanda disliked her. "I heard she's quitting work after the wedding."

"And the wedding is less than a week away." Tara pretended to thank God and they both chuckled.

For a moment, Charlie felt as if everything was right in her world again as she went back to her work. She loved her job. She loved her coworker, her friends, and she had Daniel. She thought about how lucky she was and pretty much convinced herself that everything was fine.

Of course she hadn't seen Lindy. It was just an optical illusion. Maybe a reflection from the snow and Christmas lights that made her think that was Lindy's face, Lindy's pale eyes, Lindy's smile.

Taking her cell phone, she went to the ladies' room to find it empty and placed the call. It had been years since she'd been given the emergency telephone number to call if she was ever in trouble again. Again she got voice mail.

"It's Charlie again. I'm sorry about calling earlier. I feel so silly. I'm fine. It was nothing. Just my overactive imagination. Sorry to have bothered you."

She disconnected. She didn't need any help. Her horoscope had been wrong. She hadn't seen Lindy. If it wasn't for the pain in her skinned knee, she could pretend she hadn't fainted.

Charlie took a deep breath and she left the ladies' room. She assured herself that her good luck wasn't so fragile that one little thing—like thinking she'd seen the dead woman she'd gotten killed—could destroy it.

CHAPTER TWO

HOURS LATER, CHARLIE glanced up from her work to find the office empty. This time of night, the place took on an eerie feel with all the empty cubicles and only dimmed exit lighting. She hadn't realized how late it had gotten. That often happened when she was involved in her designs. She lost all track of time.

As she glanced around for her purse to leave, she figured everyone had left at five. Stretching her tired back, she vaguely recalled Tara saying goodbye much earlier. Now she saw that the only light still blazing was in Amanda's office at the far end of the building.

The office manager had probably left her light on since she never worked late, Charlie thought as she turned off her lamp and rose. The pain in her knee reminded her of the incident that morning with Lindy's look-alike across from her apartment. For a while, she'd gotten so involved in her designs, she'd been able to put thoughts of the woman out of her mind.

The memory brought back a stomach-knotting sense of fear even as she assured herself it couldn't have been Lindy. People didn't come back from the grave either figuratively or literally. But if anyone could perform such a feat to mete out retribution, it would be Lindy Parker.

Finding her purse, she pulled on her coat and scarf and started out of the building, which meant going past

Amanda's office. She planned to turn out the woman's light on the way.

Charlie wasn't looking forward to going home to her apartment. Who knew what could be waiting for her in the dark? The thought sent a chill through her and she pulled her coat more tightly around her.

Partway down the hall she heard voices. One voice. Amanda's. It sounded as if she was on the phone. Darn, so she hadn't left.

Charlie cursed her bad luck. She had no desire to run into her. Amanda had never seemed to like her from the start. Charlie had never understood it entirely. After the morning she'd had, she didn't want to have to deal with the woman this evening.

As she hurried down the hallway, she saw that Amanda's office door was open, which would make it even harder to slip past. But with relief, she noticed that Amanda had her ear to the phone and her back to the hallway. Charlie figured with a little luck and if she was really quiet, she might be able to slip past without the woman noticing her.

She moved stealthily down the hall, keeping her gaze ahead of her. As she passed the open door, she heard Amanda nearly purring on the phone.

"Baby, I know. But I can't. I want you, too. It's been too long."

Charlie felt an eyebrow shoot up. She'd never understood what a nice guy like Greg saw in Amanda. According to office gossip, Greg had gone through a bad relationship a few years ago. When everyone had heard that he and Amanda were dating, a shock wave had gone through the building. It was far worse when they heard about the engagement.

"He can't know what she's really like," Tara had said when she heard the news. "Like on those television bachelor shows where all the women know that the man is about to make the biggest mistake of his life, but he won't listen. You should try to warn him. He likes you."

Charlie had been adamant about staying out of it. She needed this job and she had enough trouble with Amanda. The woman threw fits if Charlie was even two minutes late in the morning, not aware that Charlie was often among the last out of the place at night.

Now, if she could just get past the door and out of the building without being spotted… She did not want to hear any more of this particular phone conversation.

"Royce, I'm an engaged woman." A chuckle. "Oh, if you really can't live without me, okay. But just for a quickie. I told Greg I had to work late, but he's no fool." Another snicker. "Not that much of a fool."

Charlie felt shock and distress ricochet through her. Amanda was cheating on Greg? She increased her step, wanting to run as she tried to ignore what she'd heard, but the words were echoing in her ears.

She heard Amanda disconnect from her call, and the woman's chair squeaked as she turned around to face her desk and the hallway.

Almost to the exit, Charlie felt the woman's gaze pierce her back as if Amanda had picked up a gun and shot her. She practically ran the last few steps, shoved open the door and fought looking back for fear the woman would chase her down—literally. At the last moment before the door swung shut, she couldn't stand it any longer. She looked back.

Amanda had risen to her feet, her face completely drained of blood, her blue eyes wide and hard as ice chips. She was staring at Charlie with a deadly glare.

The door slammed shut. Charlie rushed down the street,

cursing her luck. She hadn't wanted to hear any of Amanda's phone conversation and wished she could expunge it from her memory. She had enough problems with the woman without this new information.

She couldn't help her surprise. Amanda was cheating on Greg—just when Charlie thought she couldn't dislike her more.

WESTLY "SHEP" SHEPHERD had just finished picking up his classroom for Christmas vacation when he looked up in surprise to find Judge WT Landusky silhouetted in the doorway.

Years ago, he'd found his troubled teenaged self standing before the toughest judge in Montana. To say he'd been quaking in his boots was putting it mildly. Much to his amazement, the judge had found something worth saving in the troubled youth before him and made an offer no one in that position could refuse. Landusky had saved his life and they both knew it.

"Come on in, Judge," Shep said as he finished packing up the papers he hoped to grade over the Christmas holiday. He tried to hide his shock at not just seeing the judge after all this time, but now seeing him here. He wondered when was the last time the judge had been in a middle school classroom. "You have a long addition problem you need me to help you with?" he joked, realizing he was a little nervous.

The stern older man actually smiled. "Since I'm retired, you can call me WT."

No matter what the man said, Shep couldn't see himself calling this man he respected so much by his first name or even his initials. "What brings you out to this neck of the woods?" He knew it wasn't a social visit.

"I'm here to ask a favor. I understand you're on holiday break from school? I was hoping that would give you enough time to help me with a particular problem a friend is dealing with right now."

He cocked a hip to lean against the edge of his desk, wondering if he should offer the judge a seat. "If I can help…" They both knew that he'd do whatever the judge asked him. He owed him. After going before the judge all those years ago, he'd been offered a form of boot camp that had kicked his butt good and turned him around. The judge wasn't anything if not tough.

Shep, along with the others he'd met, had been pushed to the limits as part of Landusky's second chance program. Those who hung in didn't go to jail. Those who gave up… Well, they were probably behind prison bars by now. Shep was still grateful that the man had seen his way to giving him a second chance. When he'd thanked the judge all those years ago, Landusky had said that one day he might ask him to pay it forward. Shep had said he would do anything and he'd meant it. He still did.

It seemed the judge was calling in that promise. "Though I can't imagine what problem it is that you think a middle school math teacher can help with," he said with a chuckle.

"Charlotte Farmington seems to be having a little trouble. She says she's fine now, but I suspect not."

He frowned. The name didn't ring any bells.

"I believe you know her only as Charlie."

Ding! Ding! "Charlie? Not—" He almost said, *my Charlie.*

The judge gave him a wry smile. "When she called, I thought of you."

CHARLIE HADN'T SLEPT a wink the night before. She'd gone straight from work to Daniel's but she'd found the apartment full of his friends. They'd all been drinking and playing video games. There was cold pizza on the coffee table among the empty beer bottles.

Daniel had apologized and tried to get her to stay, saying the game would be over soon and he'd kick everyone but his roommate Jason out.

She'd wanted to tell him about her unbelievable day. She'd wanted peace and quiet. She'd wanted to curl up in her boyfriend's arms, have dinner and maybe make out on the couch while watching a movie.

Instead, she'd begged off and gone home, trying not to cry. Her knees hurt and the December temperature outside had dropped. She could see her breath on the icy night air. While the walk was only a few blocks and while she'd assured herself since that morning that the woman she'd seen had just *resembled* Lindy, she couldn't help being anxious. She found herself looking into all the shadows as she hurried along the snow-covered sidewalk.

It was late enough that the streets were quiet. Only a few cars passed, their tires crunching on the frozen slush on the street. She sucked in the frosty air as she practically ran under the twinkling Christmas lights along Main Street.

While it was a beautiful winter night, she was happy when she reached her apartment. She hurried inside and locked and bolted the door, relieved beyond words that she hadn't seen the woman. There was little in the way of sustenance in the refrigerator since she hadn't been to the store. She was no better than Daniel on that count. She told herself that she wasn't all that hungry anyway. A lie. Her stomach growled but she refused to go back out.

Stripping out of her work clothes, she crawled between the sheets, too tired to even put on one of the large T-shirts she slept in. She knew she would never be able to sleep though, afraid Lindy would show up in her nightmares again.

Instead, it was Amanda who haunted her dreams.

IN THE LIGHT of morning, Charlie felt better. She'd slept well enough, even with Amanda appearing in some strange dream she couldn't quite remember. She went through her usual morning ritual from shower to robe before she padded out to her living room and opened the door to get her newspaper. She knew it was old school, getting a newspaper delivered to her door, but she liked the idea of supporting the local daily. She liked checking her horoscope and the area events.

After yesterday it was with trepidation that she flipped to the horoscope for Capricorn, already expecting maybe even a worse day than before.

Brace yourself for important information. It may be shocking, but you can handle it. All will soon be clear to you if you're open to it.

She read it again. Shocking news? Something she could handle? Was this about Lindy or Amanda or something else?

She knew she shouldn't take her horoscope so literally, but still she already had good reason to be dreading going to work. She thought of a million excuses not to go. She didn't want to face Greg this morning, let alone Amanda after what she'd heard. Not that she could stay home even if there had been food in the house and she didn't have a design presentation coming up quickly.

Telling herself to buck up, she found a bread heel in the back of the refrigerator and made herself a piece of toast before getting dressed. Daniel had promised to make it up to her tonight. She thought about a nice dinner and movie with him later. She was looking forward to it since they seldom went out.

Was he going to give her some kind of shocking news? Or was the "news" coming from another source?

Bracing herself, she checked out the front window before leaving her apartment. The Lindy look-alike wasn't standing across the street. This time of morning, downtown Bozeman was fairly quiet. She breathed a sigh of relief and walked the few blocks to her job.

As she opened the door to the building, she hoped that she could slip in unnoticed. She was early for a change. Amanda would be expecting her to be late as usual. At least that was her hope.

Unfortunately as she started past the woman's office, she heard Amanda call, "Charlie, may I have a word?"

Charlie plastered a tight smile on her face and stepped in.

"Please close the door."

She did and waited.

"You worked awfully late last night."

"I lost track of time. I have this design presentation coming up before Christmas. It's much more quiet working at night and there aren't any interruptions or distractions. It's really my creative time. I always get more work done when no one is around." She realized she was babbling and clamped her lips shut.

"I saw you leaving," Amanda said. "I was surprised. I thought you'd at least say goodbye on your way out."

"You were on the phone and I didn't want to disturb you. I had a lot on my mind so I wasn't…" she was going to say listening, but caught herself "…paying any attention. I didn't realize you were working late, too."

Amanda's gaze narrowed and locked with hers. "So you weren't eavesdropping on my conversation with Greg?"

Conversation with Greg, ha! Charlie tried to maintain eye contact, but couldn't. Looking away, she said, "Like I said, I wasn't paying any attention."

When Amanda didn't speak, Charlie sneaked a look at her. The woman's expression was carved alabaster.

"Let's cut the shit. You heard my side of the conversation."

Charlie opened her mouth, but then closed it. Since there wasn't much she could say, she said nothing and waited.

"You're probably thinking about running to Greg with some wild story." Before she could deny it—Charlie would never want to hurt her boss that way—Amanda continued, "Well, put that idea out of your simple little head. I will deny it all, tell him that you're a liar. I'll be shocked and tell him that you're jealous of us. It's the reason I've never liked you. Because I've also heard that you've said some awful things about me and him, but this… Well this is just too much. I don't see how he'll be able to keep you on with you having those kinds of feelings about us, especially since we're about to become husband and wife."

She stopped, narrowed her eyes and smiled. "You're a smart girl. You get how this is going to go, right? I'm his *fiancée*. Who do you think he will believe?"

"I have no intention of telling Greg anything."

Amanda seemed to wait as if expecting more. Maybe blackmail? The thought did have its appeal since Amanda had been riding her since she'd started work here.

"Is that all?" Charlie asked. "I have a lot of work to do."

For a moment, the woman just stared at her as if it couldn't be this easy, then she let out a hoarse chuckle. "Yes, I certainly wouldn't want you to be late for work."

She waved a dismissive hand in the direction of the door, but her distrusting gaze was still boring into Charlie.

Before Charlie reached the door, Amanda added, "You don't want to cross me. You'll regret it. I promise you that."

Charlie exited the office as fast as she could and almost collided with Greg in the process.

"Everything all right?" he asked, looking from her to Amanda and back again.

"Fine." She realized she couldn't look him in the eye. The poor guy. He had no idea what he was getting himself into. Someone should warn him about the woman he was about to marry, but Charlie wasn't going to be the one. She told herself that Amanda would screw up sooner or later and Greg would wise up—hopefully before the wedding. "I'm fine."

"Okay," Greg said, sounding as if he didn't believe her before he stepped into Amanda's office, closing the door behind him.

Charlie glanced through the wall of glass and saw Amanda's worried look before she turned her gaze on Greg and gave him a glowing smile before kissing him.

Not sticking around, Charlie hurried to her desk.

"That package was on your desk when I got here," Tara said, eyes bright with excitement. "Is it from Daniel?"

Charlie took off her coat and scarf, put her purse in a drawer and sat down before she considered the package. It was small, not much more than the size of a summer beach read. As she picked it up, she realized how light it was. So not a book. She wanted to shake it, but restrained herself.

Was it from Daniel? There was no return address. No stamp or postmark. She supposed he could have had it delivered first thing this morning to surprise her. Her pulse leaped at the thought. He'd gotten her flowers after their first meeting and had them sent to work, along with a note asking her out. But nothing like that since—until maybe now.

She tried to tamp down her growing excitement. She didn't want to be disappointed. It was probably a gift from one of her clients. They often bought her chocolates or wine or gave her a gift certificate to some restaurant that she'd said she enjoyed. This package didn't seem to be any of those things though.

With the plain paper almost off, she was cutting into the tape on the box's flap with a pair of scissors when she looked up to see Amanda standing nearby watching her. Charlie's heart dropped. Was it something from the woman so she'd keep her mouth shut? A bribe?

As she unstuck the flap, Charlie was almost afraid to look inside. She glanced at Tara.

"Come on, you're killing me over here," her friend said. "Is it sexy underwear?"

She raised a brow and laughed. "You sound so wistful."

"Because I barely remember sexy underwear. Open it!"

Charlie lifted the flap, but it was Tara who screamed.

CHAPTER THREE

"Who would send you something like that?" Greg demanded as she stood in his office, the package open on his desk. "I think we should call the police."

"No," Charlie said quickly. She would never have shown the contents to him, but Tara's scream brought everyone running.

"She's right," Amanda said quickly from where she stood. "It's probably just a prank."

"I won't have that kind of prank in this office," Greg snapped.

Charlie was still shaken after finding the small dead mouse, its little pink tongue sticking out as it lay in a pool of blood. But somehow she managed to come up with a feasible lie. "I'm sure it wasn't from anyone in the office. I suspect it's from an old boyfriend. He saw me with Daniel the other night…"

Greg gave her a sympathetic look.

"I'm sorry it disrupted the office," she said, just wanting to put this behind her.

"It's not your fault," Greg protested.

Charlie looked at the floor. "I'd like to just forget about it."

"I think that's wise," Amanda said. "Whoever sent it to you made their point. I'll call Maintenance and have them dispose of it since no harm was done."

Greg shot her a disbelieving look. "I still think we should call the police. Maybe they can get prints off the box and find this...deviant."

Did Amanda flinch when he said deviant? "Can we just forget it?" Charlie said. "Amanda's right. It's over. No harm done. Message received."

"See? That's the best plan," Amanda said, pulling out her cell phone and calling Maintenance. "Herb is on his way up," she said after making the request. "We should all get back to work."

Greg was still looking at Charlie as if wanting to say more.

As Amanda ushered Charlie out of his office, the woman's fingers bit into her arm. Once out in the hallway, Charlie shook off the office manager's hand, but not before Amanda whispered, "I had nothing to do with that. Do you hear me?"

"I hear you." But she wasn't sure she believed it.

Charlie tried not to think about the package as she worked. Or who had sent it. Or what it meant. She wanted to believe it was from Amanda because otherwise who did that leave? Her friends would never do something so disgusting—even as some kind of sick practical joke. Daniel wouldn't do anything so mean. *Who* did that leave?

Lindy. The thought was ridiculous. It was one thing for Charlie to believe she saw a dead woman. But there was no way Lindy's ghost could send packages. She tried to push away such irrational thoughts. There was only one person who could have sent the dead mouse—Amanda, the Enforcer, as she and Tara called her. Message received.

She tried to concentrate, determined to get as much done as she could today. Once her presentation was over, she was taking a few days off for the holidays. Daniel had told her that he had a special Christmas surprise for her. He'd hinted about plans for the two of them.

"He's going to give you a ring!" Tara had cried when she'd told her.

"No," Charlie had argued, heart pounding that Tara might be right. "We've only been dating a few months."

"Didn't you say it was love at first sight?"

According to Daniel. He said he spotted her across a crowded bar and had fallen at once. He said he'd been terrified as he crossed the room, knees knocking, to talk to her, because he'd been afraid she would get away before he could reach her. Or worse, that she wouldn't go out with him. It was the kind of story parents told their children about their first meeting.

Thankfully, he'd never asked if it was like that for her. In truth, she'd been startled when he came over to her table where she was sitting with her friends. She'd thought he wasn't her type and while she'd given him her number, she hadn't planned to go out with him. When he called, she'd put him off for a couple weeks. But he'd been relentless and she'd finally agreed to meet him.

There hadn't been a jolt of chemistry on their first date. The first time they kissed, there weren't fireworks. But the kiss had been nice. She liked him and felt…comfortable with him. That's why she was hoping he wasn't planning on asking her to marry him. She didn't feel ready to take that next step and wasn't sure when she would be—if ever with him.

She'd never told Tara or her other friends any of this. Everyone wanted to believe it had been love at first sight for both of them.

She'd once questioned love at first sight while having coffee with her friend Becky.

"You are so cynical," Becky had said, mugging a face. "Why can't you believe that a man could fall for you in an instant?"

Charlie could only shrug, unable to explain. Was it her resistance in believing that good things could happen to her? She didn't talk about her childhood or her past and certainly not her shameful secret. Only one person knew how bad things had been—Lindy.

But as she tried to work, she realized that she was tired of expecting the worst. Maybe her friends were right. Maybe it was time she forgave herself for the past and started believing in happy-ever-after. Maybe that's why she'd thought she saw Lindy. Because it was time to put the past behind her.

Christmas wasn't that far away. She and Daniel would maybe do something fun with no mention of marriage. Work might be better now that she'd cleared the air with Amanda. And she hadn't seen Lindy again. All in all, things could be looking up.

If only she hadn't made that call to the emergency number. She'd been in a panic, terrified at the time. She'd overreacted. Fortunately, she'd called the judge back to cancel it.

She was pretty sure that the woman she'd seen hadn't even looked that much like Lindy. After all, it had been years. Who knew what Lindy would look like now—if she'd still been alive. The last time Charlie had seen Lindy, her stepsister had been seventeen, Charlie fourteen. They both would have changed.

Meanwhile, she tried to concentrate on the positive. She had a date with Daniel tonight. She'd gotten through work without any more packages or visits from The Enforcer. And she'd managed to leave work when everyone else did, avoiding Amanda on her way out.

On the sidewalk outside, she saw that it had started to snow. Flakes hung in air, sparkling in the city's lights and decorations. There was something about falling snow that always felt magical to her even without the occasional sound of Christmas music.

Despite the holiday cheer, Charlie felt a strange prickling as if someone was watching her. She tried not to look behind her. Surely Amanda was going to let this go now. Charlie went a half block before she dared look back, afraid Amanda might be pursuing her with something sharp like a letter opener.

She felt a moment of relief not to see Amanda coming after her.

Until she saw something even worse.

Lindy Parker stood under one of the street lamps, a silver bell ornament above her head, a shopping bag in one hand, a cell phone in the other, the device against her ear. She was saying something into the phone and wearing a fluffy blue scarf over her coat—the same color and style as Lindy's favorite one.

Not paying attention to where she was going, Charlie plowed into a group of shoppers who'd stopped on the sidewalk. Off balance, she found herself falling again. Fortunately, this time, a couple of the women in the group steadied her and she managed to stay on her feet.

But when she looked back again, the woman was long gone.

Charlie hurried toward her apartment, wanting only to get inside and lock the doors. The woman had looked so much like Lindy. But ghosts didn't shop or talk on cell phones, Charlie was pretty sure of that.

Still, she was shaken. Was it possible Lindy was alive? She recognized the blue scarf—just as Lindy would know she would. But if she was alive, then where had she been the past fifteen years? And whose body had been found if not Lindy's?

The idea was preposterous that the cops had gotten it wrong. The woman she'd seen had to be someone who looked like Lindy. But if true, how did she explain the scarf or the woman's expression when she'd seen her? Charlie had had the feeling that Lindy had been waiting for her to walk past.

As she neared her apartment, winter darkness settling around her with a cold that reached her bones, she couldn't wait to get inside. She was digging out her key when she saw something that made her slow her walk to a crawl.

Someone was sitting on her front steps. From the size, it was a man. For just an instant, she thought it might be Daniel.

Then she saw the backpack on the step below him. As she stepped tentatively closer, she saw that he was leaning against the railing, his legs spread out in front of him on the step and what appeared to be a cowboy hat tilted down over his face as if he'd dozed off.

She took in the breadth of his broad shoulders, the length of the denim jeans to his cowboy boots. He looked like a man perfectly comfortable in his own skin and one who hadn't minded waiting even in the cold.

As if sensing her, he slowly pushed back the hat and lifted his head, his blue eyes pinning her to the spot as her heart dropped.

WESTLY "SHEP" SHEPHERD couldn't help but stare. The rebellious, adventurous, outrageous girl he'd known had turned into a knockout-gorgeous young woman. His surprised gaze met Charlie's even more surprised one and shot off sparks.

"The judge sent *you*?" Her voice broke. "I told him I was fine. Why would he send *you*?"

Shep pushed to his feet, settled his Stetson on his head of dark hair and shrugged. "You know the judge. He does what he does and for some reason he seemed to think you needed my help."

She scoffed at that and tried to step past him, but he grabbed her slim wrist, wrapping his fingers around it, stopping her. He felt a tingle move from his fingers up his arm.

"Charlie, you know how this works. The judge asks and we do whatever he wants because he saved our lives. He wants me to help you and that's what I'm going to do, with or without your approval."

She flipped her hair back. Snow crystals had settled in her dark curls like tiny fairy lights. "I should have never called the judge. It was a mistake. I'm fine. You can go back and tell him—"

"The judge wouldn't have sent me unless you were in trouble. So you're not fine. Remember, I know you." His gaze locked with hers. He'd forgotten the warm honey of her eyes and what looking in them did to him. "I'm not going anywhere."

She laughed. "I'd forgotten how pigheaded you are."

Her pulse pounded beneath his fingers as her laugh floated around him. He'd also forgotten that infectious laugh. It took him back to their first encounter all those years ago and what had followed. The memory sent a sharp stab of longing racing through his bloodstream. The girl had gotten under his skin all those years ago. He couldn't imagine the kind of damage the young woman standing before him could do. He let go of her wrist.

"You need to go back to the judge and tell him that I'm

fine," she was saying. "It was a mistake. I thought I saw someone from my past but—" She glanced over her shoulder across the icy street and shuddered.

He heard her breath catch in her throat. Her brown, soulful eyes had widened into saucers. She swayed on the step next to him, then grabbed hold of his biceps, her fingers digging in as she tried to steady herself.

"That's her." The words came out in a low croak.

Shep followed her gaze across the street. Through the falling snow, he caught sight of a slim, dark figure in the shadow of a light pole. He had only a glimpse of long blond hair before the figure dissolved back into the darkness of the alley.

In those fleeting seconds, several cars roared past before he could pry Charlie's fingers from his arm and race across the street, his boots slick on the gleaming black ice. By the time he reached the alley, it was empty.

When he returned to the stairs leading up to her apartment, Charlie was sitting on the step where he'd been. She looked up at him, snowflakes caught on her lashes, her brown eyes dark with fear.

"It was her," she said, voice cracking. "It's Lindy Parker. She's come back to make me pay for what I did."

SHEP HAD NO idea who Lindy Parker was. But whatever Charlie had seen, it had scared her. From what he knew of the incredible girl she'd been, scaring her wasn't easy. By the time he'd met her at the judge's boot camp—her sixteen and him seventeen—she'd already been toughened by life. She had that way of looking at a person as if she'd already seen too much, been through too much. But she'd never talked about it. Neither had he.

"Who's Lindy?" he asked now.

Charlie stared at him in surprise. "The judge didn't tell you?"

"The only thing he told me is that you needed my help."

"And you agreed without even knowing what was wrong?" She looked as skeptical as he felt. "Why you?"

They were back to that? He shrugged again. "He said I was the right person for the job."

"Are you a detective, a cop or something?"

Something. "I teach."

She waited, obviously not letting him get away that easily.

"Middle school math."

Her expression said it all.

"I believe the judge asked me because I'm a problem solver." He figured that might be part of the reason. He didn't want to speculate on the other. "I'm also reasonable and logical."

Charlie scoffed at that as she started to get to her feet. "Like I'm not?"

Shep wasn't about to touch that one. He reached out his hand to pull her up. She took it, but her gaze was on the other side of the street. Whoever had been there was gone but far from forgotten, given the fear still in her expression.

"Why don't we go inside where it's warm and you can tell me all about it?" he suggested.

She turned and started up the stairs, seeming dazed as she led the way to her third-story apartment. Apparently there was no elevator, he gathered after the climb.

He watched her try to unlock the door with trembling fingers until he gently took the key and opened the door. Following her inside, he took in the place.

It was compact. Small kitchen, living room, bedroom, bath. Everything looked clean and neat, and the walls were decorated with what he knew were some of her drawings. He remembered how she was always doodling every chance she got—even when the rest of them were exhausted from the physical and mental requirements of boot camp. He'd thought she had talent. He'd been glad to hear from the judge that she worked for a design company and had done well for herself.

"So who is Lindy?" he asked again as he closed the door behind him.

Her cell phone chirped in her purse. Still seeming distracted, she pulled it out, checked the screen and let out a cry. "I forgot all about my date. Daniel is on his way. He could be here any minute."

"Daniel?"

"My boyfriend." Her eyes widened in alarm. "You have to leave." She rushed toward him to open the door he'd just closed behind him. "Go! Hurry!" But even as she said it, he heard the door on the ground level open. A gust of winter air rushed up the stairs along with the sound of someone stomping snow off his boots.

"Sounds like it's too late," he noted.

Charlie looked around frantically as if searching for a place to hide him. From what he could see, there was only one other apartment on this floor and that door was closed. The only exit other than a rickety fire escape he could see through a window were the stairs that Daniel was now plodding up.

"Where would you suggest I go?"

She seemed to have come up with the same conclusion he had as she quickly pushed him back inside her apartment and slammed the door behind them.

Shep saw her panic. It was only a matter of minutes before her boyfriend would reach her door. "What's the big deal?" he asked, curious about her boyfriend as well as her reaction. What kind of guy would this grown-up Charlie be into?

Charlie's expression made it clear she wasn't going to let them meet. "He doesn't know about Lindy."

"That makes two of us," Shep said.

"You have to hide."

"Wouldn't it be simpler if you just introduced us?"

She shook her head. "I'm not ready for that."

"Perhaps I could hide here in your apartment? Unless you want me to go out the window." She actually glanced at the kitchen window. "That was a joke. I'm not going out the window."

"Fine. Find a place to hide while I get dressed." She rushed into the bedroom, threw open the closet door and pulled out a slinky red dress. When she turned, he was leaning against the doorjamb watching her.

"There isn't much place to hide," he said. It had taken him all of two seconds to realize that.

She groaned. "I can't explain you without getting into all of the rest of it with him."

"Why doesn't your boyfriend know about this Lindy person?"

Charlie glared at him. "I don't have time for this. Whatever you do, don't answer the door," she said as she pushed him back out of the doorway and closed the bedroom door in his face.

He could hear someone lumbering slowly up the last flights of stairs. She'd said the man was her boyfriend. "You're not very close if you're keeping something so frightening from him that you had to call the judge," he said through the door.

The bedroom door flew open. "Daniel and I *are* close.

Maybe I have my reasons for not telling him. Not that it is any of your business," she said as she fought to get her dress zipped up.

He stepped to her and turned her around to pull the zipper up the rest of the way, trying his best not to notice the lacy black bra against her pale skin.

She spun around, flushed, her eyes bright. He stood back to take her in. The sight of her in that getup made him let out a low whistle—just before they both turned at the knock on the apartment door.

"Don't worry," he assured her. "I'll hide in the bedroom. We can talk when you get back."

"Wait, you aren't planning to stay *here*."

"Isn't this where you keep seeing this person you call Lindy?" There was a more insistent knock at the door. "By the way, you look beautiful."

Was that blush from being flattered? Or from anger? "I can't imagine what the judge was thinking sending *you*," she snapped.

Anger, he guessed. She shot him a warning look as he stepped into the bedroom. He started to close the door as she hurried to answer an even more insistent knock.

He closed the bedroom door only just enough that he could still see and hear. Yep, he definitely was curious about this boyfriend.

CHARLIE TOOK JUST a second to try to calm her banging heart before she opened the door. She plastered a big smile on her face, one she hoped said, *Everything is fine. There isn't a cowboy math teacher in my bedroom.*

But as it was, she didn't have to worry about Daniel taking one look at her and knowing something was wrong.

He barely glanced at her as he pushed past, breathing

hard from the climb. "I was beginning to wonder if you had stood me up." He stopped in the middle of the living room and turned toward her. "Charlie," he said, still sounding winded and annoyed. "You have to move in with me. I'm not climbing three flights of stairs every time I want to see you."

She waited for him to notice the dress, but his gaze had gone to the kitchen.

"I really could use a beer," he said as he took a step toward the refrigerator. "You have beer, don't you?"

"No, I'm out." It was a fib. But they weren't staying here while he had a beer—not with Shep in the bedroom probably listening to every word. "Let's get a drink at the restaurant," she said, anxious to get him out of the apartment as quickly as possible. As she reached for her purse where she'd dropped it when she got home, she saw that the bedroom door wasn't closed all the way and cursed under her breath.

Moving to the door, she grabbed the knob and slammed it hard. Her nerves felt frayed. Which explained why when Shep had grabbed her wrist earlier, she'd felt a tingling. Seeing Lindy again and finding Shep sitting on her apartment steps had her more shaken than ever. She wouldn't be able to relax tonight until she was away from this apartment in some quiet, safe restaurant with a glass of wine in her hand.

"About dinner," Daniel said. "I was thinking we could have a little something here instead of going out. Maybe watch a movie on TV."

"There's nothing here to eat or drink," she said quickly. "I was really looking forward to a nice dinner somewhere before the movie."

He groaned. "I've had a really rough day."

Daniel had no idea what a rough day was. She doubted

he'd gotten a package with a dead mouse in it or seen his dead stepsister. "Do you like the dress?" she asked, trying to change the subject as she twirled around. "I bought it with you in mind."

He nodded and closed the distance between them, cupping her bare shoulders with his hands. "It's a great dress. Another reason to stay in tonight." He slipped one strap down her arm. "Why don't we get you out of it—"

She pushed the strap back up. "I'm starved. We can talk about my dress later. I have my heart set on dinner and a movie just like we planned."

Daniel groaned again. "You're killing me. All right," he said with a heavy sigh. "It's freezing cold outside but if you're determined…" He sighed. "You drive a hard bargain." He put his arm around her and they headed for the door.

She'd been looking forward to this date, but she felt as if she was juggling not only her job and the Amanda problem and Lindy and Shep but also now Daniel.

Of course Shep was right. She should just tell Daniel everything and then she wouldn't have to keep secrets from him.

Why was she so worried about how Daniel would take the news? If he loved her as much as he said, he would understand. He'd probably be protective and concerned about her.

Was she demented? Of course he wouldn't understand. She'd had years to think about it and she didn't understand. Anyway, he'd just said he'd had a rough day. This wasn't the time to tell him about the worst thing she'd ever done in her life.

CHAPTER FOUR

WHAT A JERK, Shep thought as he heard the two of them leave. He opened the bedroom door to peek out. He'd gotten enough of a look at Daniel to know he didn't like him—even before the man had opened his mouth.

Going to the window, he looked down on the street in time to see them drive away. No surprise, Daniel drove a muscle car with a muffler that made it sound more souped up than it was. As the two sped off, Shep studied the spot across the street where Charlie had seen the figure she thought was this Lindy person.

There was no one standing there at the moment, but he could see how it was a perfect spot for someone to appear—and disappear—quickly.

He turned from the window and looked around the apartment, aware of how much it reflected the Charlie he'd known. The place felt cozy, lived in, loved. He stepped to one of the pen-and-ink drawings on the living room wall. It was a girl standing at the edge of a lake, the water shimmering with the last of the day's warmth as the sun set off to one side of it. On the other side of the girl, black clouds gathered for what appeared to be an oncoming storm.

The one side of the painting radiated hope. The other... fear of something approaching? Maybe he was reading too much into it, but it made him wonder about the woman who'd drawn it. He couldn't help the disturbing feeling that came over him. He thought of the girl he'd known. Whether or not she was the woman in the painting, he feared trouble wasn't coming for Charlie. It had already found her.

Opening the refrigerator, he found a beer in the far back and helped himself as he wondered what else Charlie had lied about to her boyfriend. Taking the beer into the living room, he settled on her turquoise couch. All of the furniture he noticed was brightly colored. Somehow that seemed like a good sign, he thought, like the sunshine in the drawing.

The place had been tastefully decorated. No clutter. Just a few books and some photos of what appeared to be Charlie with young women friends. He took a sip of his beer and noticed a worn leather binding facing him on the bookshelf. Recognizing it, he rose and went to it.

Pulling out the old leather-bound photo album, he ran his fingers over the soft cover. At the judge's boot camp, everything of value that they had was stored in lockers for the day they either returned to society or the police bagged their personal possessions and took back to jail.

Shep recalled Charlie saying she had only one thing she would never part with—a family photo album. He'd gotten the impression it was her only valuable possession. While she'd never let him see the photos inside it, he wasn't surprised that she still had it.

Plopping down on her couch, he slowly leafed through the pages. There was Charlie as a baby with her mother and father. Apparently she'd been named after her father, Charles Farmington. He continued through the album until he realized there were no more photos of Charlie's mother. Just a teenage, sad-looking Charlie and her father.

After that, there were only a few photos. One of Charlie's father with another woman. It appeared to be a wedding photo. It had never been tacked down.

Like the wedding photo, the last photograph was also loose on its page. It was of Charlie about the same age as she was in the photo with her and her father. But in this one, she stood next to a blond girl. The other girl looked older. Neither girl appeared to be happy about having her photo taken. They stood just far enough apart that he suspected they weren't friends. Charlie especially seemed wary of her.

He started to put the album away when another single photo fluttered to the floor. Stooping to pick it up, he was surprised to recognize a much younger version of himself. The shot had been taken at the boot camp the judge had sent them to. It was a photo of the two of them, both grinning, both sunburned and looking tired—but also happy.

Shep couldn't help but smile at the young Charlie and Shep. Fraternizing with the opposite sex at boot camp was prohibited. But still, they had, even knowing what it could cost them because they couldn't seem to stay away from each other. This photo alone could have gotten them kicked out.

That she'd kept the photo sent a wave of warmth through him. They'd broken the judge's rules that day by slipping away and going skinny-dipping in the icy creek. He chuckled, remembering the foolish chance they'd taken even before they'd dressed and were heading back and asked a kid from a neighboring boot camp to take the photo with his instant snapshot camera he'd snuck in. If they had gotten caught... Where would they be now if the judge had kicked them out of the program?

And yet the judge had asked him to help Charlie as if... Shep smiled. As if he'd known about the two of them.

At the sound of a key in the lock, Shep quickly slipped the photo into the photo album and put it back where he'd gotten it. He glanced at his watch as he picked up his beer. What was Charlie doing back so soon?

He rose as she came in the door. One glance at her and he could tell that she'd been crying.

He opened his mouth to ask what had happened, but quickly closed it when she said, "Not one word. I do not want to hear it. First someone sent me a dead mouse and then I find you of all people on my front step and I see…" Her voice broke.

Shep would bet that Daniel had been a bigger jerk after they'd left. "Have you had anything to eat?"

She shook her head.

"I'm ordering Chinese because I'm starved and you really don't have anything to eat in your refrigerator."

She nodded and went into the bedroom, closing the door behind her as he pulled out his cell and made the call.

CHARLIE TOOK HER time changing into jeans and a T-shirt. As she hung up the red dress she'd bought with Daniel in mind, she felt both sad and angry. All he'd wanted to do was get it off of her. She tried not to cry. She didn't want to even think about her so-called date.

Daniel hadn't wanted to go to dinner and a movie. He'd suggested fast food and going back to her place because a couple of friends were still staying at his. With Shep at her apartment, that wasn't happening. She'd made excuses when in truth she'd just wanted a quiet dinner in a real restaurant and a sappy movie—just as she'd told Daniel.

"What? A rom-com?" he'd demanded. "I hate to pay good money for a movie that we could watch at your place and be more comfortable, you know what I mean?"

She knew what he meant. They'd argued and he'd brought her home. Before that, she'd even considered telling him about Lindy at dinner—and about Shep. But it was clear that he had only one thing on his mind and it wasn't food. Nor was it hearing anything about her day. Or taking into consideration what she wanted and needed.

She knew she wouldn't have argued with him if her day hadn't been such a disaster—and his apparently as well. She'd been glad when he'd taken her back to her apartment, then sped away after she made it clear that he wouldn't be coming up.

Still she didn't like leaving things the way she had. She would call and talk to him tomorrow—once she got rid of Shep.

Seeing Shep again on top of everything had thrown her for a loop. All those old feelings had come rushing back at the mere sight of him. He'd saved her all those years ago at Judge Landusky's boot camp in more ways than one.

But the big one had been on the obstacle course one day. Exhausted, covered with mud, sick and tired of everything, she'd fallen from a rope fence and lay facedown in what smelled like a pigsty when she'd felt someone grab her by the waist of her jeans and haul her to her feet.

She'd thought it was one of the judge's wardens and had been ready to tell him what he could do with his boot camp. To her surprise, it was Shep. Their first meeting hadn't gone well so this was very unexpected. He'd insisted she go first through the rest of the course and when she'd faltered, ready to give up and go to jail, he hadn't let her. He'd met her gaze and said, "I'll be right behind you. You can do this."

Charlie had found some inner strength and finished the obstacle course. True to his word, Shep had stayed behind her, watching her back. He'd picked her up at a time when she'd needed it desperately and here he was again.

With a curse, she knew she was going to have to tell him

about Lindy—all of it. He was the last person she wanted to confess to about the horrible thing she'd done. Just the thought of telling him made her stomach twist. Why had the judge sent him of all people?

Unfortunately, he wouldn't leave until she told him, and he proved Lindy was dead and she was seeing things, she realized with a groan. He was bound and determined to pay his debt. That she got. But apparently, he also hadn't gotten any less stubborn over the years either.

Leaving her feet bare, she padded back into the living room to find him in the kitchen. He'd gotten out plates and napkins, saying the food was on its way. She really was hungry and knew eating would help her not feel so desperate. Also it would delay telling him about Lindy.

At the knock at the door, he told her to have a seat and he'd get dinner. The scent alone made her stomach rumble as he came back with it.

"I wasn't sure what you liked so I bought a variety," he said as he put down the sack and began taking out the small white boxes.

"It smells so good," she said, watching excitedly. Her stomach was growling loudly and she knew he heard it. She was thankful that he hadn't asked about her so-called date.

"Kung pao shrimp, sweet and sour pork, orange peel beef, fried rice and lo mein, how does that sound?"

"Wonderful." She could actually work up a smile. "Thank you."

They ate in a companionable silence, making her remember how easy it had been to be around Shep all those years ago. She wasn't sure she would have made it through that whole ordeal of the judge's boot camp if it hadn't been for him—and not just that day on the obstacle course. She'd been self-destructive back then, wanting to punish herself for what she'd done but still unable to admit it to anyone but herself.

When they finished dinner, she put the leftovers in the refrigerator and dumped the empty containers in the trash. She felt full and content and better than she had all day—until Shep asked, "You're going to have to tell me about Lindy, you know."

"Do we have to do it tonight?"

"I can't help if I don't know what's going on, Charlie."

She doubted there was any help for her—let alone from Shep. He said he was a middle school math teacher. How he could help, she couldn't even imagine.

"Charlie, do you trust me?"

Looking into those familiar eyes, she realized she did. This handsome man had been the sweet boy who'd stolen her heart at the tender age of sixteen.

Now just when she thought she'd finally put the past behind her...

She padded into the living room to plop down on the far end of the couch. He took the other end. Tucking her feet under her, she turned toward him.

"Lindy was my stepsister and I killed her."

CHAPTER FIVE

"YOU *KILLED* HER?" Shep said, thinking he'd either heard wrong or Charlie was exaggerating. "*You* killed her?"

Charlie jumped off the couch and headed for the kitchen. "If I'm going to do this, I'm going to need wine."

He was still trying to understand as he watched her go into the small kitchen and come back with another bottle of wine and two glasses. Charlie was no killer. He'd stake his life on that.

She made a production of opening the wine until he couldn't stand to watch her struggle anymore. Taking the bottle, he uncorked it and poured them both a glass. "You're going to have to be more specific. When you say you killed her…"

He watched her take a gulp of her wine before dropping back onto her spot on the couch. Cupping the glass in her hands, she looked down at the dark red liquid and said, "My mother died when I was thirteen. My father remarried within months of my fourteenth birthday to a woman named Kathryn Parker. Kat had a daughter who was seventeen named Lindy."

He saw pain in her expression and knew that whatever had happened, it had been haunting her for years. Which made him wonder why she was only now seeing the person she thought was Lindy. Unless this wasn't something new. He asked as much.

"I've never seen Lindy—except in my nightmares—until this week." Charlie took another swig of her wine before she began again. "Lindy hated me from the beginning. I remember how disappointed I was since I thought the only good thing about my father remarrying was that I'd have a sister.

"I didn't realize at first just how much she hated me. Our parents were in love and lost in their own world. So it was just Lindy and me a lot of the time. Once, she offered to cut my hair not long after we'd moved into this large old house on the edge of town. She said she'd cut all her friends' hair where she used to live. My father liked my hair long and insisted my mother do nothing more than trim it. I was ready for a change and I'm sure I was partly angry with him for marrying so soon after my mother's death, so I agreed." Charlie let out a laugh. "I also wanted Lindy to like me. I wanted to bond. I trusted her."

Shep nodded, seeing where this was headed.

"When Lindy finished and handed me the mirror, I saw the look of triumph on her face and I knew she'd done something awful to me." She grimaced in memory. "She'd butchered my hair. It took months to grow out. I got grounded because my father blamed me for letting her cut my hair. I just remember the snide smile Lindy gave me when I got grounded and she didn't. Her mother did little more than tell her she was disappointed in her."

"I'm guessing that wasn't all she did to you."

Charlie shook her head. "She put awful things into my food when I wasn't looking, she ruined some of my clothing, always my favorites, she started rumors about me at school."

"Didn't you tell your father what was going on?"

She nodded, her eyes filling with tears. "He pleaded

with me to try to get along with Lindy and not make trouble. He said she was having a rough time of it because she was having more trouble after moving to another town, another school and leaving behind her friends than I was."

"It must have been just as hard on you. And you were hurting as well. Your mother had died."

Charlie stared down into her wine. "He always took Lindy's side, something else she rubbed in my face. The rest of the time he was enjoying his new wife. He thought that Lindy and I were old enough to work things out for ourselves."

Shep snorted. "He didn't want to upset his wife by stepping in, you mean."

"I think he was still hurting from losing my mom and Kat was a distraction."

He let that go, knowing how much Charlie had loved her parents.

"Whenever I fought back, Lindy had a way of turning things around so it looked like I was the problem."

"It must have been hell for you."

Charlie let out a bitter laugh. "That's putting it mildly. I thought about running away. I even thought about killing myself—not seriously. I knew that if I could stick it out, Lindy would be leaving, going away to college and I would be free of her. As it was, she'd been held back a year and I'd been advanced a year at school so we were in a lot of the same classes."

She sipped her wine. "There was this senior at school that I liked. Lindy often went through my things since we had to share a room and she found a note from a friend about the boy, Andy Walden. The day Lindy died, she came home from school to tell me that he'd asked her out. I thought I couldn't hate her more than at that moment. She

said he told her he thought I was a freak. I couldn't understand why she tormented me so. We argued."

"Where were your parents?"

"They'd gone out, as usual, and weren't expected back
until late. They'd joined the country club and had gone to
a party there." She took a breath and let it out slowly. He
could see that she was working herself up to tell him the
rest. "For the first time, Lindy told me that she hated me.
That I wasn't the sister she wanted and that she would torment me for the rest of my life."

"Charlie—" He started to reach out to her, to touch her,
but pulled back his hand when he saw the anguished look on
her face as if she only wanted to get though this. He feared
if he tried to comfort her, it would only make it harder.

"That day, Lindy pushed me too far. She didn't even like
Andy, she said, but she wasn't about to let me have him.
She was berating me, saying he said I was ugly and child-
ish and…" She swallowed. "Something snapped inside me.
I opened the front door as if I was going to leave, but instead grabbed her and pushed her out. It was late and very
dark that night. I knew she was afraid of the dark. I did it
out of meanness." She stopped to pour herself more wine.

"Compared to what she did to you—"

"She was screaming for me to let her back in. Our house
was on the edge of town with several empty lots between
us and the neighbors on one side and open wooded land
on the other with a house back off the road away from us.
On the other side was an old industrial area with lots of
huge abandoned buildings with broken windows. It was really dark out there and the wind was blowing, making the
nearby trees groan and moan and creak.

"I could hear her begging me to let her back in before
getting angry and threatening to tell when our parents got

home. I knew she would tell and I would get in trouble again but I didn't care. I wouldn't let her in. I wanted her to go away. I wanted her mother to go away, too." Charlie took a sip of her wine.

Shep realized he hadn't touched his he'd been so involved in her story. Now he picked up his glass, giving her time. He could see how hard all of this was on her. Whatever she'd done, she'd been living with it for fifteen long years.

"Lindy pounded on the door, threatening me with what she was going to do to me, what my father would do to me. I wouldn't relent. She began to cry, saying she was scared, that she'd heard something out in the trees, heard someone moving toward the house." Charlie scoffed. "I didn't believe her. She'd tricked me too many times. I wasn't even that sure she was really afraid of the dark. I knew if I opened the door and let her back in, she'd mock me for being so gullible and then she'd be on the phone to her mother. They would come home early, angry, and I would be blamed for everything."

Charlie stared down into her wine for a few minutes without speaking. Her fingers trembled, holding the glass. When she looked up, her eyes were bright with tears. "I'd never felt so hateful in my life. I don't know how much time passed. It's all kind of a blur."

He waited.

"There was a long period of silence. I thought maybe she had left. Then she was screaming, these horrible high-pitched piercing screams. I still hear her screams in my sleep. I remember standing on the other side of the door with my hand on the knob. I wanted her to suffer but she sounded so pitiful and yet I still thought she was faking it just to get me to open the door. I could just see her laughing, mocking me. I didn't open the door."

Charlie finished her wine, set down the glass and got up to walk to the window, her slim back to him as she hugged herself. "Then the screaming stopped. In its wake there was nothing but this unnerving silence inside the house and the wind in the trees outside. I waited for a while longer, still thinking it was a trick before I opened the door."

Shep found himself sitting on the edge of his seat, half-full wineglass in his hand.

Charlie came back to the couch and sat down. "Lindy was gone. I called for her, but there was no answer. I thought about going out to look for her, but I could imagine her out there hiding, waiting to jump out and scare me. I left the door unlocked and went up to my room. I could imagine what she would tell our parents and how much trouble I would be in even for leaving the front door unlocked. I heard her come into the house and start up the stairs. I was waiting for her to come up to our room and start threatening me when I heard a car pull up out front. I looked out my window and saw a police car. An officer climbed out and headed for our front door. I ran downstairs. I still thought that Lindy was somewhere in the house, but I didn't see her."

He held his breath.

Charlie turned to look at him, her face wet with tears. She made a swipe at them. "The police officer gave me the news. There'd been a car accident. My father had missed a curve and crashed into the river. He'd been trapped in the car and had drowned. My stepmother was missing. I was in shock. There was a sound toward the back of the house. I figured it was Lindy. The officer heard it. He asked if I was alone. I told him my stepsister was in the house. He insisted on talking to her.

"The two of us looked around the house, calling for her. She was nowhere to be found. But we found the backdoor was standing open. I had locked it earlier. I figured Lindy had come in the unlocked front door and gone back out when she'd seen the cop. The officer got his flashlight and went out back to look for her..." Again her voice broke.

"He found her back by the creek. She had been attacked and brutally murdered—at least that's what I heard later. The police thought it might have been some vagrant staying in one of those old abandoned buildings nearby next to the railroad tracks. I just knew that she was dead and it was my fault."

"No," Shep said too sharply. "You couldn't know that there was a killer outside. Anyway, you heard her come back in and go out again."

She shook her head. "The policeman said she had been dead for some time. I couldn't have heard her on the stairs."

He didn't know what to say for a moment, but she didn't give him a chance anyway.

"I could have opened the door and it wouldn't have happened," she rushed on. "As it was, I never told anyone what I'd done, especially the policeman. At first I was in shock. Later I couldn't bring myself to tell the truth."

He sighed. "You were *fourteen*."

She nodded.

"You were just a kid. What happened to you after that?"

"Foster care."

He did the math. "You were sixteen when we met the first time."

Her smile was full of regrets and guilt. "I had started

acting out in foster care, getting into real trouble until I was caught and had to go before the judge."

"It's understandable after everything you went through. Did you ever talk to anyone about what happened? Get some help?"

"You mean like a psychologist? I know what you're thinking. That I'm seeing Lindy again out of my guilt for getting her killed."

"That's not what I was thinking."

"I felt like I deserved whatever bad thing happened to me. I'd killed Lindy—"

"You didn't kill her."

She gave him an impatient look. "She would be alive if I had opened that door."

"You said you heard her come back into the house. She wasn't locked out then."

"Maybe I'd just imagined that I heard her come in and start up the stairs."

"I don't believe you imagined it. Someone was in the house. If the cop hadn't arrived when he did… Charlie, it could have been the killer. Maybe he knew that there was only the two of you home that night."

She paled. "I'd never thought of that. If it wasn't Lindy…"

"The killer could have been in the house with you." He raked a hand through is hair. "You could have been his next victim."

"Maybe I deserved it."

Shep let out a curse. Why hadn't she told him all this years ago when they'd first met? He couldn't bear that she'd been living with this all these years. He put down his wineglass and reached for her, taking her hands in his.

"Listen to me, you can't think that way. You were un-supervised teenagers. Your stepsister was terrorizing you and you had no one to go to for help. You have to stop blaming yourself."

Tears filled her eyes again. "How do I do that?"

He pulled her into his arms. "Admitting what happened that night is a beginning. But you need to talk to a professional. You didn't cause her death." He smoothed her hair as she cried quietly in his arms for a minute.

She gave him a pained smile as she leaned back to look into his face. "What about now? Are you telling me that I only imagined seeing Lindy out of guilt?"

"You've been through so much. I think you haven't dealt with the past, but I don't think you imagined what you saw any more than you imagined hearing someone come back into the house that night and start up the stairs. Have you told *anyone* what happened?"

"Not even the judge knows the whole story."

He nodded, again wondering how the judge thought this was something Shep could handle. "What I don't understand is why now? Why are you seeing Lindy after fifteen years have passed. What's changed?"

"I don't know unless…" She got up again as if she couldn't sit still. Couldn't stay in his arms. "I'm happy with my life, with my job. I have my own apartment. There's… Daniel."

He groaned inwardly, remembering what a jerk the man was. "Anything else?"

She seemed to think for a minute before she shook her head no. "I'm happy and I love my job. I don't see how that would make Lindy suddenly show up."

He cocked an eyebrow. "She tried to make your life miserable. You think if she were alive she wouldn't still torment you if she could?"

"Except she's dead. Maybe it is all in my head and if I'd told the truth that night, I wouldn't be seeing her now."

He shook his head. "You didn't imagine someone across the street."

"But you went after her and didn't find anyone, did you."

"No, but…" He frowned, just now remembering. "I smelled something. Perfume. Did Lindy have a perfume she wore all the time, like what do they called it, a signature perfume?"

She nodded. "Her mother told her she wore too much of it, that she could smell her a half mile away."

"I'm betting that the woman you saw across the street was wearing that same perfume."

"What are you saying?"

"That someone wants you to believe that Lindy has come back to haunt you."

She stared at him. "Who?"

He shook his head. Then he had a thought. "Possibly the real killer. He was never caught, right?"

CHAPTER SIX

CHARLIE COULDN'T BELIEVE that she'd confessed everything after all these years—and confessed it all to Shep. She shuddered at the thought as she picked up the wineglasses on the way to the kitchen. Worse, she'd been taking care of herself pretty much since she was fourteen. She didn't need Shep to come save her.

But to her surprise, she felt better. After rinsing the glasses, she stood in the kitchen, leaning against the counter and thinking about what he'd said.

Was it possible the killer had come into the house looking for her and if the cop hadn't shown up—that the killer might be behind Charlie seeing Lindy after all this time. She'd been so scared she was imagining it. She thought it was karma coming to make her pay for her sins. Why wait fifteen years though?

What if Shep was right? If she hadn't imagined it, then it was someone trying to scare her. Or make her think she'd lost her mind? But if Lindy's killer was behind it… She realized with another shudder what that could mean. That the person who killed Lindy wasn't some vagrant passing through like the police had finally decided when they couldn't solve the case.

If Shep was right, then fifteen years ago, Lindy's killer hadn't just been in the house that night. She'd heard him start up the stairs toward her bedroom. That's when she saw the policeman drive up. She couldn't shake the chill that raced along her spine. If true, she'd come that close and now...

She jumped as she heard Shep come into the kitchen. Turning to look into his handsome face, she was reminded of the first time she'd seen him at boot camp. His hair had been longer back then and tousled. It was still tousled, only now one lock dropped low on his forehead, making him look all the more beguiling.

Charlie had already noticed the way his body had changed. He'd filled out in the shoulders and arms, making him look strong. She'd been in his arms and had felt that strength. He'd been the best-looking boy she'd ever seen. He'd known it, too.

"You were such a jerk at boot camp," she said, smiling at the memory of their first meeting.

He laughed. She liked that laugh. It was sexy—just like him. "You came on to me."

"You rejected me."

"The judge had made it clear that there would be no fraternizing or we'd be sent to jail. He seemed pretty serious about that."

"You were so law-abiding," she joked as she stepped to him. She placed her palm on his chest, not surprised to find it as hard and muscled as it appeared. Earlier, when she'd been in his arms, she'd breathed in his male scent. It had felt as if the years hadn't passed.

As she looked up into his dreamy eyes, she blamed fear and wine for her lowered inhibitions. But whatever she did now, she would have to live with it tomorrow in the light of day. Not to mention the fact that she was Daniel's girlfriend. She'd proven that she didn't do guilt well.

"I kept us both out of jail." His gaze bore into her. She'd

seen something in those eyes all those years ago. She hadn't imagined it anymore than she did now. She swore she could feel the quickening thump of his heart under her hand.

"I didn't really want anything from you." Not then. And not now either. She wished she hadn't called the judge. She especially wished he hadn't sent Shep because the man had a way of weakening both her knees and her resolve.

"I know," he said as he lifted her hand from his chest.

Did he? Had he known even back then how fragile she was? She'd felt so strong after the boot camp and she'd grown stronger with the years, with college, with her career.

Until she saw Lindy standing across the street. "I was just—"

"Acting out," he said, and kissed her palm and gave it back to her. "I wish I'd known about what had happened to you, Charlie. Now I understand a whole lot more than I did then. The acting out, it was what we all did when we were afraid. Like now."

His words brought tears to her eyes. Why did the man have to be so damned in tune to her feelings?

She looked down at her palm where he'd kissed it and turned away from him. "It's late. You should get some sleep. I have to work tomorrow." A thought struck her. She turned to face him again. "Where will you—"

"I'll crash on your couch." He cocked his head. "If that's okay with you."

Her mouth was dry and bitter from not just her story but the wine. She felt vulnerable and scared and she hated it.

She tried not to think about any of it, especially Shep, as she got him bedding before going into her bedroom and closing the door behind her. There wasn't a lock. Not that she would need it. She knew Shep. He was too much of a gentleman. The only way he'd come to her was if he was invited.

Worse, he knew *her*. He now knew everything about her—even the horrible secret she'd kept all these years.

She stumbled to the bed and lay down without undressing. It wasn't like she was going to be able to sleep.

SHEP LAY ON the couch, staring up at the ceiling as he went over everything Charlie had told him. His heart ached for her and what she'd been through. He wished there was more he could do. He hated how aware he was of the young woman only yards away in the next room. For a moment in the kitchen, he'd seen the old Charlie, the one he'd known at boot camp. The one he'd fallen helplessly in love with as a teenager.

Shoving that thought away, he tried to concentrate on her story. Pulling out his phone, he typed in Lindy Parker murder.

The murder had made the front page of the *Bozeman Daily Chronicle*. Charlie and her family had been living in the old Drummond house on the north edge of town not far from the tracks only a few months, according to the article.

It wasn't the first tragedy at that house apparently. Jonathan Drummond had the Victorian house built in the late 1800s for his wife to be, Mary Margaret White. The two moved in after their marriage in 1901.

Tragedy struck four years later when their oldest daughter died after falling down the stairs. A few years after that they lost their two-year-old son to an accident in the yard involving a wild dog. Six months later, Mary Margaret was found hanging from the rafters in the basement.

According to the article, Jonathan lived the rest of his life in the house alone as a recluse. After his death, the house went to a nephew who sold it. Occupancy changed over the years, with no one staying long. It had become a rental back in the 1960s.

Shep stared at the headshot of the victim, the young blonde he'd seen in the photograph in Charlie's album. He knew he was biased and passing judgment after hearing the whole story from Charlie, but she looked spoiled, entitled, a little too sure of herself and certainly not as pretty as Charlie.

He hated that Lindy had been unhappy and had taken it out on her. He felt angry and a little sick to his stomach. Charlie had been so alone in a situation where she was being bullied until one day she refused to take it anymore.

For fifteen years, she'd lived with the consequences of her actions the night Lindy had died. He read through the newspaper article and the ones following. The killer had never been caught. The police speculated that she might have been murdered by a vagrant passing through town because of the closeness of the railroad tracks to the house and the abandoned buildings.

What nagged at him was why now? Why fifteen years later was Charlie seeing a woman she believed to be Lindy? Maybe the killer got picked up on some other criminal charge and had been locked away for fifteen years. But why come after Charlie? Did the killer think she knew more than she did?

Which brought up the question of where the killer would have found someone who resembled Lindy Parker so closely to terrify Charlie all over again. What was the purpose? To push her mentally over the edge? Charlie had always been a little bit eccentric—but in a good way, he thought, smiling.

He couldn't help but question what she'd seen. Not Lindy

Parker, that much was certain. But someone who looked so much like her that Charlie was running scared.

CHARLIE WOKE WITH a start to see daylight peeking through her curtains. She sat up, surprised that she'd fallen asleep in her clothes. Picking up her phone, she saw that it was still early. For a moment, she lay back on the bed and closed her eyes again. Just before she awakened, she'd had this tantalizing dream…

She tried to get the dream back, wanting to finish it. Remnants of it teased her memory. A man. The two of them lying naked on a blanket beside a small creek. She could still feel the warm breeze on her bare skin. The man was kissing her, caressing her. She felt a sharp stab of desire at the memory. She wanted this man desperately, wanted equally as desperately to finish this dream. So why had she awakened the way she had from the dream?

The reason came to her with a start. Her eyes flew open. The man wasn't Daniel. Nor was it a stranger. It was Shep.

She flung her legs over the side of the bed and rose, trying to shake off the dream and the ache still burning at her center. In the bathroom, she shed her clothing and stepped into the shower. But the dream had followed her. She could still feel an aching need. Still feel Shep's hands on her body. Still feel his mouth on hers, his tongue moving over her bare skin.

Holding her head under the spray, she tried to wash the emotions away until the water grew cold.

After getting dressed for work, she fiddled with her hair until she couldn't put it off any longer. She would have to face Shep sooner or later. It wasn't like he'd really been in her dream last night. Still she felt as if she'd cheated on Daniel. Or worse, had wanted to.

Shep was right about one thing. She hadn't dealt with her past. She hadn't dealt with Lindy. But she also hadn't dealt with Shep himself. When boot camp was over, she'd been the one to hightail it. He'd tried to contact her once, but she hadn't returned his call. She wanted no part of that slice of her life. They'd been too young. Not that she hadn't thought about him more times than she wanted to remember.

Groaning at the path her thoughts had taken her, she pushed open her bedroom door and put on a brave face. It was bad enough that she'd confessed her worst secret to Shep last night, that she'd let him hold her in his arms, that she might have even flirted with him, but that darn dream. Her cheeks felt flushed still.

When she stepped out of her bedroom though, she saw that the couch was empty. Shep and his backpack were gone. She looked in the kitchen, not quite believing it. Had he bailed on her after hearing her story?

Just then, her apartment door opened and Shep came through carrying two large, bulging grocery bags and his backpack looked full as well. He leaned down and picked up the morning newspaper before entering the apartment and closing the door behind him.

"Good morning," he said, appearing to do a double take of her before heading into the kitchen.

She looked down to see what she was wearing, confused at his reaction. Then she remembered she'd had a sweater in this same style and almost same color when he knew her before.

In the kitchen, he put down the bags and backpack, tossing the newspaper onto the table. "I bought a few things since you didn't seem to have any food on hand."

She bristled, wanting to tell him she'd been fine before

he'd showed up. But then that wasn't entirely true, was it? "Thank you. That was thoughtful of you, but Shep—"

"Don't worry. I'm only here temporarily. You made it clear years ago how you felt about me."

Had she? "I need to get to work." But first she had to read her horoscope. She moved into the kitchen and pretended to glance at the front page of the paper before flipping to the horoscope section and moving to the window.

Just as she feared, Shep joined her at the window to look out.

"She's not out there," he said and went back to putting away the groceries. But she could still feel his breath on her neck. "I checked first thing this morning and again on my way back."

Charlie felt a wave of relief at that news. After last night's confession, the last person she wanted to see was the Lindy doppelgänger again. If that's what she was. Charlie looked over her shoulder. Shep had his back to her. She quickly scanned for her sign.

"You don't have to hide it from me," he said behind her. "I'm not surprised you still read your horoscope every morning. I remember at boot camp when you used to steal the warden's newspaper and rip out the horoscopes." He turned to grin at her.

"You think it's silly. Go ahead and make fun of me."

He shook his head. "I think it's you. There is nothing silly about you. So what does it say?"

She started to tell him that it wasn't anything, but he took the paper from her and read the Capricorn blurb out loud. For a moment, she'd been too surprised that he remembered when her birthday was that she wasn't listening.

"…time to make bold choices that will positively impact your future. Trust," he read and looked up at her, "in your own judgment. It's time to collect on all that you sowed. Any idea what that means?"

"I have a big design project I've been working on," she said without looking at him. "I'm sure that's it."

"Hmm," he said. "My horoscope is interesting this morning, too." He glanced up at her. "But then as I recall, we've always been compatible."

She wasn't about to touch that, especially after the dream. "I need to get to work," she said again.

"What, no breakfast?" he asked and handed her a banana.

"Thank you." At the door, she asked, "Will I see you later?"

"If you're asking if I am going to abandon you, I'm not. The judge asked me to come here to look into your problem and that's what I intend to do. Which means I will be staying with you until I find the answer." He rushed on before she could speak. "Also I'll be dogging you until I figure out what's going on."

Dogging her? "Why the judge thinks a math teacher can save me, I have no idea," she muttered.

He chuckled. "Don't worry. You won't know I'm even around."

"Not likely," she grumbled as she left.

On the walk to the office, she didn't see Lindy. Relieved, she pushed open the door into the design office, anxious to get to work so she could get her mind off everything. Especially Shep.

"Charlie?"

She groaned inwardly. She'd almost gotten past Amanda's office. She had no choice but to turn back.

Amanda stood in the hallway outside her office smiling. "Are you free for lunch today?"

Excuses bubbled up, all of them so ill formed that they never reached her lips. "Lunch?"

"You are familiar with the concept, aren't you?" Amanda laughed. "Let's go early, say 11:30? Somewhere fun. My treat."

Fun? Nothing about lunch with Amanda could be fun, she told herself as she hurried to her desk. She hoped dead mouse wasn't on the menu.

"Did The Enforcer just invite you to lunch?" Tara whispered, eyes wide with wonder. "What horrible thing have you done now?" she joked.

"You don't want to know."

JUDGE WT LANDUSKY hadn't been to Bozeman since he'd graduated from Montana State University many years ago. He'd settled in the Whitefish area after he retired, spending his winters in Florida fishing and golfing. Often he felt like a cliché, his life had become so predictable. *He'd* become so predictable.

As he drove into Bozeman, he wasn't surprised at how much it had changed. Over the years, he'd been aware that it was often one of the fastest growing cities in the state— rivaling the Whitefish area.

Driving down Main Street, he was flooded with memories from the time he'd spent here in his youth. Blanketed in the latest snow and decorated for the holidays, downtown looked as it always had. The light on the Baxter Hotel was blinking, signaling that there was fresh snow at Bridger Bowl. He thought of all the days when he should have been in class during the winter when he'd been up on that hill enjoying the powder.

To be young again, he thought, catching a glimpse of his graying hair in the rearview mirror. Where had the years gone? He sighed, knowing that his melancholy was due to hearing from an old love recently. She'd proven to him that anyone could have a broken heart and at any age. Unfortunately, it had put him into a what-if-I'd-done-things-differently mood, one he was tiring of quickly.

Not one to spend time looking back, he parked in front of one of the stately brick buildings along Main Street and climbed out. He knew that Charlie Farmington lived just a few blocks from here, but he assured himself that Shep would get to the bottom of her problem. If needed, WT would assist, but he wasn't in town because of Charlie. She was in good hands. He on the other hand was in uncharted waters.

The envelope with its cryptic note was in the breast pocket of his coat as he crossed the icy sidewalk and entered the building. A short elevator ride to the fifth floor and he was standing at the closed door to Judge Margaret Kane's office. He'd come this far and yet he hesitated.

"You going to stand there all day?" A woman's voice came from behind him, making him start. He turned to see a slim, petite woman with a head of shoulder-length, wiry red hair streaked with gray. Her big blue eyes had tiny laugh wrinkles around them.

"Hello, Meg."

She broke into a radiant smile that made him feel as if the sun had just come out. "It's been a long time."

"Too long." He'd had his doubts about coming here, but was now glad that he had.

"Come in, Billy," she said, stepping past him to open the door.

He followed her in. The office was like the woman, startling in its contrasts. The furnishings were eclectic; a blend of old and new, polished wood, glass and chrome dotted with soft, comfortable chairs and a couch in bold colors. Like the woman, it felt comfortable.

She waved him into one of the overstuffed chairs and busied herself removing her coat and boots. He'd forgotten how small she was because her personality was so large.

"I wasn't sure you would come," she said, shooting a look at him. "I'm glad you did."

"Me, too." He reached into his pocket and brought out the envelope. "Your note was…intriguing."

She smiled as she put on a pair of black high heels and smoothed down her suit skirt. Like him, she'd retired but still did pro bono work and mentored youth in a program much like the one he started years ago.

"Coffee? You still take yours black?"

He nodded and she pressed a button on her desk phone. "Two coffees, both black. Thanks." She disconnected and instead of taking her chair behind her desk, sat down in the opposite overstuffed chair and folded her legs at the ankles. She'd always had great legs. That, too, he noticed hadn't changed.

"I was sorry to hear about Hal," he said, remembering his manners. He'd met Meg at law school in Missoula. She'd already been married to Hal by then. Her husband had been older than her, a professor she'd met as an undergraduate.

"I got your card. Thank you. It's been over a year now." She settled that blue gaze on him. "You never married."

He shook his head, rather than say that the right woman had never come along. He suspected she had, but she'd already been married.

"It's not too late," she said with a grin as she rose to answer a knock at the door. He laughed. She came back with two cups of coffee, handing him one and settling back into her chair.

"Is that what this is about?" he asked, holding up the envelope. Inside was the note written in her beautiful sweeping script: *Remember the promise I made you?* That's all it had said. She'd signed it, *Meg.*

She laughed softly, for the first time seeming a little unsure of herself. It looked good on her, added color to her cheeks. Nothing dimmed the spark in those blue eyes though. Meg had always been a firecracker, first as a law student, then a lawyer and later as a judge. Anyone who crossed her path never walked away without knowing they'd been in the presence of one exceptional human being.

"I do remember your promise," he said, remembering what a cocky young man he'd been.

"Do I need to remind you what you said?" she asked, tilting her head mischievously.

He shook his head. Now he was the one feeling off balance and a little embarrassed. "Bold as brass, I remember asking you out only to learn that you were married. Then I said, 'Well, if you're ever free, give me a holler.'"

She smiled. "'What is it you have in mind?' I said and you responded—"

"'I'd take you to dinner and then I'd take you dancing.'"

"'Dancing,' I said. 'You're assuming I dance.'"

"'It would just be an excuse to hold you in my arms,' I said."

She nodded slowly. "I said, 'William Landusky, I promise that if I'm ever free, I'll holler.'"

"I've been waiting." He laughed, remembering the bunch of law students who hung out together, studying all hours until they were bleary-eyed and exhausted. Meg would joke around with the best of them, but ultimately she would go home to her husband.

"Hal was the love of my life," she said.

WT nodded. "You were married a lot of years."

She looked sad for a moment before she said, "I have a lot of wonderful memories that have helped me through this past year. But life goes on and I don't want to miss another moment of it. And you, William Landusky. You owe me a dance."

AFTER TAILING CHARLIE to her job and making sure she got there without any trouble, Shep decided to follow up on what information he'd been able to get on his phone last night about Lindy Parker's unsolved murder. A woman who lived in the closest house to the family had been quoted as saying she'd heard the screaming, but hadn't thought much about it since the two daughters were always arguing.

He looked up her name the old-fashioned way in the phone book and was surprised to find out that she still lived in the same house—just down the way from where the murder had happened. He also wanted to see where Charlie had lived—and Lindy had died. But as he drove by the spot where the old Victorian house should have been, he saw that the lot was now covered with a multi-unit condo complex.

Down the street he found Edna Trenton's two-story cottage-style house. The sidewalk had been freshly shoveled after last night's snowstorm. Christmas lights stretched across the front of the porch and a brightly painted wooden Santa sat on the top step.

Shep's knock at the front door was answered by a woman wearing yoga pants and a matching top. She appeared to be in her late seventies with snow-white hair that looked freshly permed into a halo on her head. Two keen hazel eyes took him in as she opened the door to him. "Yes?"

He introduced himself, making it sound as if he was an investigator rather than a middle school math teacher. He hated that Charlie had made a good point this morning at the door. Even though he'd been military police in the service, he felt out of his league investigating a fifteen-year-old murder. But that had never stopped him before.

It must have worked. She ushered him into her neat-as-a-pin living room and offered him coffee and a chair. He took a seat but declined coffee, noticing the yoga mat on the floor by the window.

"I wanted to ask you a few questions about the night Lindy Parker was killed," he said. "If you remember—"

"Do I remember?" Edna cried. "If only I could forget." She perched on the edge of the couch. There was a nervous energy to her. He suspected she'd been working out when he came to the door. "I swear even after all these years, I can still hear that poor girl screaming for help."

"But you didn't call the police?"

Edna shook her head sharply. "Those two girls were always going at it— screaming, yelling, arguing. It just sounded like another night over at that house with the parents gone. It always sounded as if they were killing each other." She realized what she said and blushed to the roots of her white hair. "You know what I mean. How was I to know that the girl was in real trouble?"

He could say the same for Charlie and yet she had blamed herself all these years. "What were the parents like?"

"Busy." She looked away for a moment before lowering her voice in confidence even though there was no one else to hear. "It was a second marriage, I heard." She raised an eyebrow as if that said it all. "They were never home. Those girls were just allowed to run wild. I felt sorry for them. No wonder they were always fighting. It was clear that the older one, the blonde? She was always picking on the other one, the dark-haired one."

He found it interesting that a woman who lived a half block away had noticed but Charlie's father hadn't. "Any idea who might have wanted to harm the older one?"

She shook her head. "The police said it was probably just someone coming through town. We're so near the train tracks in this part of town. It used to be even more industrial out here. Lots of old warehouses standing empty. Could have been some hobo living in one of them."

Hobo. The word made him smile to himself. "The father was killed that night in a car accident. Did you ever see the mother again?"

Edna nodded. "Came back after she got out of the hospital just long enough to pack up her things. Had some man with her."

"Did they appear to be a couple?"

"Not at all. I suspect she'd hired him to help her."

"How did she seem?" he asked.

"Upset, crying, throwing things into what looked like a rental truck. I got the feeling she couldn't wait to get out of that house and who can blame her after what happened there. After that, the house was rented to a lot of different people, college students mostly. The police gave up looking for the killer. Everyone just forgot about all of it."

Not everyone, he thought, reminded of what Charlie must have been going through all these years.

"I often wondered what happened to the little dark-haired girl," Edna said. "I saw her that day when social services took her away. Poor child. She looked devastated. I remember she was wearing this rust-colored sweater and had her arms locked around a large book." The photo album and that rust sweater he later saw her in at boot camp. "How does a child get over something like that?"

"Sometimes they don't," he said. "But in her case, I hope she is able to put it behind her."

AFTER WT LEFT, Meg smiled to herself. She hadn't been sure that he would even remember their conversation. It had been years ago. They'd been so young, so full of themselves, so sure they were going to make their mark in the world. WT had. She'd followed his career. She'd even started a program like the one he had, to give youth that came before her a second chance.

She'd felt bold and brazen on the bench and off. But she'd felt vulnerable and a little scared when she contacted WT. Mostly because she wasn't sure he would remember—let alone reply. Yet he'd driven to Bozeman, her note in his pocket and he'd remembered their conversation just as she had as if he'd thought of it long after—just as she had.

From her desk, she picked up the photograph of Hal. He'd been her English professor her freshman year. A good thirteen years older, he'd been her first. She'd spent her high school years with her nose in a book, and Hal had brought out the shy girl she'd been. He'd always been there for her, encouraging her, taking care of her and yet never holding her back.

She could smile back at the man in the photo instead of cry, but it had taken a full year. Having always advised others to wait a year before making any big decisions, she'd taken her own advice. And was now glad that she had.

Hal was her past. She had no idea what the future held—but she had a date tomorrow night and that was a good place to start.

At a tap on her door, she turned to see her assistant with an armful of papers. "You asked for these?"

Meg took them, thanking the young woman. Hannah

was studying criminology and getting a second degree in criminal law.

"Was that WT Landusky I saw leave your office?" Hannah asked.

"It was."

"He's a legend," Hannah said, getting stars in her eyes. "Good-looking, too."

"I hadn't noticed," Meg joked. She almost blurted out that he'd asked her out. Instead, she stepped to her desk to put down the papers.

"He was a guest speaker in one of my classes. He's tough."

"Yes. But I believe he's saved more than he's sent to prison. He and I went to law school together."

"Is he in town for a conference?"

"No, I think it's personal."

CHAPTER SEVEN

"I FEEL AS if I misjudged you," Amanda said the moment she and Charlie were seated at the table. The office manager had chosen an expensive, upscale restaurant for their lunch. "Thank you for accepting my invitation."

Charlie nodded, afraid of what this might be about. "If you're worried that I'll—"

"No, it's not that," Amanda said quickly and picked up the wine list. "Let's splurge on something expensive." She motioned to the waiter and started to order a bottle of wine.

"None for me," Charlie said quickly. She had to keep her wits about her. "I have too much work to do this afternoon."

Amanda was clearly disappointed. "Fine, then I'll take a scotch. Make it a double on the rocks. The good stuff." She smiled at Charlie. "Our boss is picking up the tab."

"And you, miss?" the waiter asked her.

"A diet cola."

Amanda shot her a withering look. "One drink wouldn't . hurt you." She sounded offended, as if Charlie's not drinking alcohol somehow reflected badly on her.

"I still have a lot of work to do this afternoon," she said again.

"Whatever," Amanda muttered.

They both busied themselves looking at the menu until the drinks arrived. Amanda took a healthy gulp of hers and seemed to relax a little. "I wanted us to have lunch because

I don't think I've been…fair to you." She let out a nervous laugh. "If I'm being honest, I'm jealous of you."

Charlie frowned. "Why would you—"

"Because of the way Greg had to have you."

"I beg your pardon?"

Amanda must have seen her confusion. "When he hired you. He saw some designs you did, he said, and he was determined to get you to come to work for him."

"But he didn't contact me directly," Charlie said.

"No," Amanda said. "I don't get it but he had a friend of his who's a headhunter to contact you. I guess he thought it was more professional or something. I don't know. But he was definitely obsessed with hiring you."

Charlie had had no idea. "That's flattering but I'm sure he was the same way with the others on his team."

Amanda laughed again. "Yeah right. Well, anyway that's why I was jealous." She drained her glass and ordered another. "I thought, who is this woman that he would go to that much trouble to get? She can't be that talented. No offense, but I just didn't see it. I mean you're good, don't get me wrong. But to go to extremes to make sure you were working for him? You can see why I would be suspicious."

Not really. Though Charlie thought Amanda might be suspicious because she was a cheater and thus expected to be cheated on. But she kept that to herself as the waiter came over to take their meal orders.

Amanda ordered a lobster roll.

"I'll take the lobster roll as well," Charlie said, only to have Amanda look at her in surprise as if she expected her to order the cheapest item on the menu or maybe not eat at all.

She closed her menu and handed it to the waiter, wishing this lunch was already over. Tension thick as pea soup settled between them.

Amanda sipped her second drink and leaned forward conspiratorially. "So, do you have a boyfriend?"

Oh, so they were going to do girl talk now? Charlie nodded. She really didn't want to share confidences with this woman.

"Is it serious?"

Was it? "Maybe. Too early to say."

"I wasn't sure either when I first met Greg. I mean, he's good-looking enough but maybe a little too...nice and he is older than me. We met at a bar and I practically had to pick him up, he was that shy."

Charlie frowned. "I thought you met at work."

Amanda laughed and finished her drink. "Greg doesn't like people to know his business." She waved a hand though the air as if it wasn't important. "I worked for him at his last design company in Denver."

That was news. "I didn't realize he had a company before this one."

"Oh yeah, several. Made money on all of them. He gets them up and running and then sells them and moves on." Seeing Charlie's concern, Amanda quickly assured her, "He isn't planning to do that again. Not now that he has you, I'm sure. He says it's hard to get good talent." She shrugged. "But after we're married, he's going to help me start my own business, anything I want so I never have to sit behind a desk again. I want to do something where I can work from home, you know? Start my own empire. Call my own shots."

"Do you have something in mind?" Charlie asked out of politeness.

"Not really. I like to leave my options open."

The good news was that Amanda planned to quit her job as soon as she tied the knot. The bad news was that Greg had no idea what he was getting into. But how could the man not see it? He was a nice guy, just as she'd said, and he deserved so much better.

Charlie realized that Amanda was staring at her as if reading her thoughts. "You like him, don't you?" Amanda asked.

"Greg?" Charlie felt herself flush at being so easy to read. "He seems to be a good boss."

"You don't think he's handsome?"

"Sure, but he's too…" She realized she was about to put her foot in her mouth but couldn't think of how to get it out.

"Old for you?"

Yep, that had been the word she'd been planning to say. Greg was forty. Amanda was probably midthirties—not that much younger—while Charlie was twenty-nine.

"Too taken," Charlie said as she pointedly looked at the huge diamond on the woman's finger. "He's in love with you. The two of you are getting married right after Christmas."

Amanda drained the rest of her drink and licked her lips, her gaze becoming vague and distant for a moment. "Yes, we are getting married. You must think I'm a real shit for running around on him."

Charlie couldn't deny it. "It isn't my place to—"

"I just wanted one last fling, you know? I plan to be married to Greg for the rest of my life. So why not enjoy myself before I vow to love him forever?"

Charlie didn't want to answer that and was relieved when their orders arrived so she didn't feel forced to respond. She felt guilty even dreaming about another man, not to mention that weak moment when she'd flirted with Shep. She certainly had no right to judge.

They ate in silence. The two drinks Amanda had downed seemed to have made her so mellow she was no longer interested in talking. Charlie was thankful for it.

"I really need to get back to work," she said once they finished eating.

Amanda didn't even look at her as she began glancing around for the waiter. Charlie assumed she was flagging him down for the check. But as she rose and excused herself, thanking Amanda for lunch even though Greg was picking up the bill, Charlie heard her order another drink.

She doubted they would be seeing Amanda the rest of the day.

SHEP WAS CURIOUS about Charlie's stepmother. He wasn't sure how she could be behind these Lindy sightings, but he had to find out if she knew about them. Apparently she'd never reached out to Charlie while in the hospital or searched for her afterwards that he was aware of. Whatever the judge's thinking for asking him to look into this, Shep was going into it like he would a math problem—one step at a time. When he tried to locate Kat and came up empty, he called for help.

The judge answered on the second ring.

"You said if I needed any assistance…" Shep began. "I need to see what the police had on Lindy Parker's death, autopsy photos, what evidence including any DNA that was recovered from the scene. Fifteen years ago, they would have saved everything, right?"

"I'll make a call and get back to you," the judge said with his usual efficiency.

Five minutes later, Shep's cell rang. "Talk to a retired cop by the name of Danny Mulvane. He has agreed to give you what you need." Landusky rattled off the man's number.

Shep wrote it down and said, "I'm also having trouble finding the stepmother, Kat Parker Farmington."

"I'll see what I can find for you."

Retired homicide detective Danny Mulvane lived in Gallatin Gateway, a town outside of Bozeman. Mulvane told him to give him an hour so he could get copies of the information Shep needed.

After Shep disconnected, he realized he was starving. He hadn't bothered with breakfast, but now looked for somewhere to grab a bite before meeting with Mulvane. He found a burger drive-through, ordered the works and ate it in the parking lot as he thought about Charlie.

For a moment last night, he swore she'd been flirting with him. He knew it didn't mean anything. Especially after baring her soul to him. Anyway, she had a boyfriend. Daniel.

Shep groaned and took a bite of his burger. Still, he'd thought that for just an instant... It had been something he'd glimpsed in her eyes... But then again, he thought she'd been as enamored with him as he had been with her at boot camp. He'd thought they had something special, even though they were just kids. Way too young to be serious. And yet...

His cell phone rang, bringing him back to earth with a thud. It was the judge.

"She changed her name. It's now Ramsey. Kathryn Ramsey. She lives up Bridger Canyon." Landusky rattled off the address and was gone.

Shep looked at the time. As anxious as he was to talk to Kat, he didn't have time. He had to meet with the retired cop.

But he found it interesting that she hadn't moved very far away. Also that she'd remarried. He wondered how soon that had happened after her daughter's death.

CHARLIE WAS STILL thinking about what Amanda had told her at lunch as she headed back to the office. Why had Greg not wanted anyone to know that Amanda had come with him from another company he'd owned? Why did it matter?

Unless he didn't want anyone to know how short a time he'd had the other businesses before selling and moving on. But if that was the case, then he shouldn't have brought Amanda with him. Surely he knew that she wasn't good at keeping secrets—other than her own.

Then again, he didn't know a lot about her, including that she also had a lover on the side.

If Amanda had been telling the truth, then Greg had hired a headhunter friend. Had he really wanted to recruit Charlie that badly? She felt honored. Why hadn't Greg ever mentioned that he'd done that? Amanda had thought Greg was obsessed with his new creative artist, but other companies did the same thing to get the personnel they wanted.

However, it did explain at least why Amanda had disliked her from the get-go.

Charlie chuckled to herself. At lunch, Amanda had made it clear she didn't think Charlie was that talented. Was she? She loved what she did, but it wasn't like her last boss had praised her all that much. She was glad that Greg had seen something in her work that he liked enough to go to the trouble of getting her to come to work for him—and with a much better salary. The trouble was Amanda's jealousy.

She was stewing over all this as she came into the building and found Greg waiting for her. He looked concerned.

"Is something wrong?" she asked.

"I just didn't want to miss you," he said. "Why don't you step into my office where we can talk?"

Oh boy. She had absolutely no idea what to expect now—and went with her old standby, expect the worst.

"I'm sorry, have I done something?" she asked as Greg offered her a chair.

He took his behind his desk and waved the suggestion away. "Did I hear you went to lunch with Amanda?"

She nodded, a little surprised he hadn't known. Apparently his and Amanda's pillow talk hadn't included lunch today.

"How was it?"

"Lunch?" She swallowed down the lump that climbed up her throat. "We had lobster rolls."

He nodded. "Amanda's favorite. I've never known if she loves lobster or if she just likes to order the most expensive item on the menu. So they were good?"

"Delicious. I just ordered what she did." Charlie wanted to call the words back the moment they were out of her mouth. She sounded like a kid making excuses for her behavior by blaming someone else.

But Greg didn't seem to hear her, which told her that this wasn't about lunch or the bill. "I'm worried about you," he said, leaning back in his chair to study her.

That was the last thing Charlie wanted. "Because I've been showing up for work early rather than late?" she joked, hoping to lighten the tension she felt in the room.

"I'm serious, Charlie. This old boyfriend who you think sent the dead mouse… He sounds dangerous."

You have no idea.

"I think you should go to the police."

She was already shaking her head. "Really, that isn't necessary. I'm sure he'll never do anything like that again."

"You talked to him about it?" Before she could answer, he continued, "Is he the man I saw watching you come into the building this morning? I got the impression that he followed you." Greg went on to describe Shep. "Could he be stalking you?"

He thought Shep was her old boyfriend who she'd said had sent the dead mouse. She started to say no, but sensed he wasn't going to let this go. "You have the wrong idea," she said. "I can promise that Shep and I now have an understanding."

"Shep? That sounds like a dog's name," Greg said. "No offense."

She had to laugh. "I said the same thing to him when I first met him. His last name is Shepherd." She shrugged, then she clamped her lips shut, realizing she was only getting in deeper.

"He isn't someone you dated since you went to work here?"

"No, it was a long time ago." A very long time ago. She frowned. "Why would you ask that?"

Greg looked embarrassed. "Amanda was with me this morning. She said he wasn't the one who's picked you up from work in that muscle car of his." Daniel. "She thought he might be someone new. She keeps track of these kinds of things. I have to admit, it isn't something I ever notice."

Amanda, of course. Charlie wondered what other things the woman had told Greg about her. "Amanda definitely has a lot of interests."

"I wouldn't ask about the man. It's just that you seemed upset this morning."

It surprised her that he'd noticed. "You know how old relationships are. Often those feelings are still there." She meant that as a throwaway, not realizing how close to home she'd hit until she saw his expression.

"I guess the staff have been talking about my old girl-friend," he said quietly. "I did make a fool of myself over her. And you're right, it's often hard to get over, especially your first real love."

She wanted to swallow her tongue. How had they gotten on this conversation? She didn't want to share confidences with her boss anymore than she had wanted to with his fiancée.

"Well, if you ever want to talk about it…" Greg rose, dismissing her just as a clearly drunk Amanda appeared in his doorway.

"What do you have here?" Amanda said, slurring her words as she took in the two of them.

"Running a business," Greg said stiffly. "Nice of you to join us."

Charlie made the fastest exit of her life, fearing another dead mouse. Or worse.

RETIRED HOMICIDE DETECTIVE Danny Mulvane offered Shep a cold can of beer and a chair at the kitchen table. He took both. Mulvane was a big man, broad-shouldered with thick legs and a belly that preceded him wherever he went. The man seemed comfortable with himself and his retirement.

"Lindy Parker," Mulvane said with a sigh and shook his mop of graying dark hair. "Have you seen a photo of her? Beautiful girl. Had her whole life ahead of her. What a waste."

"You talked to the neighbors at the time?"

He nodded.

"What about boyfriends?"

"She was seventeen," Mulvane said.

"Exactly."

"The neighbors said they'd never seen her with a boy. The mother was in a coma in the hospital, the stepfather was dead and the sister said no boyfriend, but she wasn't the most reliable witness, even if she hadn't been in some kind of state of shock."

Shep was surprised by his take on Charlie but asked, "Were you the one who found her?"

Mulvane nodded. "I was in the office when the call came in. I offered to go with the new patrolman to deliver the bad news about the parents to the family. The father was dead. The mother was missing somewhere in the river. It was the last thing I wanted to tell the family. The moment the one daughter opened the door, I felt like something was wrong. You know when you just have a feeling you can't shake. The girl… What was her name?"

"Charlie Farmington."

"Right, the stepsister. She said Lindy was in the house, but when we called for her, she didn't answer. I insisted we find her. Turns out she wasn't in the house and hadn't been for some time. When we found the back door standing open, I told her to stay and I stepped out back. Found Lindy Parker only yards from the house. She'd been brutalized. Definitely a crime of passion. I figured, like you, a boyfriend. At first."

"At first?"

"Turned out that according to the sister—Charlie? Odd name for a girl, don't you think?"

Not if you knew the girl, Shep thought.

"Anyway, it seemed that Lindy didn't have a boyfriend. A little hard to believe that she wasn't involved with anyone, as pretty as she was in her picture. So that left the sister. The neighbor said the two fought like cats and dogs.

Then the sister answers the door acting completely out of it, you know?"

Shep felt a start. Charlie was "out of it" before she opened the door and found out about her father's death? "How so?"

"Ditzy, like she was confused and didn't know what was going on. And she lies about her sister being somewhere in the house."

"Wait a minute." Shep remembered what Charlie had told him. "Are you telling me you actually suspected Charlie of killing her stepsister?"

"I sure as hell did. If you had seen how strange she was acting... Then I find the sister's body. By then the kid was catatonic."

"Shock does that to some people." Shep was still trying to digest this. "Was Charlie questioned as a suspect?"

Mulvane shook his head. "The forensics guys found footprints out by the creek where someone had hidden like they were watching the house. Once they found blood in the same shoe track near the body and disappearing into the woods behind the house, they figured they had their killer. So it's always been believed that some vagrant hanging out in those buildings killed her." He shrugged. "We found a bloody baseball bat back in the woods but couldn't get any DNA off it other than the young woman's."

"You must have tried to find the man who'd made those tracks," Shep said.

"There was the neighbor kind of kitty-corner from the Farmingtons' place, an old farmhouse way back off the road. Paul Wagner. I think he still lives there. He said he hadn't heard anything. Had his television turned up because he was half deaf. I asked if he lived alone. I already knew he had three older stepsons. But he said his stepsons hadn't been around all night. Turned out that they didn't know the girls at all. The media was quick to blame some homeless psycho traveling the rails near the old house and my boss was happy to go with that. No one wanted to believe there was a killer in town that might come after his or her daughter next."

The former cop sighed and finished his beer. "Social services took the sister. The mother was found in the river a day or two later, barely alive. Once she got out of the hospital, she buried her daughter and that was that. The killer escaped justice."

Shep left with a large manila envelope with copies of the file on the murder. He felt shaken that Mulvane had ever believed that Charlie was that killer. What struck him was the question of who else might blame her and be looking for justice?

CHAPTER EIGHT

WHEN CHARLIE RETURNED to her apartment, she found Shep poring over stacks of papers strewn across her kitchen table.

"What's all this?" she asked as she shrugged out of her coat and boots. She padded in her socks into the kitchen.

"You may not want to look at these," he said, trying to shield her from what she realized were copies of the murder investigation and what might have also been copies of autopsy photos. There were also copies of what appeared to be newspaper articles on the case.

"All this is about Lindy's murder?" She couldn't help her surprise. The table was covered several inches thick.

She felt a stab of guilt. Her foster care mother wouldn't let her follow the news about the murder. But in truth, she hadn't wanted to know. She knew what had happened. Lindy had been killed behind the house. It didn't matter who'd done it or how. Charlie knew who the real guilty person was.

"The original stories were pretty sensational so it's no surprise that they went national," Shep was saying. "Since then, your stepsister's story keeps coming up whenever the area papers do stories on unsolved murders."

She stepped past him to pick up a page-one newspaper article and recognized Lindy's high school photo. She'd forgotten how beautiful her stepsister had been and said as much.

Shep made a not-that-beautiful sound.

"Seriously?" she demanded. "Look at this girl."

"You're more beautiful than she ever was," he said without looking at her.

She eyed him suspiciously. "If you think flattery will get you—"

"It's the truth," he said, looking up at her in a way that sent fissures of pleasure through her. "Your face is more interesting."

Charlie laughed nervously. "Okay, I'm going to take that as a compliment." She put down the newspaper article without reading it. She knew what had happened. Well, enough of what had happened. She'd lived with it every day for fifteen years. "I'm sorry, but how is this going to help?"

"I'm not sure, but I have to start somewhere and I need to know all the facts."

"I already told you what happened."

"You didn't mention that you told the police she didn't have a boyfriend. Did she?"

"What? You think I lied to the police? She didn't have a boyfriend. Did she have a crush on someone?" She shrugged. "But there wasn't any boy who took her out on dates, if that's what you're asking."

"Was there anyone at school who was interested in her?" Shep asked.

"Other than Andy, the boy I liked?" Charlie thought for a moment. "There was this one boy she argued with a lot at school. This can't have anything to do with her death though."

"Tell me about this boy."

"Fletcher. I've forgotten his first name. Everyone just called him Fletch. I saw Lindy with him a few times, always arguing. Lindy said all the boys at school were too immature. She couldn't wait to graduate and find a real man. Fletch," she repeated as he came into view in her memory. "I remember this one time, he grabbed her arm roughly. She fought back and got him in trouble. He was kind of a bully. I thought they were perfect for each other."

"I'll check him out. What about boys in the neighborhood?"

She shook her head. "There weren't any. Not boys anyway. There were some guys in their twenties around that older man's house down the road. I did see Lindy wave to them once, just fooling around. She liked to think that any man alive would want her. It was probably true."

"Did you ever meet the twentysomethings?"

"I know it seems strange, but Lindy didn't have time for boys—or men. Her full-time job was making my life miserable."

"It certainly sounds that way. I'm sorry." He surreptitiously shoved some copies of photos under a pile of newspaper articles.

"Are those the autopsy photos? Let me see them."

He shook his head. "You will never unsee them, trust me."

"They're that bad?" She shuddered. "I heard my foster mother talking about the murder. I knew it must have been awful."

"It wasn't your fault," he said.

"You and I will always disagree about that. If I had just opened the door—"

The buzzer sounded. "Another date with what's-his-name?" Shep asked.

"His name is Daniel and no, not until later." She frowned as she moved to the intercom. "Yes?"

"Hey, I'm starved. I thought you might have finally gotten to the store?"

"I'll be right down." She turned to look at Shep. "He's going to get suspicious if I keep sending him away."

"I'm not leaving you alone in this apartment. I promised the judge I would find out what was going on and make sure that nothing happened to you. Why don't you just tell your boyfriend about Lindy and that I've been hired to investigate?" He grinned. "You don't have to tell him that—"

"Tell him that you're a middle school math teacher?"

"True, but I'm good at it and I have other talents." He sounded defensive enough that it made her smile.

She remembered some of his other talents. He'd probably picked up a few more in the past fifteen years too.

"I think we'd better keep your...talents a secret for now." With that she was gone, slamming the door after her.

SHEP SWORE TO himself as she left. But she did have a point. Did he really have any idea what he was doing? He'd gone into this as if it was a math problem. So far, he hadn't figured out anything. At least by staying in her apartment and dogging her every step, he could make sure she was safe. If there was another Lindy sighting, he would be there.

He wondered what was happening downstairs. He moved to the window and peeked out—first across the street. No Lindy. Below the window he could make out Charlie and Daniel talking.

She was right. Her boyfriend was suspicious. He could tell they were arguing. Daniel was all wrong for her anyway. But Shep didn't want to see her hurt. If she had real feelings for this guy...

He stepped away from the window and picked up the newspaper article with Lindy's high school photo. He thought of the stories Charlie had told him. There'd definitely been something dark inside Lindy. Too bad the judge didn't get hold of her. But then again, not everyone came out of the judge's boot camp changed.

Staring at her stepsister, he wished the photo could talk. What had happened that night outside the house? It seemed too coincidental that the one time Charlie locked Lindy out, a killer came along. He supposed it could have been random. They were close to the tracks and a lot of empty warehouses. A derelict could have heard Lindy yelling and come out to see what was going on.

Still…if that wasn't what had happened, then what were the other options? Someone who'd been stalking the girl without her knowing it? The shoe tracks the police had found at the edge of the creek… Someone from school? Or someone from the neighborhood? He thought about the boy named Fletch. He also thought about the twentysomethings from down the street who Lindy had waved at.

He felt as if he was clutching at straws.

He realized he had a lot more investigating to do. Christmas was almost here and he had to get back to teaching after the first of the year. Even if he found the killer—unlikely after all this time—it didn't explain why Charlie was seeing Lindy in someone who looked like this girl had fifteen years ago.

But at least he did know something. Lindy hadn't come back from the grave. Though it did give him a chill to think that if she had, would it be to torment Charlie—or demand that someone find her killer?

The door to the apartment flew open and quickly slammed shut. He turned to look at Charlie standing there madder than an old wet hen, as his grandmother used to say. "He thinks I'm avoiding him."

"You are."

She rolled her eyes.

"He's just annoyed that you don't drop everything for him when he snaps his fingers. You can do better."

"I should have known you would be understanding," she said, her voice dripping with sarcasm. "I don't want to fight with him. He thinks I'm breaking up with him, avoiding him, ghosting him."

He met her shiny gaze. "Would that be so terrible?"

She stared him as if in shock. "This is really none of your business."

Like that was going to stop him. "Charlie, tell him what's really going on. That's all you have to do. I'm sure he'll be understanding since he knows that you're being stalked by someone." She shook her head. "What are you so afraid of? What's so special about this guy anyway?"

"He's...nice looking, easygoing and he likes me."

"You could be describing a golden retriever."

"We're in a *relationship*. If you'd ever been in one—"

"I was in a relationship for three years."

CHARLIE STARED AT him in surprise. *Three years?* She always thought of Shep as the love-em-and-leave-em type— even though she'd been the one to leave him all those years ago. "Three years? The same woman?"

"That is how a relationship works, isn't it?" He turned back to the kitchen table and the papers on it.

She stepped in and pulled out a chair. Curling her feet under her, she sat. "Tell me about her."

He gave her an are-you-serious expression. "She was nice."

"Three years is a long time." She swallowed the lump

in her throat at the thought before she asked, "Were you serious about her?"

"I thought I was." He went back to his papers.

"Did you…did you ask her to marry you?" She felt an ugly twist of jealousy turn in her stomach. Even though she'd been the one to break things off, she always thought of Shep as being hers. That he'd never forgotten her, maybe had even yearned for her over the years. That their connection had been so strong, that he'd not found her in anyone he dated and that's why he was still single. He was single now, wasn't he?

He didn't look up. "I did."

"You asked her to marry you? Did you buy her a ring?"

He dropped the handful of articles he'd been looking through to give her his full attention. "I asked. It was kind of spur of the moment. I didn't have a ring yet."

"Did she…say *yes*?"

He seemed to study her for a long moment. "She said yes."

Charlie felt her eyebrows shoot up. "Did you—"

"We didn't get married. End of story." He started to turn away.

"She dumped you." She felt guilty because that make her feel a little better.

"She didn't dump me. I realized it wasn't going to work. All right?"

"Oh, Shep, I'm so sorry."

He shook his head. "You don't look sorry."

"Wait. *How* long ago? Did you meet her right after me?"

Sighing, he said, "Charlie, you and I were kids when we met, just like you said."

"Not kids exactly. Teenagers."

"I met JoAnn at college and no, I didn't go from you right to her. In fact, after you, I didn't date at all for a while."

Her heart floated up. "You didn't?"

He smiled. "No, I didn't. I knew I'd never meet anyone like you again."

She felt her lips turn up in a smile of their own accord. "That is so sweet."

He laughed. "Sweet, right. You dumped me without a word after boot camp, left me with a huge hole in my heart and made me compare every woman I dated with this troubled teenage girl I met at a court-required boot camp."

"Oh, that is even sweeter when you put it like that."

"I'm serious, Charlie. You broke my heart."

She could see that he wished he hadn't shared that with her. "I didn't mean to hurt you. I had my reasons for taking off the way I did."

He seemed to be waiting to hear them.

"We were too young. Who believes you can find true love at that age?"

"I did."

She stared at him. So had she. "The truth is… I couldn't bear the thought of you breaking my heart." There, she said it.

"I wouldn't have broken your heart."

"You don't know that."

"I do know that. Charlie, I was serious about you."

Her throat had gone dry even as her eyes burned with tears. She tried to swallow. "You never said—"

"That I was crazy in love with you? That I knew a love like that came around only once in a lifetime? That I had this insane idea that you and I could figure out a way to stay together against the odds?"

She was seldom speechless.

"It was a pipe dream, Charlie. I realized that after you left. How could we have made it without money or an education?" He shook his head. "It was best that you left the way you did because I would have never been able to let you go otherwise." He brightened. "But look how it turned out. I got my GED in the military, went to college, became a math teacher and you became a graphic artist. I remember how much talent you had even back then. Now you have a job you love and…and Daniel."

She nodded numbly. Clearing her throat, she said, "I do have all of that."

"Your boyfriend will get over it, but if you're serious about him, you really should tell him what's going on," Shep said and turned back to what he was doing.

"I will," she said, wondering if she would. Rising, she mumbled that she was going to change clothes.

She felt off-kilter. She'd been so content with her life. Then she'd seen Lindy and now, like a line of dominoes, one thing after another was happening as if leading to total destruction.

THE MOMENT SHE left the room, Shep glanced at her closed bedroom door and swore under his breath. He'd never planned to tell her that she broke his heart all those years ago. He'd thought he would take the hurt to his grave. Then again, he never thought he'd see Charlie again.

He smiled at the memory of the girl he'd pulled out of the mud that day on the boot camp obstacle course. What was it about her that made it so he couldn't have left her that day any more than he could now? She'd made him want to do something important with his life—all because of her, he thought with a chuckle. Maybe being a teacher wasn't the be-all or end-all, but he loved what he did. He loved his students. He believed that what he was doing mattered.

And yet his teenage self still ached for Charlie. Why hadn't he told the judge that he couldn't do this? Clearly, he had no idea what he was doing. Wouldn't it have made more sense for the judge to hire a private detective to dig into this?

Even as he thought it, he knew why the judge had chosen him, and it wasn't for his logical reasoning abilities. The judge had to have known about the way he and Charlie felt about each other at boot camp. And yet the crusty old man hadn't kicked them out. Instead, he'd shoved them together years later.

Shep pulled out his phone. "I need to know why you picked me for this job," he said the moment the judge answered.

"Nice to hear from you, too, Shep. Why do you think I chose you?"

"You aren't seriously playing matchmaker when Charlie's life could be in danger."

The judge scoffed at that. "I don't play games. I chose you because I knew you would take this seriously. You care about Charlie and I have faith in your ability to get to the bottom of whatever is going on. You stick with what you start, have an inquisitive mind and you balance out Charlie. It's just that simple. Good night, Mr. Shepherd." The phone went dead.

Shep turned as Charlie came rushing out of the bedroom.

"I just saw Lindy!" she cried. "She's right outside."

CHAPTER NINE

BY THE TIME Shep reached the street, whoever Charlie had seen was gone.

"I swear I saw her," she cried when he returned to the apartment. She'd been standing at the window looking out at the snowy night when she'd seen her.

"I'm not doubting you," he said quickly. "But there was no one there by the time I got downstairs." He could see how upset she was. It was clear that she'd been hoping she wouldn't see the woman again.

He'd known better. Someone wanted her to believe that her stepsister was alive. Because they wanted Charlie to suffer? Or some other reason? Shep was more determined than ever to find out who was doing this and why—right after he put a stop to it.

"Why don't I make us something to eat?" he suggested.

She nodded. "Let me help."

"You cook?"

Charlie mugged a face at him. "You make it sound as if it's hard to do."

He was glad to see some of the color come back into her face. "What's your favorite meal to cook?" He could see the wheels turning. He laughed. "Charlie, you can't lie to save your life. You don't cook."

"I've made things before," she stammered. "Okay, I can

scramble an egg, make toast. I once made pancakes at my foster parents' house."

He shook his head. "Come on. I'm going to teach you a few tricks I've learned."

She raised an eyebrow.

"*Cooking* tricks." Taking her shoulders, he steered her toward the kitchen. Fortunately, he'd picked up a variety of items at the store earlier, including two rib eyes, potatoes, onions and a bag of green beans.

He set her to work snapping the green beans while he fried up some bacon, then peeled and sliced the potatoes and onions. As he fried the potatoes and onions in the bacon grease, he helped her finish snapping the green beans.

"You're making my stomach rumble," she said as he put them on the stove to cook.

He made a salad and broke the crisp bacon over the top, then whipped up a simple vinaigrette dressing. "I thought we'd start with this." He handed her a salad and a fork before sitting down at the table next to her.

"How did you learn to do this?" she asked, so impressed that he had to smile.

"I like food. If I wanted to eat, I had to cook. Once I started, I realized that I enjoyed it." He shrugged.

"They don't have restaurants where you live?" she joked. "Where *do* you live? I know nothing about you while you know everything about me."

"Not quite. I live and teach in Stevensville, Montana. And I don't know near enough about you. For starters… tell me what you know about your stepmother after she was found," he said as he watched her dig into her salad.

CHARLIE SWALLOWED THE bite of salad as he got up from his chair to see to the fried potatoes. She had no idea her apartment could smell this good. Her neighbors would think someone new had moved into her unit. The thought amused her and for a moment, she forgot about what she'd seen out her bedroom window not thirty minutes ago.

"My stepmother? I only know what one of the cops told me," she said, fiddling with her fork. She hated to even think about Kat, about any of it. "She was found downstream, half drowned and injured, and taken to the hospital. When she was told about her husband's death and Lindy's, she became hysterical and had to be sedated."

He sat back down at the table. "Did you ever talk to her?"

"No. By the time she was released from the hospital, I was in foster care down in Billings."

"She didn't try to find you? She could have gotten you out. Legally she was your stepmother."

Charlie shook her head. "She told social services that she wasn't up to taking care of me. Anyway, I was fine. It wasn't like she and I were ever close. With Lindy gone… I doubt she wanted to see me anyway. I'm sure she felt that I was the trouble in the house, not Lindy. Like with the haircut, Lindy told our parents that I begged her to cut it even when she kept saying she didn't really know how."

"I can't imagine what you went through back then and in the years since she died. Even in foster care, you had to be better off without your stepmother."

"I used to have dreams where I would wake up and Kat would be standing over my bed with a butcher knife saying, 'I know what you did.'" She swallowed the lump growing in her throat and looked away for a moment, remembering how terrifying the nightmares were. In her dreams, Kat had known about the lie. She'd known why Lindy had been outside. "She'd plunge the knife into my chest, screaming,

'You killed my baby girl!' I woke up drenched in sweat every time, unable to breathe."

When he said nothing, she looked over at him. "You think she might be involved in this?"

"It's a thought."

"My father hadn't gotten around to changing his will so I inherited everything—not that I could touch it until I was twenty-one. But I used some of it to pay off my college tuition and other expenses. The lawyer who explained everything to me told me that Kat had made overtures to overturn the will but their marriage had been too short that she would have failed."

Charlie thought of the woman who always left the house dressed to the nines on her new husband's arm. "I got the feeling that money might have been one of the reasons she married my father. He wanted to give her whatever she desired. It's why he sold the house where I grew up and rented the old Victorian. It was going to be temporary. My father was building Kat a new home. They'd already hired an architect and were just looking for the right lot.

"Kat didn't like the neighborhood where we were renting. She thought it might be dangerous and wanted us out of there as quickly as possible. As it was, we were there only a few months. But she was right."

"WHAT ABOUT YOU?" Charlie asked as they finished the meal he'd cooked. "What happened to you after Landusky's boot camp?"

"I got my GED, enlisted in the army, put in my time, came back and went to college. I realized while in the army that I had a talent for math and teaching." He got up to take their dishes to the sink. "Pretty dull, huh?"

"I can't imagine you ever being dull." She rose to join

him at the sink. "I might not cook, but I can handle dishes. I'll wash."

"I guess I'll dry then," he said. He turned on the old-fashioned radio she had on a shelf in the kitchen. It looked like an antique and he marveled at this young woman who still got a printed newspaper delivered to her door. She had the radio turned to a country station, and a slow song came on. "But first, do me the honor of a dance."

She laughed as he pulled her into his arms. "I didn't know you danced."

He met her gaze. "There's a lot you don't know about me, but you know everything that's important." He pulled her close and she relaxed into him and the song.

When the song was over, they cleaned up the kitchen and he challenged her to a game of gin rummy as he pulled a well-used deck from his backpack.

"I knew you were a card shark the moment I saw that worn deck you carry around with you," she said hours later. Tossing in her hand, she yawned.

"I'm just lucky at cards and unlucky at love," he said, putting the cards away. She looked exhausted. "Tomorrow's another day. Maybe you'll get lucky."

She smiled as she rose from the table, but it never reached her eyes. He could see that she was afraid her luck had run out. "Thank you."

"No problem. I'll be happy to beat you at any card game you pick."

"Thank you for being here."

He saw how hard that was for her to say. He was messing up her relationship with Daniel. He'd also forced her to relive the worst time of her life. "I'm glad to be here. Don't worry, I'm going to get to the bottom of all this if it's the last thing I do."

"Don't get crazy," she said. "Seriously, be careful."

"Always." He watched her head for her bedroom.

She hesitated at the door and turned back to him. "You're going to look for Kat, aren't you?"

He nodded and thought about telling her that he already knew where she was. He would talk to Kat Parker Farmington Ramsey tomorrow if he could catch her at home. He wasn't sure she was going to want to talk to him though. "Don't worry," he said, although he could see that just the thought of Kat made Charlie uneasy.

"She hates me. Just like her daughter did. Not even knowing the truth about what I did, I'm sure she blames me for Lindy's death—as she should."

"You need to stop blaming yourself. You were fourteen. Lindy was tormenting you. I shouldn't have to tell you that teenagers sometimes make bad decisions. You could have just as easily died that night at the hands of the killer."

He hated that she blamed herself. Lindy's bullying had led to her death. The parents held some culpability as well. They weren't around enough to care about what was going on in their own home.

"Are you all right?" he asked.

Charlie hugged herself and nodded.

"Let me see your phone."

She hesitated a moment before she handed it over.

"I want you to have my number in case you ever need me." He looked up at her. "And I want yours as well."

He finished with both of their phones and handed hers back. "It's going to be all right."

She didn't look as if she believed that. "Good night, Shep."

"Night, Charlie. Get some sleep."

Not ready for sleep, he picked up the pile of papers he'd

cleared off the table earlier. The day's newspaper on top opened to the horoscope page. He read his.

Aries, it's time for a change. Be careful how you react. Don't be fooled by matters of the heart.

He laughed as he took the papers to the couch. *Don't be fooled by matters of the heart.* That was clear enough. *Keep your distance from Charlie.* Yep, he definitely needed to maintain his guard. But seeing her again had stirred up all those old feelings. He'd never forgotten her, had often wondered what had happened to her. Years ago, he'd given her his heart. He feared he'd never gotten it back.

Focusing on the information about the murder, he read through everything again. Something was bothering him. Something he'd seen but hadn't thought much of at the time.

It was someone quoted in one of the articles. He found the article and the name. Paul Wagner. He had lived down the block and off the road, but he'd been in clear sight of the old Victorian apparently—and he'd been home that night. Shep made a note to try to find the man tomorrow—after he talked to the stepmother.

But first, he had to make sure Charlie got to work safely the next morning and every morning. It would be tougher to tail her when she got off work since she seemed to work odd hours. He would figure something out. At least now she had his cell number if she needed him.

He couldn't let anything happen to her. Something bad already had—and long before the night Lindy was murdered. Maybe if he could get to the truth… Why was someone doing this to her? More important, what did they plan to do next?

Finally exhausted, Shep put away the papers and lay

down on the couch. As he stared up at the ceiling, he thought of Charlie in his arms, dancing to the radio in the kitchen.

CHAPTER TEN

KAT RAMSEY LIVED up Bridger Canyon not far outside of town. From her large home, she had a magnificent view of the snow-covered Bridger Mountains. Shep parked in front of the sprawling log house with its bank of windows and four-car garage. Christmas lights shone from the eaves and a large Santa complete with sleigh loaded with skis stood in the front yard.

The drive and sidewalk had been plowed so he had no way of knowing if Kat was home. He'd thought about calling first, but had changed his mind. He wanted to see how she'd recovered after losing her husband and daughter. If the house was any indication, she'd bounced back—at least financially.

The bell chimed out a tune he couldn't quite place before the door opened. He'd been expecting Kat, who he figured would be an older version of her daughter Lindy. Instead, the leggy girl standing in the doorway was about twelve with dark brown hair streaked with blue. She had her mother and Lindy's blue eyes, if not the blond hair. She wore ripped jeans and a short T-shirt that said she was cute.

"I'm looking for Kat." He cleared his voice. "Kathryn Ramsey."

The girl turned and yelled, "Mom!" over her shoulder. "There's some man to see you!" With that, the girl turned and disappeared up the stairs.

Shep stepped into the foyer from where he could see the massive living room under a huge vaulted ceiling. Everything was done in whites, grays and tans from the rugs to the fireplace to the furniture. The only splash of color came from the Christmas tree standing twenty-five feet tall at the other end of the room. An assortment of white balls and feathers adorned the limbs twinkling with tiny white lights. There were so many presents already under the tree that they spilled out onto the white furry rug.

It took a few moments before Kat appeared. Like her daughter, she wore holey jeans with only a lightweight sweater that accentuated her slim body. He had to look closely to see that she'd aged at all from her wedding photo fifteen years ago. But on closer inspection, she appeared to be fighting aging with every procedure available.

"Yes?" She didn't look happy to see this stranger who'd come into her house and closed the front door behind him. He was sure her daughter would hear about it for having let him in.

Now that he was here, he wasn't sure how to approach the woman. "My name's Westly Shepherd." He decided to dive right in. "I'm here about your daughter."

Kat frowned. "My daughter?" She glanced toward the stairs before turning back to him. "Cara?"

He assumed Cara was the one who'd opened the door. "No, Lindy."

Kat swayed slightly and frowned. *"Lindy?"*

"If you could spare a few minutes?" He had taken off his Stetson and now wiped his feet on the foyer rug before he took a step toward her.

She didn't move, holding her ground. "Why would you want to talk to me about Lindy?" she demanded, crossing her arms over her chest, eyes narrowing. "You're not a reporter, are you?"

"No, ma'am." It was clear he wasn't going to be offered a seat on her expensive white furniture. "I'm a friend of Charlie Farmington's."

The name instantly soured her expression. "I really have nothing to—"

"You haven't seen Charlie since the...incident."

"Incident?" she snapped. "My daughter was brutally murdered."

"And your husband was killed and you were injured. Still, I'm curious why you never reached out to Charlie. She was your stepdaughter."

Her voice sounded strangled when she spoke. "As you said, I was injured and in the hospital for—" She stopped herself. "I don't have to explain myself to you, whoever you are. *I lost my daughter.*"

"But not your stepdaughter."

She shook her head, anger flaming her cheeks. "Not a hair on Charlie's head was touched, was it? I've never been able to get anyone to tell me exactly how that happened when the two of them were supposed to be in the house together. How my daughter died and Charlie survived. She didn't even know that my Lindy was outside lying in a pool of blood."

If Shep had wondered how Kat felt toward Charlie, he knew now. "When was the last time you saw Charlie?"

She looked surprised by the question and then angry. "The night my daughter was murdered. I left Lindy in the house with her and look how that turned out."

It was hard to hide his dislike for this woman. She wanted to blame Charlie? A fourteen-year-old whose mother had died and whose father had forsaken her for his new wife?

He made a show of taking in the house with his gaze. "You seem to have done all right since then though."

Just as he anticipated, her anger reached the boiling point. She pointed toward the door. "Get out! You have no idea what my life has been like. How dare you judge me! That girl did nothing but cause problems in my marriage. She resented me and was jealous of Lindy and did everything she could to get her into trouble."

She was like a machine gun of resentment and bitterness. It was as if she couldn't get the words out fast enough. "Charlie." She said the name like a curse. "I want nothing to do with her or her...*friends*. Now get out before I call the police."

"Not a problem," Shep said calmly as he started for the door. Out of the corner of his eye, he saw the daughter, Cara. She'd come to the top of the stairs. "Now I have a pretty good idea what the problem was in that house."

Breathing as if she'd run a marathon, Kat seemed to have difficulty speaking. "People wanted to blame me. That old bag down the block saying I was never home, that I let the girls run wild, that I was a bad mother." She choked on the spilled words for a moment before she got control again. "As if they knew anything about what went on in that house."

"Did *you*?" He couldn't help himself. He opened the door to leave but turned back to Kat, feeling his own anger bubble over. "Did Charlie's father really know what was going on? Charlie was *fourteen*. She'd just lost her mother. And all the while, your daughter was *tormenting* her, making her life miserable to get back at you, I suspect. And you want to blame Charlie? Is that why you're stalking her now?"

"*What?* I'm not stalking anyone, certainly not Charlie. I haven't given that girl a thought in fifteen years. How dare you come to my house and accuse me." Kat jabbed a shaking finger at the door as she pulled out her phone. "I'm calling the police. If you ever come back here…" Her voice broke. "Or if Charlie ever comes here…"

"Why would she?" With that, he turned and walked out, slamming the door behind him. He heard her rush to the door and lock it.

CHARLIE COULDN'T BELIEVE how well her design presentation had gone. She had breathed a huge sigh of relief when Greg had given her a thumbs-up at her conclusion. The client had loved it. She'd left Greg to finish the deal and had gone back to her cubicle, feeling as if her feet weren't touching the ground.

"How did it go?" Tara asked and then grinned. "Never mind, you look like the cat who ate the canary. You wowed them, didn't you?"

"I think it went well."

Her friend laughed. "Play it down, like you always do. What are you going to do to celebrate?"

Charlie hadn't even considered celebrating. Shep was staying in her house. Daniel was barely talking to her. Her dead stepsister was haunting her.

Before she could answer, Greg appeared next to her desk. "I'm taking you to lunch," he announced. "You knocked that one out of the park, Charlie. Come on, it's a little early but we'll avoid the rush."

Charlie hadn't realized that Amanda was right behind him until the woman said, "We need to take her somewhere special." Greg even seemed surprised that Amanda was tagging along.

Lunch with Greg and Amanda. Charlie couldn't imagine anything worse, but she also didn't know how to get out of it without being rude.

"Didn't you have a lunch date with your boyfriend?" Tara spoke up and gave her an I'm-doing-my-best-to-save-you look.

"She can go out with her boyfriend anytime," Amanda said to Greg before turning to Charlie. "Wouldn't it be more fun to celebrate with him at dinner tonight? Much more romantic, too. Let us treat you. You deserve it."

"Charlie?" Greg asked. "I understand if you have plans that you can't change. I just thought since your presentation went so well…"

She could see how disappointed he was. "No, it's a great idea." She looked to Tara, gave her a grateful smile, but couldn't bring herself to tell a bald-faced lie. It would be too easy to get caught up in it since Daniel wasn't taking her to lunch. "Daniel will understand." That, too, felt like a lie though. He didn't understand what was going on with her at all. Not that she could blame him. He didn't have all the facts. "I'd love to go to lunch with you to celebrate. Let me text him."

As she texted a thank-you to Tara instead of texting Daniel, Charlie desperately wished her friend could come along, but Greg didn't invite her. Finished, she followed Greg and Amanda toward the exit.

"Won't this be fun, just the three of us?" Amanda was saying as she hooked her arm in Greg's.

SHEP LEFT THE Ramsey property and drove back to Bozeman half expecting to run into the police on his way. But Kat hadn't called the cops. She'd lied about that. Just as he suspected she'd lied about her lack of knowledge about what had been going on in that house fifteen years ago.

Had she also lied about not giving a thought to her step-daughter in that same amount of time? What if she was behind the stalking? He suspected that if she'd found someone who resembled her daughter to torment Charlie, she would have lied about that as well. Which always came back to the question of what was the endgame?

Somehow though, he thought Kat might be telling the truth about putting Charlie out of her life—and her mind. She'd obviously married well, even better than she had with Charlie's father. She had a daughter with the man. She had a shiny new life. Why would she risk it to torture Charlie after all this time?

He still felt angry. Kat had to have known what her daughter was doing to Charlie. Just as Charlie's father surely had. Why else would he have pleaded with his daughter to get along with Lindy? Did he really think Charlie and Lindy could work it out among themselves? Lindy was older. Did he know his daughter at all?

It made Shep want to punch something. But he couldn't change what had happened to fourteen-year-old Charlie. All he could do was find out who was tormenting her again. From Kat's reaction to his visit, he didn't think she was behind it. She had too much pent-up anger. He figured if Kat ever let that fury out, she would do more than get someone to quietly stalk Charlie.

Also, she had too much to lose for something so trivial as revenge—even though he wouldn't put anything mean-spirited past Kat. He suspected that Lindy's cruelty might also run in her mother.

He decided to swing by Paul Wagner's. Still, as he drove into Bozeman, he couldn't quit thinking about how Kat had gone on with her life. She'd had another child. *Another* daughter. To replace the one she'd lost? Had Kat been disappointed when the girl had looked nothing like Lindy?

Kat's attitude toward Charlie though came as no surprise. The woman blamed her fourteen-year-old stepdaughter. He was just thankful that Charlie never told anyone about locking Lindy out of the house. She had enough guilt on her plate.

CHARLIE FELT AS if the lunch would never end. At first Greg and Amanda were in a celebratory mood. But the more Greg talked about what a talent Charlie was, the more despondent Amanda became. Charlie feared that Amanda would drink too much and then say or do something they all would regret.

"How is your lunch?" Charlie asked her the first chance she got. Greg seemed determined to talk business. He apparently didn't notice how many drinks his fiancée had consumed or how bored she had become. It had been Amanda's idea to come along on this celebratory lunch, not Greg's, although he'd accepted her inviting herself graciously enough.

Amanda looked down at her nearly empty salad bowl, as if unable to remember tasting it. She reached for her drink.

"I have another client I want you to work with," Greg was saying. "Speaking of clients…" He put down his napkin. "Would you excuse me for a minute?" He rose from their table and worked his way through the restaurant to a table at the front that had just been seated.

Amanda's gaze had been on the liquid in her glass, but now it slowly rolled up to pin Charlie to her chair. "If I have to hear how wonderfully talented you are one more time…" She was already slurring her words and from the look on face, trouble wasn't far behind.

"This wasn't my idea," Charlie pointed out, then added, "And you didn't have to tag along."

Amanda let out a brittle snort. "Aren't you the innocent one. Like I'm going to let you have lunch with Greg alone."

"That's your problem, not mine." Charlie put down her napkin and rose. "I'm going to the ladies' room," she said, not wanting this to turn into an ugly scene.

"Sure, why not? Maybe you and Greg can hook up in there and he can continue to tell you how wonderful you are," Amanda muttered into her glass before draining it and looking around for the waiter.

Charlie hurried toward the restroom. She had eaten way too fast, but she couldn't help it. She'd been so nervous that she just wanted the meal to be over. Now she needed a quiet place to escape this endless lunch.

Stepping into a stall, she sat down, wishing she could stay in the restroom until the restaurant closed. Knowing she had no choice but to go back, she took her sweet time washing her hands and drying them before she returned to the dining room.

To her surprise, the only one at their table was Greg. She couldn't help her relief even as she worried about why Amanda wasn't there and where she might have gone. She hadn't come into the ladies' room or Charlie would have seen her. And she didn't seem to be at the bar.

"Amanda had to leave," Greg said, no doubt seeing Charlie look around for her. He got to his feet to help her with her chair, always the gentleman. "Wait until you try this dessert."

Dessert was the last thing she wanted as she took her seat.

"Chocolate mousse," he was saying. "It's the restaurant's specialty and Amanda made me promise that I would make you at least try it." He picked up his own spoon and waited

for her to do the same. "I know she's a bit…much sometimes. But her heart is in the right place."

Charlie nodded, seriously doubting that, and picked up
her spoon.

"Isn't it delicious?" Greg said, smiling over at her.

Charlie tasted hers. It was good. She could see that he
was waiting for her to take another bite. She took a larger
one, even though her stomach was still roiling from her
lunch.

Greg chatted about the company and his plans for the
future as he finished his mousse.

After another bite, she put her spoon down. The first
couple of bites hadn't been bad, but the last one had a
strange taste to it she didn't like.

"Is yours all right?" Greg asked.

"It's really good, but honestly, I'm still so full from my
meal. It's going to be hard enough to stay awake at work
this afternoon," she said, making a point of looking at her
phone and the time. "Which reminds me…"

"You should take the afternoon off," Greg said, quickly
warming to the idea. "Have you ever been to the Museum
of the Rockies? I heard they have a wonderful new dino-
saur display. I would love to see it."

Charlie felt her mouth fall open. He wasn't suggesting—

"We could play hooky. You definitely deserve it."

Yep, he was suggesting. Amanda would have a cow if
they went to the museum together. "It's a lovely idea, but
I can't, thank you anyway. I have some calls I have to
make back at work." She pushed up from the table. "I really should get back, but thank you again for everything."

Greg looked disappointed. "How did I get so lucky to
have you on my team?"

Yes, how did you? She thought about saying something

about the headhunter who'd come after her, but her stomach was roiling even worse than earlier. She felt...nauseous. If she didn't get back to work soon, Amanda might come back looking for them.

Charlie smiled at his compliment. "That goes both ways," she said and left the restaurant.

The office was only a few blocks away, but her nausea had gotten so much worse that she had to duck in an alley and throw up in a garbage can. She thought that would make her feel better, but clearly she was wrong. She felt dizzy and sick and reached for her phone.

Shep answered on the first ring.

CHAPTER ELEVEN

"I'M SURE IT was just something going around," Charlie said after Shep had tucked her into bed. "Or something I ate during a lunch from hell. The mousse had kind of a funny taste."

He doubted it was food poisoning, which he knew usually hit two hours after a person ingested whatever had gone bad. Charlie had said the stomach cramps hit right after she ate some of her dessert.

"What happened at lunch?" he said. He carefully folded a cold washcloth and laid it on her forehead. "Charlie? You aren't just sick, you're upset. What happened?"

She swallowed and closed her eyes. "It has nothing to do with Lindy."

"If I'm right, someone doctored your food at lunch. You said you were with your boss and the office manager?"

She said nothing, her eyes still closed.

"There wasn't anyone else? Why would one of them put something in your food? More specifically, in your mousse?"

Charlie slowly opened her eyes. "Amanda."

"That's the office manager?"

She nodded.

"Why would she want to make you sick?"

"I can't believe she would."

A lie. "You mean you don't *want* to believe it."

"No, I don't, but the mousse was her idea, Greg said."

"Greg, your boss?"

"Amanda's his fiancée."

"Wait," Shep said. "Are you saying she's jealous?"

"*Very*—not that I've given her any reason. Greg likes my work. Apparently he saw some of it and sent a headhunter after me because he wanted me to work for him at his new design company. He and Amanda had been an item before that, so she knew all about it and apparently resented it."

He waited, sensing there was more.

With a sigh, Charlie said, "I overheard a phone conversation one night when I was working late. She's cheating on him and now she knows that I know about it. I think she's afraid I'm going to tell him."

Shep saw her hesitate. "What else?"

She groaned. "It's all so silly. After she warned me not to tell Greg about what I'd overheard, I received a package at work."

"A package?"

"It had a dead mouse in it. Amanda swore she didn't send it, but when I said I didn't want the police involved, something Greg wanted to do, Amanda jumped in and agreed with me. She also agreed that whatever message someone wanted sent, that I'd received it. Then she called Maintenance and got rid of the package."

"Maybe the police could have gotten prints off the package."

"What was the point? I know who sent it."

Shep gave that a moment's thought. "If so, then I guess it wouldn't be that out of character for this woman to doctor your dessert. But why would she do that?"

"Spite. Jealousy. Meanness. Pick one or all three. Amanda wasn't getting enough attention during lunch, had drunk too much and had started saying stupid things. She's just really insecure and needs a lot of reassurance. Or maybe with the wedding coming up so quickly, she's panicking." Charlie shrugged. "Anyway, Greg stepped away from the table to talk to a possible client. I got up to go to the ladies' room to get away from Amanda and when I came back she was gone. But she apparently ordered mousse for Greg and me and told him to make sure I tried it."

"So she had opportunity."

Charlie nodded. "I have no idea how long she was at the table alone. Earlier, Amanda was furious that Greg had been complimenting me on the presentation I did for our client. The lunch was supposed to be a celebration of how well it went."

"Congratulations," Shep said, smiling at her as he adjusted the cool cloth on her forehead. "I keep wondering about her motive. You haven't done anything to make her think—"

"Make her think I was after her fiancé? I can't believe you just asked me that."

"Sorry."

They both fell silent for a few moments. Charlie had closed her eyes again. He wondered if she'd fallen asleep and was about to get up and leave the room when she asked, "Did you find Kat?"

He watched her take a deep breath before letting it out slowly.

"She hates me, right? Blames me? Not that she shouldn't."

"Lindy died because someone killed her. If anyone shares blame, it's Kat. I have no doubt that she knew her daughter was torturing you. She and your father weren't there for you or Lindy. There are a lot of factors that play into what happened that night. The only one truly to blame is the killer."

She smiled at him as she opened her eyes, then cupped

his stubbled jaw. "I've always known you were a nice guy. It's why I dumped you after boot camp. I didn't want to drag you down with me."

He chuckled. "So that was your thinking?"

She removed her hand. "Maybe I didn't want to steal your heart so I ended it before I could."

He laughed. "Sorry, you were too late. You already stole my heart."

She looked at him as if trying to see if he was serious and apparently decided he wasn't. "So back to Kat…"

"I don't think she's behind this. She's married, has another daughter—"

"*Another* daughter?"

He saw the instant fear in her eyes. "She looks nothing like Lindy or her mother. Dark brown hair with blue streaks. Her name's Cara."

Charlie nodded mutely. "I think I'm going to be sick again."

Shep helped her up and followed her into the bathroom to hold her hair back as she upchucked.

Once he had her back in bed, she said, "If not Kat, then who?"

He shook his head. "But don't worry, I haven't given up." He rose from the edge of the bed. "Try to get some sleep. You should feel better in the morning."

"Shep?" she called before he could reach the door. "Thank you."

He nodded and stepped out, closing the door behind him. All he could think about was the woman who'd made Charlie sick. Did she know about Lindy's murder? Was she motivated by more than jealousy? He couldn't for the life of him see a connection between Charlie's past and Amanda.

But that didn't mean there wasn't one.

WT COULDN'T HELP being nervous. It was one thing to flirt with Meg years ago in law school—back then it had been safe. He'd known she was happily married, so it was all in good fun. Not that he hadn't meant it. He'd been attracted to her—just like most of the other male law students.

Meg had always had that extra special something that made her stand out. She wasn't classically beautiful. She was interesting, full of life and a challenge intellectually. She'd finished in the top five of her class, along with him.

But now there was no husband. No safety net. It would be just the two of them. What if they found out they had no sparks?

Meg had laughed when he suggested that after asking her out.

"What do we have to lose, WT, at our age?" she'd asked. "One dance. That's all I'm asking."

When he picked her up at her house for their date, she opened the door in a drop-dead gorgeous fire-engine red dress. She twirled, spinning the skirt out and exposing some damn good-looking legs.

"Wow." That's all he could say. He was seldom tongue-tied. Until now.

She laughed. "You look pretty good yourself, Judge."

"Retired," he said. "Thanks."

"We never really retire," she said and winked at him. "We're too young."

He had to admit, he felt young as long as he didn't try to remember the last time he'd been out on a real date. He'd felt that all of that was behind him for some time now and he'd been okay with it.

She grabbed her wrap and they headed out to his pickup.

"Sorry for the Montana transportation." He hadn't brought his sports car because he felt it would be broadcasting the wrong message. He wasn't sure exactly what that message was. He feared that he'd look like a man going through a late midlife crisis, which he suspected had been the case when he bought the damned thing.

"It won't be my first truck ride," Meg said as he opened the passenger side door.

He took her elbow to help her in, but she didn't really need it. She hopped in as if she was a teenager and he closed the door. The cold winter night air seemed to invigorate him. His step felt lighter as he walked around and slid behind the wheel.

"I didn't know what restaurant to pick so I asked around," WT told her. "I understand we can't go wrong with this one."

"You really think what food we have will matter?" she asked, clearly amused.

Was he trying too hard? He just wanted this night to be everything she expected. Unfortunately, he really had no idea what her expectations were—if any.

They talked about the weather, Christmas holidays and an update on her grown children and so far, lack of grandchildren, until they reached the restaurant.

Once seated, they caught up on people they'd gone to law school with and how many of them had stayed in the profession. He ordered a good bottle of wine.

"To old friends and lovers," she said, clinking her glass against his, her summer-sky-blue eyes dancing with mischief.

"Why do I get the feeling you're paying me back for the way I behaved in law school?" he asked.

"What? You think I'm flirting with you, WT?" She laughed. "I am." She opened her menu and disappeared behind it, leaving him surprisingly a little flushed with the attention.

When the waiter returned, WT ordered salmon and salad for himself and closed his menu. Meg turned to the waiter and shook her head. "I know what I want, but we're going to need a moment."

"Why did you just send our waiter away?" he asked, confused.

"Because you aren't having salmon and salad. Tonight we're having beef, rare, with a big fat loaded baked potato."

"I haven't eaten red meat in five years, and if I eat all that, I won't be able to move, let alone dance," WT told her.

She grinned. "We'll see," she said, then signaled the waiter over and ordered them both rib eyes, rare, loaded baked potatoes and side salads. "You still like blue cheese?" she asked him but didn't wait for a reply. "Throw some blue cheese on them both," she said, picking up their menus and handing them to the waiter.

"If you're trying to lead me astray—"

"How am I doing so far?" she asked, leaning toward him, elbows on the table. Her eyes sparkled in the candlelight and he felt a tug on his heart.

"You definitely have my attention."

Meg laughed. "What more could a girl ask?" She seemed to study him for a long moment before she asked, "How have you been, Billy, really?"

No one had ever called him Billy—no one but Meg. Even when he was young, he was Will. "Tolerable."

She shook her head. "I was surprised when I heard that you retired."

"It was time." He looked way, but he could feel her gaze on him. Slowly, he turned back to her. "I keep my hand in some with helping my protégés when they need it. But there are times when…" He'd never put the feeling into words because he hadn't let himself even think it.

"When it isn't enough?"

He nodded, realizing it was the first time he'd admitted it to himself—let alone anyone else.

The waiter brought their salads and poured them more wine. The rest of the meal passed easily. They found they had a lot in common so there were no tense silences. WT couldn't remember a time when he'd enjoyed a meal more. Over dessert—Meg had insisted on the crème brûlée for two—they continued talking and sharing confidences like old friends.

"What are you doing tomorrow?" she asked when their plates had been cleared.

He'd planned on driving back to Whitefish—unless Shep needed him here in Bozeman. "What did you have in mind?"

AFTER SLEEPING MOST of the afternoon and night before, Charlie felt well enough the next morning to shower and dress for work. She'd convinced herself that it was the mousse that had made her sick—and that Greg had probably been as deathly ill as she had. Amanda was unstable, but surely she didn't carry around something in her purse to make people wretch like that. No one was that crazy, were they?

"Where are you going?" Shep said when she walked into the living room. He was sitting on the couch and appeared to have been up for some time. He had his laptop open and had been reading something. She could smell coffee.

As she moved into the kitchen to get a cup, she saw that he had also made oatmeal. She hadn't had oatmeal in years.

"I thought something bland might be best for your stomach," he said from the other room. "You aren't really going to work, are you?"

She poured herself a cup of coffee before turning to him. "I have to. I'm sure it was the mousse."

"So am I."

"I need to find out if Greg got sick as well. If he did, then...mystery solved." Shep said nothing, but she could read him only too well. "I jumped to conclusions yesterday. It couldn't have been Amanda. It's too off-the-wall even for her."

"You should have some oatmeal."

She shook her head. "I appreciate the thought but I can't eat a bite yet."

Today's newspaper was on the kitchen table, opened to the horoscope page. She quickly read hers.

Your love life going nowhere? Maybe you haven't held the bar high enough. Let your intended rise to your level. You deserve more.

"When that coffee hits your stomach..." Shep came into the kitchen. She gave him an impatient look, and he held up both hands in surrender. "Sorry, none of my business. Let me put my boots on and I'll follow you to work."

"Is that really necessary?"

"Yes. I do it every day. You just don't know I'm there. I wish you'd call me when you get off work each day."

She groaned and headed for the door. "Shep, since I haven't seen Lindy again, don't you think it's time you went home? I appreciate everything you've done but I really think you should—" She let out a gasp and stumbled back in horror at what lay just outside her door.

A pair of blank dark eyes stared up at her from a doll's mutilated face. Its curly chestnut hair, once so like Charlie's own, had been hacked into a hideous cut. The dress it wore was soiled. But what had been done to its face was what had Charlie's stomach roiling again.

Someone had applied gruesome makeup to the doll, smearing bright red lipstick sloppily over the mouth so that it appeared to be grinning insanely.

She heard a high-pitched sound and realized it was coming from her. Shep was there in an instant, pulling her away. She saw him look from the revolting looking doll lying on her doorstep to her in confusion.

Tears filled her eyes as she gulped air and found her voice. "It was a gift from my father. A doll that looked like me. It was the one thing that Lindy knew better than to touch."

Shep pulled her into his arms and kicked the door closed with a boot heel. He buried one hand in her hair and cradled her back with the other.

She closed her eyes, soaking in the warmth of his body. Only moments before, she'd been ready to send him away. Now, she was never more thankful that he was here for her—just as he'd been last night.

"I'm not going anywhere until I find out who is doing this," he whispered as he kissed the top of head. "I'm going to find them, Charlie, stop them and make this end. That's a promise."

WHILE CHARLIE FORCED down some of the oatmeal he'd cooked, Shep took care of the doll. It was evidence, so he treated it as such, bagging it carefully for the judge. He'd called WT, concerned that it might be time to call in the police. But the judge had assured him that they couldn't do any more at this point than what Shep was doing.

"There really hasn't been a threat against Charlie. I'll take the doll to the local lab," the judge had promised. With luck, there would be fingerprints on it or something else about the doll that would put an end to this quickly.

"I feel as if Charlie's in danger even if a threat hasn't really been made," he told the judge when he called again from the sidewalk just outside the apartment. His breath came out in white puffs as he brought the judge up to date on what had been going on. He talked fast, wanting to get back to Charlie as quickly as possible. He'd come out here because he hadn't wanted her to overhear his conversation.

"I've sent someone to pick up the...evidence," the judge said when Shep finished. "He should be there any minute. Keep me up to date on what is going on."

"I'm trying not to let Charlie out of my sight, but she's determined to go to work. You know how she was at boot camp. She hasn't changed. Are you sure we shouldn't let the police handle this?"

"Let's wait and see if we get any prints off the doll. We need something more before we go to the police."

"I'm just afraid of what that more might be." Shep waited for the driver of the car the judge had sent to pick up the bagged doll, then ran back upstairs to the apartment. Charlie was standing at the sink, washing out her empty bowl.

"I ate the oatmeal. It was good, thank you," she said, leaving the bowl to drain. She glanced at him. "Did you—"

"I took care of it. The judge has someone taking it to a lab. Maybe we'll get lucky and there will be a clear print on it."

"Even if that was the case," Charlie said, "destroying my doll isn't enough to get the person arrested."

She had a point—just as the judge had said. So far, who-ever was behind this hadn't made a direct threat. "When was the last time you saw the doll?"

"Fifteen years ago, at the house. I kept it on the top shelf near my bed."

"You didn't get to take it with you?" The moment the words were out of his mouth, he realized how foolish they were. Of course she hadn't.

"I was taken straight into foster care with nothing but the clothes on my back. But I did refuse to go until I grabbed my photo album."

"Then you have no way of knowing what happened to the doll."

Charlie shook her head. "I forgot all about it until I saw her lying outside my door."

He thought about who had access to the doll. Charlie had been taken away after her father's death and Lindy's. Kat had been in the hospital, but at some point she would have come back for her belongings, right? The house would have been a crime scene until the investigation was over, but then anyone could have come in and taken the doll.

Unless Kat had taken it out of spite.

After seeing what had been done to the doll, it had to have been someone who knew about the haircut Lindy had given Charlie. That certainly narrowed it down. "Did any-one else know about the time Lindy cut your hair?"

She shrugged. "Maybe Lindy bragged about it at school. I don't know."

He thought it was a long shot that someone from school had taken it. The obvious suspect was Kat. But why would she have taken the doll that looked so much like Charlie, given how she felt about her stepdaughter? It would have been a constant reminder of the person she blamed for her daughter's death. How macabre, if true.

Charlie's cell rang. She checked it. From her expression, he could tell it was Daniel.

He stepped out of the room to give her some privacy, all the time swearing under his breath. Maybe it was time to see what he could find out about Daniel along with Amanda, the office manager.

"I need to get to work," Charlie said behind him.

He turned. "That was a short call. Everything all right?"

She pulled a face. "What do you think?" She stepped to the door, took her coat from the hook and tugged on her boots again. This time when she opened the door, it was with obvious apprehension.

"I'll be right behind you all the way," he said, reaching for his own coat.

"That's ridiculous. Walk me to work. I won't have you skulking behind me."

"I don't skulk."

CHAPTER TWELVE

CHARLIE'S THOUGHTS JUMPED all over the place from the doll to Daniel's call to Shep walking beside her to work. She hated how glad she was that he was here with her—even though it was causing problems between her and Daniel. And not just because she hadn't told him about what was going on. Having Shep here... Well, it had messed with her in other ways she didn't want to think about. That, too, had put distance between her and her boyfriend.

Seeing her once treasured doll had traumatized her. The person who'd done this was so...hateful. It frightened her. But she also felt guilty that she'd forgotten about the doll her father had bought her. What she couldn't understand was what the person who'd done this wanted from her. Scare her? Or let her know that this wasn't over. There would be more hateful things coming.

When Daniel had called earlier he'd sounded...strange. Almost as if he was sorry, until he lost his temper when she told him not to come by her apartment on his way to work because she was leaving right away.

"You can't spare a few minutes?" he'd demanded. "Fine. Whatever. When you decide to let me know what's going on, you call me."

By the time she reached her building and left Shep standing out in the snow, she decided it was time to tell Daniel everything and let the chips fall where they may, as one of her foster mothers used to say. What did she have to lose? Daniel. But if she kept this up, she was going to lose him anyway.

She pushed open the door to the design office and stepped inside. For a moment she'd forgotten about yesterday's lunch and the horrible stomach problems that had caused her not to return to work.

"Enjoy your afternoon off?" Amanda asked sarcastically as Charlie started past her office. Apparently Amanda *had* returned after lunch—even though she was quite drunk the last time Charlie had seen her. Had it been an act so she could doctor dessert and leave? Charlie found herself questioning the woman's every action now.

"Something I ate made me sick," she said, wanting to ignore Amanda and the jab, but thinking about Shep's suspicions. "But you wouldn't know anything about that, right?"

"I can't imagine what you're insinuating," Amanda said and rubbed a temple with her fingers as if in pain. She did appear to be suffering from a hangover, but then that, too, could be a ruse. If Amanda had put something in Charlie's mousse yesterday, a hangover wasn't near enough punishment.

Glancing toward the office next to Amanda's, Charlie asked, "Greg isn't in yet?"

"He called in sick yesterday. Said he would be in later today. Apparently it was something he ate, too." Did that smug smile mean what Charlie thought it did? Or was Amanda questioning if she and Greg had both used the same excuse so they could get together yesterday afternoon?

It was enough to make Charlie's head ache. "I think it was the mousse."

"That's what Greg said. I suppose you're both going to blame me since I was the one who insisted you try it."

Charlie stared at her. Was it possible that Amanda had doctored both of the desserts to make them sick? Or had the mousse turned and made not just the two of them sick but everyone else who'd had it at the restaurant?

Charlie moved down the hallway to her cubicle. The oatmeal had helped settle her stomach somewhat, but she still felt weak. Her muscles ached from all the heaving and she still felt a little light-headed.

"How was your lunch?" Tara whispered, looking at her in alarm.

"I got food poisoning. Or something."

Tara gasped. "That's horrible. Where did Greg take you?"

Charlie told her the name of the restaurant. "I suspect everyone who had the mousse got it. Greg called in sick, too, I guess," she said, lowering her voice.

On impulse, she looked up the restaurant online and called the number. "This is a crazy question and one you might not even honestly answer, but did you get any complaints about the mousse making people sick?"

"The chocolate mousse? It's our specialty. No one ever complains."

"So no one called to say it made them sick?" Charlie prodded.

"No, but you're welcome to speak to our manager."

She was looking at Tara who was now wide-eyed. "No, thank you." She disconnected. "I think Amanda put something in my dessert that made me deathly ill. It's possible she doctored Greg's as well. She was drinking and upset because she wasn't getting enough attention from Greg."

Tara rolled her eyes. "You'll have to tell me about it before the shower."

For a moment the word *shower* didn't make any sense. "Oh, your baby shower."

"You forgot."

"No, not exactly." Charlie groaned. "Yes. I'm sorry. I've had so much on my mind."

"It's all right. On top of that, you ate something that made you sick."

"What does anyone carry in her purse that could cause that kind of nausea if mixed with a food like mousse?" Charlie asked.

Tara, whose whole family was involved in the health profession, thought for a moment. "Something small that anyone might carry…" She burst into a grin. "Eye drops."

"Eye drops?"

Her friend shook her head. "I know it sounds odd, but my uncle the pediatrician was telling me about a toddler who got into his mother's eye drops. Made him sicker than a dog."

"Eye drops," Charlie repeated, wondering how she could get a look inside Amanda's purse. Maybe at the shower. That's when she realized she had also forgotten her baby shower present. She'd purchased it weeks ago. She'd have to go home and get it. "I am sorry I forgot about your shower."

"Don't be silly." Tara hugged her huge protruding belly. "You haven't been lugging around a constant reminder like I have. Charlie, I'm worried about you. If you're right…" She made a motion toward the front of the office.

"It's fine. I'll deal with it."

"Well, at least you have job security. Greg seemed over the moon about your presentation. Are things with Daniel okay?"

Charlie shrugged. "It's a long story." She knew she had to tell Tara something. The woman was one of her best friends. "An old boyfriend has come back into my life. Literally. He's…staying with me."

Her friend's eyes widened. "What does Daniel think of that?"

"He doesn't know yet. I'm trying to figure out how to tell him."

Her expression said *good luck with that*. "This was a serious boyfriend?"

Charlie nodded. The explanation wasn't completely true but it covered at least part of it. "Daniel knows something's wrong, but not all of it."

"You're going to tell him, aren't you?"

She swallowed the lump that had formed in her throat. "I'm worried he won't understand."

"I guess it depends on how serious things are with the old boyfriend now."

Just then Amanda walked through on her way to the ladies' room.

Charlie turned back to her desk and so did Tara.

"Come to the shower early if you want to talk about it," Tara whispered over her shoulder.

BACK AT THE apartment, Shep looked up the design company where Charlie was employed. Under Contact Information, he found the names of the administrative staff. Gregory Shafer, CEO and owner. Amanda Barnes, office manager. At the top of a list labeled Creative Design Team was Charlie Farmington.

He felt a wave of pride. Charlie had succeeded against odds that someone half as strong would have crumbled under. The woman amazed him.

He studied the photograph of Amanda Barnes for a moment before going online to see what he could find out about her. He found nothing in her background on social media to raise any red flags. She appeared to come from a middle-class family and had majored in history and English. She'd taught one year, English as a second language at an alternative school. The job apparently hadn't worked out, and she'd fallen into administrative jobs until she went to work for Greg Shafer at a design company in Colorado as an office manager.

There was much less information available on Greg Shafer. He appeared to be a self-made man, majoring in design at Colorado State, opening his first company right out of college. By Shep's count, the Bozeman design company was his fourth. On paper, he appeared to be a successful man. The kind a woman would be attracted to, maybe especially a woman like Amanda.

Shep looked up the restaurant where Charlie had been served chocolate mousse. The call went through. He inquired about anyone calling in to say the mousse had made them sick. A woman assured him that they'd had no report of anyone getting sick.

Placing another call, this one to Paul Wagner, the man who had lived down the street from Charlie fifteen years ago, Shep's mind buzzed with worry about her. Someone had doctored her mousse. If not Amanda, then who did that leave?

A thin elderly voice answered the call. "Hello?"

Shep introduced himself and then said, "I need to talk to you about the murder of Lindy Parker. Do you mind if I come over?"

"I'll be here," Wagner said and Shep headed for his pickup.

Like Edna Trenton, Paul Wagner still lived in the same house he had fifteen years ago. Having an unsolved murder just doors away hadn't seemed to worry either of them. Probably because most everyone believed the killer had been a vagrant passing through town. Except for Mulvane. And possibly Kat Ramsey.

The farmhouse back off the street had seen better days. It looked odd with all the new development around it. Bozeman had always been a desirable city to live in, hitting a lot of the Ten Best Places to Live lists over the years. Recently the city had taken off again with home prices shooting skyward.

Shep wondered why Wagner hadn't cashed in yet. His large piece of property was worth a small fortune.

A mangy mutt of a dog limped out, barking as Shep parked and started to get out. The dog began to growl in warning.

"Bruce!" a man called from the sagging farmhouse porch. "Knock it off!" The dog skulked away and Shep got out onto the unplowed drive.

"Paul Wagner?" he asked. The man was small and wiry with a shock of white hair and a scraggly beard that dropped clear to his protruding belly.

The man leaned on his walker, craning his neck to look at Shep. "Who's asking?"

"My name's Shepherd, Westly Shepherd. I called earlier. I'm looking into the murder of Lindy Parker." The man's brown eyes took him in as Shep climbed the steps to the porch. "It happened fifteen years ago in that old Victorian that used to be down the road from here."

"So you're the one who called. Wondered when you'd be getting around to me. Heard you were asking questions around the neighborhood. Best come inside," Wagner said, and he opened the door and led the way in.

As Shep followed the man, he realized that time and possibly disease had whittled the man down to just the potbelly.

"Pay no attention to the mess," Wagner said as he slid his walker along the worn wood floor. "I live alone and I'm used to it. It's my mess, as I keep telling my well-meaning stepsons who want me to tidy up. Well, the ones who bother to visit, that is."

Shep followed him into the small living area. It was a mess, cluttered with newspapers and magazines and books piled everywhere.

"You're a reader," Shep said, noticing the books that took up most of the wall space as well as the floor. "I've read a lot of these."

"Takes a reader to appreciate another," the man said as he carefully lowered himself into a well-worn recliner. He motioned for Shep to take a nearby chair.

But Shep had gotten distracted by a framed newspaper article on the wall titled "Local Hero Saves Girl's Life." A nine-year-old girl had fallen into a pond near Wagner's house. He had jumped in when he realized she didn't know how to swim and dragged her out to save her life.

"That was right before the murder," the man said. "Back when I was capable of saving someone. Not much hero left in me."

Shep took the chair he'd been offered. "Did you know the Farmington family?"

Wagner shook his head. "Never met 'em. Just saw 'em coming and goin'."

"I'm sure the police already asked you this fifteen years ago, but did you hear anything the night of the murder?"

Shep asked. He noticed that Wagner now wore hearing aids in both ears.

"Had the TV turned up too loud to hear myself think back then. Was convinced I didn't need these damned things." He pointed at the hearing aid in his left ear. "Got so bad I finally bit the bullet. I was shocked when the cop came to my door and told me what had happened."

Shep was beginning to wonder why he was bothering with asking the neighbors. It wasn't like they had anything new to offer. He glanced around the room. Everything looked well-worn. On a bookshelf in the corner, he spotted an assortment of what appeared to be a variety of sports awards. He pointed at them. "Yours?"

Wagner shook his head. "Mostly from two of my stepsons. A couple of them are mine from back in my heyday." He grinned. "I may not look it but I was fast on my feet, and good with my hands."

"Did any of your stepsons know the teenage girls down the road?"

"The boys had moved out long before that family moved in, but they visited occasionally." Wagner winked. "They weren't apt to miss a pretty face so I'm sure they'd noticed. But they were all in their twenties, way too old for those schoolgirls."

"Did any of your stepsons stop by that night?"

The old man shook his head. "The only time they came around back then was when they needed a meal or money. Damn shame what happened. You know I saw her that night."

"You did?" Shep's ears perked up.

"I'd gotten up during a commercial on TV to go into the kitchen for a snack. That window in there looked out on that big old house. All the lights were blaring. I figured the parents were gone. Can't imagine what their electric bill was each month."

"So you saw Lindy?" Shep asked, hoping to get Wagner back on track.

The elderly man nodded. "That girl had the prettiest blond hair. Shone like a lamp that night even though it was pitch-black out."

"You saw her outside the front door?"

"That's where she was the first time I saw her. She seemed to be poundin' on the door like she was locked out. But when I looked again, she'd gone around to the back."

"Did you tell the police this?"

"I suppose I did since the way the house was, I could see her at the back. I saw her bend down and pull something out from under a flowerpot at the edge of the house, then she disappeared back inside. I watched for a moment, but she didn't come back out."

So she hadn't been locked out the whole time. "She didn't put the key back?"

"Not while I was watching."

Shep leaned back in the chair, trying to make sense of this. Lindy had never been locked out? So why the hysterics at the front door? Had Charlie been right that Lindy was playing her?

"You're sure you told the police this?"

He saw the man's hesitation. Wagner hadn't told the cops. They hadn't looked for the spare key. If Lindy had come out of the house to put the key back… Was that when she was attacked?

Shep realized that even if Wagner had told Mulvane what he'd seen, it wouldn't have meant much to the cop. He didn't know about Charlie locking Lindy out.

"I felt bad for that dark-haired one to have something

like that happen, just the two of them alone in that house."
Wagner nodded, smiling from his skeletal face. "She was
so lucky that night, wasn't she?"

"Yes, she was." Shep rose. "Thank you for all your help."

"Not sure I was any help," the man said as he tried to
struggle to his feet.

"Please, don't get up on my account. I can see myself
out." Shep had a thought as he remembered Charlie saying that she once saw Lindy wave to the stepsons. It was
a long shot, but he had to follow any and all leads at this
point. "Would you mind if I spoke with your stepsons?"

"Not sure they have anything to add, but you're welcome
to it." Wagner picked up a pad and pen next to his chair
and labored to write down their names and phone numbers.

Shep took it and glanced at it in the dim light. The man's
handwriting was almost unreadable, but there appeared
to be three first names on the paper with telephone numbers after them. He stuffed the paper into his pocket and
thanked Wagner again as he left. The man had been more
helpful than he knew.

CHARLIE LOOKED UP from her desk to find Daniel standing
over her. Startled, she tried to rise from her chair when she
saw that Amanda was right behind him.

"Look who's come to see you," Amanda said and gave
her a huge smile, eyes glinting maliciously. Charlie remembered Greg telling her that the woman had seen her with
Shep—not that she'd known his name. She'd thought it was
another, newer boyfriend. So the smile meant that she was
hoping for fireworks.

"Daniel." Charlie met his gaze. He looked upset. What
had Amanda said to him? She could only guess. "What are
you doing here?"

"I figured if I wanted to see you, it was going to have to be here," he said.

She could hear anger in his voice. "I was going to call you."

He looked as if he didn't believe that. She could see that Amanda was hanging onto their every word.

Charlie's cell phone rang. She fumbled it out, meaning to simply turn it off, but then she saw who it was. Shep couldn't have picked a worse time to call. She hit Accept, quickly put the phone to her ear and turned her back to Daniel and Amanda. "I can't talk right now."

"Bad day?" he asked. "Sorry. I have some good news and thought you might need some."

"You have no idea."

"Can you take a break? Meet me at that coffee shop on the corner near your office and I'll tell you everything."

"I…I can't. I'm sorry."

"I get the feeling there's someone standing next to your desk?"

"Uh-huh, but thanks for calling." With that she disconnected and turned to Daniel, pasting a smile on her face. "I can take my break. Why don't we go next door to the coffee shop?"

"There's coffee in the break room," Amanda pointed out. "You can certainly visit in the conference room."

"I could use the fresh air," Charlie said and gave Daniel a pleading look. She'd told him enough about Amanda that he had to know how uncomfortable this was making her.

"Fine," he said, and turning, he headed for the front door.

"He seems upset," Amanda noted with no small amount of glee. "Maybe he heard about…the other man." She gave Charlie a grin.

"There is no other man," Charlie snapped.

"Tell it to Daniel," Amanda said as Charlie hurried after her boyfriend, passing Greg on his way into work.

SHEP COULDN'T HELP being disappointed. He'd called on his walk down to her office moments ago hoping to share the good news with her. Lindy had never been locked out. It had been a ruse, just as Charlie had suspected it was. He couldn't wait to tell her that she wasn't responsible for her stepsister's death, just as he'd been telling her. But now he had solid evidence.

It was late afternoon, the downtown busy with the holidays so close. He'd almost reached her office and had started to turn away when he saw Daniel come storming out of the building scowling. Shep stepped back into the shadows of the building next door as Charlie came out right after Daniel. She'd sounded so harried on the phone. This could explain it, he thought.

From where he stood, he watched Charlie catch up with Daniel and, grabbing his arm, turn him to face her. Shep was only yards away so he couldn't help but hear their argument.

"Why would you come by my office knowing that I'm working and can't talk to you?" she demanded.

"I already told you. I figured this was the one place I might be able to see you. I want to know what's going on. Why have you been putting me off?"

"I want to explain, but not out here on the sidewalk."

"Well, I don't want to talk in a coffee shop. Let's go back to your place—"

"I can't."

"Can't or won't?"

"Both. I have to finish work and then—"

"Forget it," Daniel snapped. In the reflection in the shop

window, Shep saw him step back from her as she reached for him again. "Just forget it." With that he stormed away.

For a moment, Shep thought she'd go after him, but when her cell phone rang, she swore and pulled it out. Dodging shoppers on the sidewalk, she took the call. Whoever was on the other end of the line, they seemed to be asking her questions, which she answered with either a yes or a no. "I'll meet you there."

He watched her disconnect. He thought she would head back toward the front of her office building. To his surprise, she turned in his direction. He thought for sure she would see him and would be furious that he'd witnessed the scene. But she was busy wiping away her tears as she started in the direction of her apartment.

Shep was wondering who had been on the phone when he recognized the man now coming out of her office building. Greg Shafer, her boss, glanced after Charlie, hesitated, then began to follow her.

Shep waited until Greg passed before he fell in behind the man.

CHAPTER THIRTEEN

CHARLIE HADN'T GONE far through the falling snow and frantic shoppers when she realized she was headed in the wrong direction. The restaurant where the shower was being held was the opposite way. She stopped and was jostled by several shoppers. Then she remembered that after arguing with Daniel she'd decide to run home to get her shower gift. A shopper hit her in the back with one of her packages.

Clearly she couldn't just stand here in everyone's way while she debated what to do. She pushed open the door to what turned out to be a bar. But at least inside, she wasn't being snowed on or attacked by the crush of last-minute Christmas shoppers.

Tara had called and wanted her to come right away because Amanda had called to say she was headed over to the restaurant. No more explanation needed.

Charlie couldn't abandon her friend. She'd just have to give Tara her present tomorrow at work since she didn't have time to return to her apartment for the gift and still save Tara from Amanda.

Just the thought of spending the afternoon around Amanda was almost too much to bear. But she was doing this for Tara, Charlie reminded herself, and started to step back out onto the busy sidewalk when she saw Greg coming down the sidewalk.

She ducked back into the bar and was looking around for the exit when she heard the door open behind her.

"Charlie?" Greg sounded out of breath as if he'd seen her and had wanted to catch her before she got away.

Cursing under her breath, she turned and pretended surprise at seeing him. "Greg."

"Today's my lucky day," he said. "Have a drink with me."

"Actually," she said, stalling for time to come up with a reasonable excuse, "I can't. I just ducked in here to use the ladies' room," she said, lowering her voice.

He grinned. "Best go take care of that and I'll get us a couple of drinks."

She opened her mouth with an excuse on the tip of her tongue.

"Don't tell me you don't have time before the baby shower." He knew about the shower. "Amanda's gone over to be with Tara until everyone arrives, so you have no excuse. I've been wanting to talk to you about something important anyway."

"Seriously, I can't. I was on the way to my apartment to pick up my baby shower gift. I forgot it this morning."

He looked disappointed for a moment, but then brightened. "I'll walk with you. We can talk on the way. This is important. It's something I've been wanting to tell you for some time now."

She felt panic rise up in her along with bile. Walk her to the apartment? She didn't think so. She couldn't depend on Shep being there and maybe she was paranoid but she didn't want to be anywhere with Greg alone. If Amanda found out…

"You know, this is silly. I'll give Tara the gift tomorrow at work. A glass of wine might be just what I need."

"Great. I'll get us a table."

What could be so important that he had to talk to her right now? He had her cornered. There was nothing she could say at this point, she thought as he signaled the bartender and ordered their drinks.

She could sit through one glass, couldn't she? Much better than the thought of taking him back to her apartment.

"Hurry back," Greg said and paid for their drinks.

In the ladies' room, she washed her hands and returned quickly, just wanting to get this over with, whatever it was. Greg had gotten them a quiet, dimly lit corner booth. He was nursing his drink as she sat down across from him in front of her glass of wine.

"I hope red is all right. I should have asked."

"It's perfect."

"The bartender said it was a local favorite."

She smiled and took a sip. "Delicious."

Greg looked relieved and she felt guilty for trying to avoid him. She liked Greg. He'd been a good boss. Being engaged to Amanda must be horrible, let alone actually planning to go through with the wedding. Is that what he wanted to talk about?

"So you must be getting excited," she said. At his confused look, she added, "The wedding."

"Oh yes, the wedding. How could I forget that? Amanda reminds me daily if not hourly." His smile didn't reach his eyes.

She actually considered reminding him that he didn't have to go through with it, but smartly took a sip of her wine instead.

"That's kind of what I want to talk to you about," Greg said and Charlie groaned inwardly.

"I'm afraid I know nothing about planning weddings, if you're looking for advice," she joked.

He smiled as if to say he wasn't that easily fooled. "You must wonder why I'm marrying her."

Could this conversation get any more uncomfortable? She feared it could. She shook her head, trying to think of what to say to that.

"I know you and Amanda haven't gotten along all that well," he said.

She frowned. "I wouldn't say that."

He laughed. "No, you wouldn't. You're too nice. But I'm aware that she's been harder on you than all the other employees."

"She has a lot going on right now with her job, the wedding…" *Her lover.*

"Amanda likes it that way. She says she has to keep busy or she goes crazy. I suspect you're a little like that." His gaze met hers and Charlie quickly shifted her attention to her wine. She didn't want to drink it too quickly, but the sooner she could get out of here…

"I love her. But sometimes I wonder if love is enough," Greg said, staring down into his drink before glancing up at her again, his gaze intent. "This isn't my first rodeo, as they say here in Montana."

"Just because one didn't work out—"

"It's been more than one," he said, catching her gaze and holding it. "I'm sure you heard about the one before you started working at the design company."

She nodded and tried to lighten the mood. "Though I doubt she was really taken away in a straitjacket."

"No, she wasn't, though one of them might have been handy. I haven't had a lot of luck when it comes to women. The first girl I ever kissed gave me a black eye." He laughed. "It's true. I went for years afraid of girls. Then I had a string of bad dates until I found The One." He got a faraway look in his eye for a moment, then grimaced. "With her, it turned out even worse than you can imagine."

Charlie squirmed, not wanting to hear any of this.

He took a sip of his drink. "I'm making you uncomfortable."

She wasn't about to deny it.

"I like you, Charlie. You're the one person who might understand why I'm going to marry Amanda even though I know…"

Her heart seized up in her chest for a moment.

"She isn't perfect."

"Who is?" Charlie said and took another drink of her wine instead of doing what she really wanted to, which was run.

SHEP COULDN'T BELIEVE what he'd just seen. First Charlie got a call, then ducked into a bar. Her boss came out of their office and went after her, ducking into the same bar Charlie went into. He didn't think that left much doubt about the interpretation.

The two of them were meeting at the bar. It appeared part of a plan, starting with the phone call. This was unbelievable. She'd told him that Greg was engaged to Amanda, the insanely jealous office manager who allegedly put something in Charlie's food to make not just her ill but Greg as well. Knowing how jealous Amanda was, why would Charlie meet Greg in a bar so close to their office? What was he saying? Why would Charlie meet him at all?

Moving across the street so he could watch the entrance, he waited, half afraid the two might have been followed by the unbalanced fiancée. But Amanda didn't appear, fortunately. Was that the way Charlie and Greg had planned it?

He knew he was jumping to conclusions. Charlie had

Daniel. Greg had Amanda. Did Daniel suspect Charlie and Greg had a relationship outside of the office? Amanda apparently seemed to think so. Was it true?

Maybe there was a perfectly good explanation for this. And yet as the minutes passed, Charlie didn't reappear and neither did her boss.

Finally, unable to take it any longer, Shep crossed the slushy street. It had been snowing all day. Huge lacy flakes drifted down to stick to any and everything as he reached the front of the bar. Christmastime in Montana, he grumbled, feeling like Scrooge.

His boots were soaked by the time he reached the front door of the bar. He walked slowly past, looking in through the window, hoping he wasn't spotted. But neither Charlie or Greg noticed. They seemed to be deep in conversation at a back booth. As he watched, her boss reached over and placed a hand on hers.

Shep swore under his breath. There were times when he would have said he knew Charlie better than any person on earth. Right now wasn't one of them. What was she doing? How had he missed this?

Because he'd been busy trying to find out why she was seeing Lindy. Why someone had defaced a doll that looked like her and left it on her doorstep. Why someone had given her a dead mouse. Why someone had doctored her dessert to make her so ill.

The last two incidents could have been Amanda, especially if she was as jealous as Charlie said. He wondered what the woman would do if she knew that her fiancé and Charlie were meeting at a bar on a workday afternoon, but he pushed that ugly thought away.

He reminded himself what he was doing here in Bozeman. It had nothing to do with Charlie's love life. This had everything to do with finding out who the Lindy look-alike was and why she was stalking Charlie.

So where did that leave him? Standing outside a bar in the snow feeling like a fool.

GREG REACHED OVER and put his hand on hers. He looked as if he was going to bare his soul to her.

"I need to ask you something," Charlie said, desperately wanting to change the subject before he did.

He seemed surprised. "Anything."

She took her hand back. "Amanda said something—"

"Oh, great. Something mean, I'm sure."

"No, she said you had another design company before this one."

Greg nodded. "She told you that she worked for me there. I suppose you think it's silly that I hoped to keep our relationship before coming here a secret. I should have known better than to think Amanda could keep anything to herself. I thought my employees wouldn't be comfortable with me bringing my girlfriend in as office manager. But that's exactly what I did. Foolish on my part in so many ways."

"No, that wasn't my question actually. Amanda mentioned that you hired a headhunter to see if I was interested in coming to work for you rather than contacting me directly."

He took a drink, licked his full lips and then smiled at her. "Dear Amanda." He shook his head as if amused. "I did. I hired someone to find me the best and the brightest. I believe that's the way it's done in business nowadays. I had seen your work and wondered if you'd be interested. But I hired everyone through the service – not just you."

"So I wasn't the only one?"

Greg laughed. "Is that what she told you? But if that's

what she believes, it could explain her animosity toward you from the beginning. I'm sorry."

"It's all right." Charlie felt a wave of relief wash over her. It hadn't just been her. "I can handle Amanda."

He chuckled. "I wish *I* could."

Charlie downed the rest of her wine and looked pointedly at her phone. "I didn't realize it was so late."

Greg sighed, clearly disappointed. "Yes, you have Tara's shower. After that you probably have a date."

She didn't, but she said nothing as she got to her feet, feeling as if she'd dodged a bullet.

"We'll have to take this up some other time."

She hoped not. "We can talk anytime. You know where to find me Monday through Friday." She chuckled. A joke, but maybe he got the subtle message.

"This isn't something we can talk about at work. Don't worry. I had something else I wanted to tell you but it can hold. For now."

Was it as ominous as it sounded? Whatever Greg had wanted to tell her, she'd derailed him—at least for now. She just hoped he didn't want to take her into his confidence and go so far as ask her if she thought he should marry Amanda. That was the last place she wanted to be with her boss.

Fortunately she'd turned the conversation and was now going to make her exit. She didn't want her boss discussing his love life with her. She'd just have to be sure she never gave him another opportunity.

"Have a nice evening," he said and seemed to settle in as he ordered another drink.

"You, too. Thank you for the wine." Charlie walked out, telling herself she couldn't let this happen again. She would keep her distance from Amanda and Greg and their problems. She already knew too much as it was.

WHEN CHARLIE CAME through the door, Shep had barely reached the apartment ahead of her. He'd seen her leaving the bar and had taken a shortcut, moving fast so he'd be there when she arrived.

He hoped she would tell him about meeting her boss at the bar. Not that it had anything to do with him—except for the fact that he needed to believe that she was being honest with him about everything else. Not that she owed him anything.

But if she would hide a relationship with her boss, then how could he trust she was telling him the truth about Lindy and the rest?

"Hi," she said, looking exhausted. "Sorry I had to cut you off so quickly on the phone earlier. It was one of those kinds of days."

"Not sure I know what those kinds of days are," he said.

She slipped out of her boots before she said, "Just busy and odd. I forgot all about my best friend's baby shower." She shook her head, clearly disappointed in herself. "Tara. I don't think I've told you about her. She and I are desk-mates. I wouldn't be able to survive the place without her. I also forgot her present, so now I'm running late, but I decided I couldn't go without my gift." She started for her bedroom and stopped. "I'm sorry, earlier, you said you had good news?"

"It can wait."

"No, tell me as long as it's quick."

He nodded, realizing she wasn't going to tell him about her and Greg at the bar. He quickly related what Paul Wagner had told him. He'd been excited earlier, now not so much.

Charlie took the news without much enthusiasm either. "So Lindy had a key and let herself in the back door."

"Which proves that you weren't responsible. She was never truly locked out of the house. She could have come in at any time, and she did. She was still alive at that point and able to stay in the house where it was safe, but apparently she chose to go back out."

Charlie shook her head. "She went back out to replace the key and was attacked. Shep, you're splitting hairs. It always comes back to the fact that I locked her out. She was out there screaming and carrying on and attracted a killer. If she hadn't been locked out..."

He held up his hands in surrender. "You weren't responsible. I don't know how many times I have to say that. I thought you'd be more excited about the news. I'm sorry. So tell me about your afternoon. You sounded busy even before you remembered the shower."

Charlie went into her bedroom and came back out with a wrapped present. "I really don't feel like getting into it. Do you mind? I don't have time right now anyway. The good news is that I didn't see Lindy and I'm assuming you didn't find anything new on my doorstep?"

"No." He now wished he'd said something about stopping by her office, seeing her with Daniel, seeing her go into the bar and her boss coming in after her. He'd waited out in the snow until she came out. Alone. When he'd seen that she was headed toward the apartment, he'd beat her home.

Shep told himself that she probably felt it was none of his business. It wasn't, since it had nothing to do with Lindy or the past or the stalking. He reminded himself that he was only here to solve this problem for her and then it would be time for him to get back to his own life.

He watched Charlie pull on her boots to head out to her party. Then he walked to the door, pulled on his own coat and followed her, afraid of what other secrets Charlie might be keeping from him.

CHAPTER FOURTEEN

A<small>FTER HE SAW</small> Charlie safely to the restaurant where the shower was being held, Shep tracked down the boy Lindy had argued with at school all those years ago.

Austin Fletcher worked as a car salesman on the west end of town. He didn't look all that different from his senior photo in the yearbook from fifteen years ago.

He'd been a big boy. He was now a large man, thickly built with a head of blond hair, intense blue eyes and a cleft chin.

While striking, his looks were just short of handsome. When he saw Shep looking at a used truck in the lot, he came over to give him a toothy smile and a strong handshake.

"This is a nice one. I know the guy who owned it. Can't go wrong with this truck, but I do have some rebates right now. I can put you in a new one if you're interested."

"I want to ask you about Lindy Parker."

It took Fletch—that was how he'd introduced himself—a couple of moments to change gears. "Who?"

"Lindy Parker, the girl who was murdered your senior year in high school."

"That had to be—"

"Fifteen years ago," Shep said, helping him with the math. "I heard you had a crush on her."

Fletch let out a nervous laugh. "I don't know where you

heard that but…" He shook his head, seeming at a loss for words.

"But you knew her."

"Sure. We went to the same school."

"Her sister remembers the two of you arguing."

"Her sister?" Fletch said, frowning. "That dark-haired girl?"

"Charlie. She said you grabbed Lindy's arm and the two of you had words. What was that about?"

Fletch looked around as if wanting desperately to escape. "Are you serious? That was so long ago. You expect me to remember?"

"Did you see Lindy outside of school?"

The man blinked. "What did her sister say?"

"How about you tell me the truth?"

Fletch shifted on his feet. "Are you some kind of cop?"

"I teach middle school math, but I'm a friend of Charlie's. I'm just looking for answers. Anything you say is between the two of us. I'm trying to get a handle on what Lindy was like and why someone wanted her dead."

"I thought some vagrant passing through town killed her?"

"So what was Lindy like?" Shep asked. And waited.

Fletch shook his head again and looked toward the Bridger Mountains. They were white with glistening snow in the fading twilight. "She was different."

Shep continued to wait as patiently as he could. The car salesman had a gift of gab when he was trying to make a deal. Otherwise, it was as if he thought he had to pay for every word he uttered.

"She was a…challenge," Fletch said, avoiding his gaze.

"A challenge you won?"

It took Fletch a moment before he shifted to look back

at Shep. "We met a few times after school down by the creek, but not much happened. She was a tease. The more she thought you wanted her, the more she held back."

"That sounds like a motive for murder."

Fletch took a step back. "Not me. I wasn't even in town the night she died."

"You can prove that?"

"I can. I was at an away game. I threw the winning pass that night. It's funny. I was actually thinking about her on the way back on the bus. I wondered if that pass would get me anywhere with her. The bus got a flat and we didn't get back into town until like three in the morning. I heard about her murder the next day."

"Who do you think killed her?" Shep asked, disappointed.

"If not a vagrant?" Fletch scratched his head. "I guess someone she messed with like she did me. Someone who was tired of putting up with it."

"There were others she led on?"

Fletch laughed. "Lindy didn't just tempt boys. She liked to make our male teachers squirm. She was ruthless, especially with the teachers closer to her age."

"What teachers?"

THE MOMENT CHARLIE walked in the door of the restaurant where the shower was being held, her friend snagged her and drew her aside.

"Where have you been?" Tara demanded. "Amanda is in a really bad mood. I thought she might stab herself with one of the cake-cutting knives."

"Sorry I couldn't get here sooner. Is everyone already here?"

"Not to worry. We still have a few stragglers and

Amanda didn't like the way they arranged the tables so she's making everyone move them. How did things go with Daniel?"

"Not well," Charlie said, hearing Amanda barking out orders in the other room. "I... Never mind, today is about you and your baby shower."

Tara rolled her eyes. "I was hoping you would tell me that Greg wasn't going through with the marriage and that's why she's moping. I could use a day brightener."

"Why would you think Greg would share that with me?"

"Because I heard from Connie that he left the building after you did with Daniel." Connie was an artist who sat closest to the exit.

Charlie felt a headache forming at the back of her skull. She and Daniel had just been outside talking for a minute... Greg must have been watching. Then he'd followed her to the bar.

"He's taken quite an interest in you," Tara said.

Charlie groaned. Was that what the drink in the bar had been all about? She wanted to sink into the floor. "Did Amanda know he followed me outside?"

"Apparently she tried to tag along, but he waved her back."

Mystery solved, Charlie thought. "She thinks I want Greg."

Tara's eyes widened in alarm. "Why would you want Greg? You already have two men you don't know what to do with."

Just then Amanda saw them and headed their way.

"Watch your back," Tara whispered.

"I'm doing this for you," Charlie whispered back. "You and that baby."

The shower was actually fun. Tara got a lot of great

baby gifts and seemed to enjoy herself. Amanda got drunk and became more morose, sitting in the corner by herself.

So, all in all, Charlie chalked up the party as a success. But she wasn't pushing her luck. Once things started breaking up, she grabbed Tara, told her goodbye and hightailed it for the door. She was determined to avoid Amanda at all costs.

What had Greg been thinking, coming after her, following her to the bar? She couldn't care less about his intentions. Was he trying to get her killed?

THERE WAS STILL TIME before the baby shower would probably end, so Shep decided to talk to one of the teachers Fletch had told him about. Larry "Mac" McCormick taught English at the high school. Like Shep, he was out on Christmas break and easy to find. He lived in a cottage-style house on Cooper Park not far from Montana State University.

Mac answered the door on the second knock. He was holding a Christmas cookie in his free hand and was half turned, still talking to a child. Behind him came a cacophony of young voices, a roar broken only by a woman's holler.

Mac laughed at whatever was going on in the kitchen as he held the door open and turned to Shep. "Sorry, we're making Christmas cookies."

The woman, whom Shep could not see, called that *she* was making cookies and that her husband was eating them.

"What kind of rule is it that you have to decorate at least six before you get to eat one?" the teacher asked him.

"Very unfair," Shep said.

"Exactly." The man seemed to take him in just as Shep was doing the same. Mac was a nice-looking man of about forty with a great smile and two deep dimples.

"This is probably not a good time," Shep said. "But I need to ask you about Lindy Parker. She was—"

"I remember Lindy," Mac said and turned back toward to the kitchen to tell his wife they would be in his office and would be back soon. With that, he stepped out onto the porch with Shep. "It's around the side."

They followed a shoveled path around to a small building. Mac opened the door and entered what was partly an office, but mostly a man cave complete with recliners and a huge flat screen TV that took up one wall. A very small desk and chair had been pushed to a corner.

"Why do you want to know about Lindy?" Mac asked. "Did you know her?"

"I'm friends with her sister."

"Charlie." Mac smiled. "Smart girl. Not that Lindy wasn't." He dropped into one of the recliners and waited for Shep to join him. "You're looking into her murder?"

"I am. What can you tell me about her?"

"Typical seventeen-year-old. Smart, but lazy when it came to doing schoolwork. Troubled." Mac shrugged. "I see enough of them that I can spot it."

"Troubled how?"

"Just going by what I saw, I'd say it had to do with her mother. I only met her once, new marriage, new husband, new town. Lindy didn't adapt well to change."

Shep found it interesting how Mac had sized up the situation. As a teacher, Shep often saw troubled kids. Usually meeting the parents answered any questions he had.

"I heard she might have led on boys in her class."

Mac nodded. "That doesn't surprise me."

"Did she come on to you?"

The man laughed. "I teach high school English. There are a lot of raging hormones out there. Lindy was just learning to use her sexuality. I'm not susceptible to teenage charm. But I would imagine she drove boys her age crazy."

"Was Fletcher in your class?"

Mac nodded. "Was he one of them?"

"You never saw him and Lindy together?"

"Fletch had his choice of high school girls, but I guess I can see him going after Lindy. I would imagine she didn't give him the time of day so he might have liked the challenge. Poor fool."

"So you really weren't one of the poor fools?"

Mac could have taken the question badly, but he didn't. He smiled. "I was twenty-five, green, scared, right out of college and not sure I could do this. I was terrified of all of them, especially the girls. High school age students can be tough on you."

Shep chuckled to himself, thinking that middle school students could be as well.

"But I found I loved teaching and that the students were as scared as I was. There are always those students you can't reach. But the ones you can? The ones whose eyes light up when they start finding meaning in the written word? They make it all worthwhile."

"Lindy?"

"Unfortunately, she wasn't one of them. She pretended not to get it for attention. It wasn't that she wasn't smart. She just didn't care."

"She didn't come on to you."

Mac laughed. "Of course she did. But even if I hadn't been newly married and her teacher, I wasn't interested. Lindy was trouble. I felt sorry for her, but there wasn't much I could do to help her."

Shep rose from his chair. "Thanks for your time."

"Thank you for stopping by. I really suck at frosting

Christmas cookies so you saved me." Mac grinned. "You should have at least one cookie before you take off. You said you're a friend of Charlie's," he said as he got to his feet. "She was one of my better students."

"She's doing okay."

"I'm glad to hear that. If you're going to see her, take her a cookie, too." Mac led the way to the back door where he had his wife wrap up a couple of giant cookies.

"I hope you find her killer," Mac said as he handed Shep the package. "Her death must have been hard on Charlie."

"It was."

CHARLIE RUSHED TOWARD the restaurant exit, determined to escape as quickly as possible. She threw open the door, practically throwing herself out as well, and crashed into a woman who'd apparently been standing there waiting for someone. It wasn't until she looked into the woman's face that Charlie realized who this woman had been waiting for. *Her.*

With a jolt of horror, she found herself face-to-face with her dead stepsister.

Charlie was actually holding on to Lindy's arm to steady them both and looking directly into the blue eyes she still saw in her nightmares.

The shock of it immobilized her.

Lindy pushed her off and rushed into the crowd of Christmas shoppers. Charlie stared after her, mouth agape. Caught so completely off guard, for a moment she didn't even realize what she was holding in her hand—the blue scarf Lindy had been wearing. She must have grabbed hold of the scarf as Lindy pushed away from her.

The woman *had* been Lindy. There was no doubt. No

ghost. Flesh and blood. Lindy was alive—as impossible as it seemed. And Charlie was holding her scarf.

Only seconds had passed. She could still see Lindy making her way through the crowd. Maybe it made no sense, but the one person who could provide the answers wasn't going to get away. Not this time.

Charlie started after her. She'd always been faster than Lindy when they were girls. She would catch her.

But before she could get two steps away, someone grabbed the sleeve of her coat and swung her around.

She found herself looking into Amanda's angry face. The woman reeked of alcohol and seemed to be having a hard time standing without holding on to Charlie's sleeve. Charlie tried to free herself from Amanda's death grip on her coat sleeve. She was still shaken, not just from seeing Lindy, but actually colliding with her. That surprised look in Lindy's eyes… She hadn't planned on that happening either.

"I want to talk to you, bitch," Amanda slurred, grabbing hold of her again. "Now!"

"Not a chance in hell," Charlie said, and tore Amanda's hand from her sleeve. Turning, she hurried down the sidewalk, still hoping she might be able to catch up to Lindy.

But in the few blocks to her apartment, she didn't see Lindy again.

Thanks to Amanda's clawlike hold on her coat sleeve, she'd missed her chance. Lindy had gotten away. Again.

But in Charlie's hand was the scarf—Lindy's favorite. She stopped trying to make sense out of it as she reached the steps to her apartment. Her heart was thundering in her chest. *Lindy was alive.*

CHAPTER FIFTEEN

"You do realize it couldn't have possibly been Lindy," Shep said reasonably after Charlie had finished telling him what had happened.

"I have her scarf to prove it," she argued.

He'd bagged the scarf, hoping the lab would be able to get DNA from it. Now Charlie paced her small apartment, angry and upset—mostly at him. He'd never seen her this worked up.

"I was within inches of her face. I looked into those blue eyes. I was holding on to her. I have her scarf. Her favorite scarf, by the way." She took a frustrated breath. "I was so close that I could almost feel her heart beating. She was... real. Solid. Flesh and blood."

"I've never doubted that whoever you saw was a real person—just not Lindy."

"It *was* her though," Charlie cried. "They were wrong about who died behind the house that night. It couldn't possibly have been her. I just saw her and she's alive. Come on, Shep, I haven't seen the autopsy photos, but I heard that she was brutalized," she said. "Isn't it possible—"

"That someone else was killed behind your house and Lindy just took off and has now come back? Charlie... I know what you think you saw—"

"I know what I *saw*. How do you explain it?" she demanded, hands on her hips.

She looked so damned cute that he almost laughed. But as stirred up as she was, he didn't dare. "I can't explain it yet."

When she'd come in the apartment door, she'd rushed into his arms. She'd been trembling. He'd held her close and breathed in…perfume. Only Charlie didn't wear perfume. But maybe her friend Tara did. Or maybe…

He could still smell the scent on his shirt. "Smell this," he said, moving to her and holding out the collar of his shirt.

"Seriously?" she asked, as if it was some kind of trick.

"Just smell it."

She did and stepped back abruptly, eyes wide. "That's Lindy's favorite perfume."

"I had a feeling it was. You said she seemed to be waiting outside the restaurant for you. She must have followed you there. What do you know about Lindy's extended family?"

"Nothing. Neither Kat or Lindy ever mentioned any relatives."

"I was just thinking she might have had a cousin who looks enough like her to fool you when you had only got a few seconds to really study her."

Charlie shook her head, getting more angry with him as if he was only trying to distract her. "The cousin would have to be a dead ringer for her."

She stopped pacing to stare at him. He saw the change in her as if she'd suddenly shifted gears. "When I told you about Amanda confronting me outside the restaurant, you got a funny look on your face. Why were you in such a weird mood earlier?"

"Now look who's changing the subject." Shep chewed at his cheek for a moment, studying her. "Are we going to be honest with each other now?"

"I thought we were," she said slowly.

"I saw you get a call after fighting with Daniel. A few minutes later you walked down the street and into a bar. Your boss followed you."

"Wait, you spied on me?"

"When I called you, I was already at your office. I was excited about the news I had to give you. I saw you take a call and then Greg came out of the building and followed you right down to the bar."

"You thought we were what? *Hooking up?*" she demanded.

"That's definitely how it looked."

Charlie shook her head. "I thought you knew me better than that."

"So did I."

She swore, eyes narrowed. Flames could have shot from those dark depths. "The call, for your information, was from Tara, my friend from work, asking me to come early to the shower because Amanda was headed there. She couldn't bear spending any more time with her than possible. I was trying to decide if I had time to come back here for the gift I left here since I'd forgotten the shower completely or just go and save Tara. I stepped into the bar to get out of the snow and shoppers to think."

"Things didn't go well with Daniel."

She glared at him. "You said you were there, so I don't think I have to tell you how things went."

He nodded sheepishly.

"That's when I happened to see Greg headed in my direction. I stayed in the bar, waiting for him to pass. I had no idea he was following me."

"Why *did* he follow you?"

Charlie sighed. "I thought it was just a coincidence. He insisted I have one drink with him. I tried to get out of it, but he knew I had plenty of time before the shower. When I told him I didn't, that I needed to come back here for the gift, he offered to come with me. So it seemed having a drink with him was preferable to bringing him back here."

"It doesn't sound like he gave you much choice," Shep said. "Whatever he wanted to talk to you about must have been important."

"His bad choices in women? I have no idea what he was leading up to. I changed the subject, finished my wine and got out of there." She shrugged. "Unfortunately, you weren't the only one to see Greg come after me. Tara said that Amanda saw him, which probably explained her rotten mood at the shower. I hope he doesn't try to talk to me again about whatever it is."

"Sounds like he might want your advice on whether or not to marry Amanda."

She groaned and plopped down on the couch. "That's what I'm worried about. Isn't it bad enough that I have a dead woman stalking me? The last thing I need is to be caught between Amanda and Greg."

"I'm wondering why *Lindy* was waiting for you outside the restaurant," Shep said. "Maybe whoever is behind this didn't get the reaction they'd hoped for from the earlier sightings—or even the doll."

Charlie rolled her eyes, still angry with him for not accepting that the woman she'd seen was the dead Lindy. "I'm more concerned with what she'll do next. We need to find her before she finds me again."

Shep couldn't have felt more inept. "I'm trying to track down as much information as I can, but I have to admit, I'm at a loss. Maybe it's time to turn it over to the police."

"What does the judge say?"

"That the police can't do anything, probably won't take it seriously since there has been no real threat."

"Sounds like we need to do this together," Charlie said.

"You have a job. I'm off right now. You should concentrate on that."

She looked as if she was going to argue so he quickly changed the subject.

"So what are you going to do about Daniel?"

As if on cue, Charlie's phone rang. She took the call in her bedroom.

When she came back out, she was dressed in jeans and a sweater. She'd pulled her hair up and formed a messy ball of it at the nape of her neck. He didn't think she'd ever looked more beautiful.

"I'm meeting Daniel," she said. She headed into the kitchen and poured herself a glass of wine. Turning to him, she offered, "Beer?"

He shook his head. After the argument he'd witnessed, he found it hard to believe she was going out with Daniel. "How did you meet this guy anyway?"

She seemed to hesitate. "In a bar. He said he saw me from across the room and…" She looked up. "You're just going to make fun, aren't you?"

"No." He said it softly, gently. "I'm curious is all, okay?"

"Curious? Or you think he's behind the Lindy sightings? I already told you, I met him several months ago—long before I saw her the first time."

He nodded. "How much does he know about you?"

"If you're asking what I think you are, nothing. I never told him I even had a stepsister. All I've told him is that I lost my parents, ended up in foster care for a while, got into trouble and a judge turned me around."

"He never asked anything specific?"

"No. You're barking up the wrong tree. Daniel isn't behind this."

"And you know that how?"

"I just know it." She let out a frustrated sound. "It's so obvious that you don't like him and you've never even met him."

He knew the wise thing to do was bite his tongue. "I'm not impressed, if that's what you're asking. I think he's all wrong for you."

She laughed. "Really?"

"You want him to be *the* guy, but in your heart, you know better. He's not good enough for you." *Neither is your boss*, he wanted to add. Because he suspected Greg wanted more from Charlie than advice about his love life.

"You realize that you sound...jealous?"

"*Jealous?* The guy's a jerk." He wasn't sure if he was talking about Daniel or Greg or both. "Sorry, but I know one when I see one. I'm just trying to save you from a life of heartache—not that this relationship will last that long."

She glared at him. "How can you say that?"

He stepped to her and took both of her shoulders in his hands. He felt that familiar tingle. "Because ever since I got here, not once have I heard you say that you're crazy in love with him or that you love him at all. I think you want this to be the perfect love story, but you know the truth in your heart. It's why you haven't moved in with him."

CHARLIE COULDN'T BELIEVE THIS. She felt her exhaustion, frustration and anger mix into a dangerous brew. "You come walking in here and within a few days, you know what's right for me?" She opened her mouth to argue that Daniel was the one, but only ended up sputtering, she was so angry. "You know nothing about it or me. And...and what makes you an authority on relationships? From what you've told me, you've had only one and look how it ended."

"I've witnessed enough of them."

"So you aren't in a relationship."

"Not at the moment, but—"

"That's what I thought." She let out a bark of a laugh. "But you've already decided that Daniel is wrong for me based on your vast…experience?"

"I can see that I've upset you."

"You think?" Her cell phone rang. She pulled it out and saw that it was Daniel. "I'll take this in the other room since it is none of your business."

"He's calling to either cancel or ask you to pick up something on your way over to his house for the night," he said after her.

She slammed the door, the sound echoing painfully through the apartment. She heard the man who lived directly downstairs yell a curse. "I was just heading to your place," she said into the phone.

"That's why I called." For a moment she thought he was going to change his mind about her coming over to talk. "I was thinking…"

Charlie held her breath. *Don't let Shep be right.*

"I'm sorry about earlier. Not seeing you, being with you… Well, it's been driving me nuts. So I'm glad you're coming over."

"Me, too," she said, relieved.

"You'll be here soon?"

They only lived a few blocks from each other. She was looking forward to a night away from her apartment and Shep. "I'm on my way."

"Great. Hey, I just had an idea."

Don't let Shep be right.

"Would you mind picking up something for us at that takeout place you like? I've been so busy lately I haven't had a chance to go to the store so there is literally nothing to eat here. I'll call and it will be ready and paid for. Say you don't mind."

Charlie groaned inwardly, before murmuring agreement. She disconnected, angry at herself for not telling him to go get the food himself. But then why should he have to go out in the storm when she was headed that way anyway?

What made her grind her teeth was that Shep had been right. But was he right about why she hadn't moved in with Daniel as well?

She half expected to see Shep grinning when she came out of the bedroom. He'd called it, but then again, he didn't know that.

When she looked at him, she saw that he didn't seem to be pleased about anything this evening. He seemed distracted and out of sorts, which wasn't like him.

She realized that he'd thought the news he'd brought her would exonerate her from Lindy's death. He'd expected her to be happy and finally free of all of it. Shep was trying to help her. She wished she hadn't argued with him about Daniel.

"I'm sorry I snapped at you," she said, only to have him merely nod. "I shouldn't be too late." She headed toward the door for her coat and boots when she saw him get up and start doing the same.

"Where are you going?" she asked as he pulled on his coat.

"I'm going with you."

"What?"

"I told you. I'm not letting you go out in the storm alone."

"I won't be alone. I'll be with my boyfriend."

"Right. Daniel. Unlike you, I'm not sure he *isn't* involved in all this. Even if he isn't, I'm at least walking you to his place."

She shook her head in disbelief. "I told you, he doesn't know anything about my past."

"You don't think he could have done some research on you?"

Charlie groaned. "What are you going to do? Stand outside his apartment house?"

"Don't worry, you won't see me."

But she would know he was there, she thought angrily as she watched him reach for his Stetson. Once a ranch boy, always a ranch boy, she thought.

"Ready?" he asked as he snugged the Stetson down on his thick, dark hair. "Don't want to keep lover boy waiting."

She growled under her breath.

"I forgot to ask you," he said as she buttoned her coat. "Was your boss sick from the mousse, too?"

"You know, I never got a chance to ask him," she said. "But Amanda told me he'd called in sick and he hadn't come to work until the afternoon."

"Sounds like with the day you had there was no chance to ask him," Shep said sarcastically.

She shot him a look. "It didn't come up at the bar, okay?" His tone made it clear he was still upset with her. He couldn't possibly think that she was interested in Greg.

But unless she'd lost her sixth sense, it appeared that Shep was jealous not just of Daniel—but Greg.

CHARLIE ARRIVED AT Daniel's house with the food. She'd walked the four blocks through the falling snow. She knew Shep was somewhere behind her but she didn't turn around to look. If he wanted to get cold and wet, far be it from her to stop him.

She'd made a decision. After a very long day, she was ready to tell Daniel the truth. About Lindy. About Shep. She couldn't keep this from him any longer.

Common sense told her to wait until she wasn't so emotional, so exhausted, so over everything. But in her weakened state, she knew she wouldn't be able to stop herself.

"Here, let me help you," Daniel said as she stepped through the front door of his apartment. He took the food into the small kitchen while she shrugged out of her coat and boots. She'd noticed that his roommate Jason's car was gone, which meant she and Daniel would be alone.

"Baby," he said, stepping to her and kissing her. "You're nose is as cold as a snowman's. I should have gone for the food," he said as he planted kisses down the slope of her throat to her collarbone. "You're too good to me. How can I make it up to you?" He drew back to meet her gaze. "I'm not all that hungry yet. I was thinking—"

She knew exactly what he was thinking. "There's something I need to tell you first."

He froze. "You're not…"

"Pregnant?" She shook her head. "Could we just sit down?"

With a big sigh, he led the way into the living room and dropped into one of the recliners angled at the huge television taking up one wall. There was some kind of game on.

"Sit with me," she said, taking a spot on the couch. "Could you turn off the TV?"

He shoved himself up, found the remote and muted the television before coming over to the couch. She tried not to let his moaning and groaning irritate her. "I've never told you about my past."

"If this is about some other boyfriend, can't it wait? The food is getting cold."

Now he was worried about the food getting cold? "I had a stepsister named Lindy. She was murdered."

His eyes widened. At least now she had his attention.

"I've always blamed myself. She and I were fighting that night and I locked her out of the house. I'm not sure exactly what happened, just that she was screaming to be let back in and then she wasn't. I opened the door. She wasn't there. I left the door unlocked and went back upstairs. I heard someone come in. I just assumed it was her... Now I realize that it could have been the killer. That he'd come into the house for me—after he'd killed her."

"Whoa. That's horrible."

She nodded. "The only thing that saved me is that a policeman stopped by. There'd been an accident. My father and stepmother had gone off the road on their way back from a party. I don't know if they got a desperate call from Lindy when she came back into the house or if they were just headed home on their own. They'd been drinking and my father was probably driving too fast.

"Anyway, my father was killed. My stepmother was hospitalized after she was found unconscious downstream later. I was fourteen and taken by social services to be put into a foster home. I think they assumed my stepmother would take me after that. She never did."

Daniel sat back shaking his head. "Wow, Charlie, I'm so sorry. That's terrible. Thanks for sharing that. I know it must have been tough."

She could tell that he was relieved to have the story over. He reached for her, since he still had only one thing on his mind.

"That's only part of it," she said, moving so he couldn't

draw her to him. She saw impatience flicker across his expression.

"There's more?"

"The more part is why I've been putting you off lately when you called or wanted to come up to my apartment. I've been seeing Lindy, my dead stepsister."

"Seeing her?" he asked slowly.

"I saw her standing across the street a couple of times. Then I found my favorite doll destroyed on my doorstep."

"Your doll?"

"From when I was fourteen. My father had given it to me. It was a collector's edition. Anyway, today I ran into Lindy—literally. I looked into her eyes. It was her."

"So…she's *not* dead? This is good news, right?"

"I don't know. But I have someone looking into what is going on. He's an old friend from a long time ago."

"Like a PI?"

"Something like that. He's staying with me."

"That's cool," Daniel said and reached again to put his arm around her. "So we're good?"

She shook off his arm again and stood. "I don't think you understand. Someone is *stalking* me. My dead stepsister. And my boss at work… I think he has a crush on me and his fiancée is insanely jealous. So there is nothing cool about what I'm going through right now."

He sighed heavily. "What do you want me to do? You said you've got some PI looking into it. I'm sure he'll figure it out. Are you afraid I'll think you're crazy or something? I mean your story is rather unbelievable, but…hey. If you say you saw a dead woman…" He shrugged. "Now can we—"

"No, we can't," she said, hating that she was seeing Daniel through Shep's eyes. Daniel was just an overgrown kid who made a living playing video games. Who only thought about beer, food and sex and not always in that order. "This isn't working for me."

Daniel threw himself back on the couch as he swore. "I saw this coming. You've been acting so weird lately."

"I just told you why I've been acting so…weird, as you call it."

His gaze took her in for a moment. "I said I'm sorry. Whatever is going on will pass so don't blow it out of proportion just because you're upset about this stepsister of yours. You and I are good together." He stood up and moved toward her. "Maybe if you'd let me show you…"

"Forget it. I'm done." She started toward the kitchen just as his roommate came in, stomping snow off his shoes.

"Oops, looks like I came back too early?" Jason asked and laughed. He worked at the same video game company as Daniel. "Or maybe I was gone just long enough?"

Charlie wanted to slap that sneer off Jason's face. She hadn't liked him from the first. *Oh, you'll get used to him. He likes you*, Daniel had said. *He's always asking about you.*

She pulled on her coat and boots and started to leave when she saw the bag of food she'd brought still sitting on the kitchen table. Storming over, she grabbed it up and headed for the door.

"She's taking the food?" she heard Jason say. "Now that's cold. You must have really pissed her off."

"Shut up, Jas," Daniel said.

She slammed the door behind her and stepped out into the falling snow. She hadn't gone but a few feet when Shep fell in beside her.

She glared over at him. "What if I hadn't left until morning?"

He shrugged.

"You were that sure I wasn't staying long?"

"What's in the sack?"

She shoved it at him. "Dinner. On Daniel."

Out of the corner of her eye she saw Shep smile. "Even better."

CHAPTER SIXTEEN

SHEP WATCHED CHARLIE help herself to another pulled pork slider as she wailed, "You must think I'm the biggest fool on the planet." They were curled up on the couch, Friday night dinner spread across the coffee table, a home remodeling show on the television and a bottle of wine half gone.

"Do not say, I told you so," she warned him before he could comment.

He merely nodded and let her talk as he dipped French fries into ranch dressing.

"You were right," she concluded. "He was just this big, overgrown boy who thinks fart jokes are funny. How did I not see that sooner?" She groaned and pushed the last of the sliders in his direction along with her remaining fries.

Pouring herself more wine, she tucked her bare feet under her and snuggled into the corner of the couch facing him. "You still don't think I saw Lindy."

"Truthfully, I don't know what to think. I called the judge and he had someone pick up the scarf to take to the lab. Apparently he is pulling some strings until the time when we have to call in law enforcement. I noticed there were numerous strands of blond hair caught in the fabric."

"If they're Lindy's, then she's alive."

He couldn't bring himself to go that far. Lindy was dead. The police wouldn't have misidentified the body. But if it hadn't been Lindy who was found murdered behind the house, then who was it? Some random blond girl passing by?

They watched the television show for a while, making fun of the couple arguing over the size of the master bathroom.

"It's really over with you and Daniel?" he asked after a while.

"Don't sound so happy about it," she said and sipped her wine, glowering at him over the rim of her glass.

"I'm not happy. I'm sorry. Truly. But he wasn't right for you."

"And you are?"

He let out a nervous laugh. "I didn't know I was an option on the table."

Her cheeks flamed and she looked away. "Don't pay any attention to me. I don't know what I'm saying. Grief and wine. A bad mix."

"Grief?"

"I'm burying my relationship with Daniel." She started as her cell phone rang. He worried it was Daniel coming to his senses.

Charlie answered it. "She is? No, I'll be right there." She disconnected. "It's my friend from work, Tara. She's in labor. Her husband is taking her to the hospital now. I promised I would be there."

Shep put down his wineglass. "Let's take my truck. You can navigate."

Just as they entered the hospital, Shep got a call from the judge. "I'll find you," he said and stepped back outside.

"I just heard back from the lab," the judge said without preamble. "There were two sets of fingerprints on the doll, but only the one set was in the system."

Shep waited impatiently for a few moments before he said, *"And?"*

The judge cleared his throat. "The clearest set, the one in the system, belonged to Lindy Parker."

Shep couldn't contain his shock. "How is that possible?"

"She must have handled the doll."

"She's been dead fifteen years."

"Because of the surface material, the prints obviously stayed. Fingerprints can last on some surfaces as long as forty years."

Shep knew that was the reasonable explanation, but it wasn't going to be one that Charlie accepted. She was convinced that Lindy was alive.

"And the other prints?" Shep asked.

"Your guess is as good as mine until we have a suspect to compare them with."

CHARLIE WAS TIRED after a long emotional night, but still in awe on the ride back to her apartment. "It was so…incredible. I've never seen anything like that before. Did I tell you that Tara is going to name her daughter after me?"

Shep chuckled. "You mentioned that."

"I was holding Tara's hand when the baby came into the world. The doctor placed the baby girl on Tara's chest." Charlie looked over at him. "You should have seen it. I cried harder than the baby. She is just so…perfect. So small and so beautiful."

She took a breath and frowned, remembering he'd gotten a call just as they arrived at the hospital. "Did the judge call you earlier?"

He nodded and glanced over at her.

"It's bad news, right?"

"Not necessarily," he said without looking at her. He

sounded irritated that bad news had been her first thought. Wait until he got to really know her. "The lab found prints on the doll."

Charlie held her breath as she stared at him. Clearly he didn't want to tell her, which told her that she already knew. "Whose were they?"

"Lindy's."

Expecting nothing less, she still gasped.

"Now, don't go jumping to conclusions," he warned quickly.

How could she not?

"The judge said because of the doll's surface material, the prints must have been on there from fifteen years ago."

Charlie let out a snort. "And you believe that?"

"The judge told me that fingerprints can last up to forty years on some surfaces if not disturbed."

She found that hard to believe, but if the judge said it was true… "But the doll had been disturbed."

He seemed to ignore that. "There was another set of prints, but they didn't come up in the national AFIS system, he said."

Charlie fell a chill rattle up her spine. "I guess we'll know when the blond hair on the scarf comes back, won't we?"

Shep said nothing as he parked the pickup in front of her apartment and they got out. Her earlier euphoria hadn't dimmed with the news. Lindy had touched her doll. But when?

SHEP SENSED SOMETHING was wrong the moment Charlie started to unlock the door to her apartment and he saw the fresh marks in the wood near the lock.

"Don't move," he whispered close to her ear and quickly stepped past her to open the door.

It didn't take but a minute to search the small apartment. The place had obviously been broken into but the intruder was long gone. He could guess what the person had been looking for. The scarf.

He came back into the living room to find Charlie where he'd left her.

"It was Lindy," she said. "I can smell her perfume." Shep caught the familiar scent as well. "She was looking for the scarf."

"*Someone* was looking for the scarf," he said, only able to agree to a point.

Charlie sighed and took off her coat to hang it by the door. "At least she didn't make too big of a mess." She began picking up the coats that had been thrown on the floor by the coat rack.

"I'll do this if you want to see to the bedroom since it's so late," Shep said. The mess in the living room and kitchen weren't bad. Whoever had done this had also emptied out all the dresser drawers in the bedroom and ransacked the closet.

A while later, she came out of the bedroom saying she was finished. There was a knock at the door and they exchanged looks. Daniel? She motioned for him to go into the bedroom as she headed for the door.

Shep was wondering why he still had to hide when he heard Charlie say through the locked door, "Who is it?"

"It's me. Amanda. I have to talk to you."

He looked back at Charlie from the bedroom door. She groaned and motioned him away before she opened the apartment door. Like before, he left the door ajar so he could listen. If this was the woman who'd doctored Charlie's food at the restaurant, he wasn't about to leave them alone in the same room without hearing what was going on.

"Amanda?" Charlie said. "Do you realize what time it is?"

"I've been waiting for you to get home," Amanda snapped, like it was Charlie's fault she was at her door so late.

"What are you doing here?"

"We have to talk."

"It's the middle of the night. Can't it wait until Monday?"

"No."

He got a glimpse of the blonde forcing her way in before he stepped back out of sight, still leaving the bedroom door ajar.

"WHAT IS SO important that it can't wait?" Charlie said, taking a step back as Amanda forced her way in. "I just got back from the hospital. Tara had her baby. A girl." She closed the door and turned to find Amanda standing in the middle of the apartment, taking it all in with a critical eye. Clearly she wasn't impressed with what she saw.

"I figured you were out with one of your boyfriends," the woman said, completely ignoring the part about Tara and her baby girl. "One is apparently not enough for you."

Charlie shot a glance toward the partially open bedroom door before crossing her arms over her chest and demanding, "What is it you want, Amanda?"

"Something is going on with Greg, but you wouldn't know anything about that, would you?"

"No, I wouldn't."

Amanda made a rude noise. "I know about the two of you."

"There is no two of us. Greg's my boss. That's it."

"Then how do you explain the two of you in the bar down the street from the office?"

How *did* she explain that? "If you must know, I'd forgotten Tara's baby shower gift at my apartment. I stepped into the bar to get out of the snow to decide whether to go home for the gift or just go to the shower. It was that simple. Apparently Greg came out of our building and saw me. He insisted I have a glass of wine before going back out in the storm."

Amanda sneered at her. "What did you talk about?"

"Nothing exciting. I asked him if he hired a headhunter to get me to come to work for him. He said he did—along with others besides me. We talked about my latest client and my presentation." At least she thought they might have. She wasn't about to tell Amanda that Greg had been in a peculiar mood and had seemed to want to talk about his past—and possibly present—relationships.

Amanda looked hurt. "He didn't mention me?"

"He said the wedding was coming up quickly. I might have missed what else he said because I was thinking about what I would get you for a wedding present. I finished my wine, excused myself and went back to my apartment for Tara's gift."

Amanda glared at her. "That's not what the bartender told me. He said you went to the ladies' room before you had a drink with him. Were you expecting Greg to come join you maybe?"

"No!" Charlie realized she might have said it a little too sharply, a little too I-can't-imagine-anything-more-disgusting. Amanda was studying her openly. "Amanda, have you asked yourself why you are so insecure about this relationship?"

"I beg your pardon?"

"You don't seem to trust Greg. Why is that?"

Amanda tossed her hair. "Because of women like you."

She meant women like *her*. "I've told you," Charlie said. "I'm not interested in Greg. Tonight I broke up with Daniel and—"

Just then, Shep came out of her bedroom. His hair was still wet from a shower and he wore nothing but a towel wrapped around his slim hips.

"I'm sorry, am I interrupting?" he asked.

Amanda looked at him agape. Charlie was doing the same thing. She hadn't seen Shep like this in years. Everything about him appeared to have only improved since then—as if that were possible.

"I'm sorry," he said. "I don't believe we've met." He took a step toward Amanda and held out his hand.

Charlie felt her heart lodge in her throat. If he lost that towel—

"I'm Shep," he said. "Charlie's…" He looked at her as if waiting for her to fill in the blank.

"He's a friend," Charlie said.

"A good friend, apparently," Amanda said, clearly flustered. "I should go and leave you two…at it." With that, she walked to the door.

"I hope this answers any questions you have about me and Greg," Charlie said. "I kind of have my hands full as it is."

"I can see that." Amanda looked past her to where Shep was still standing before she left.

Charlie closed the door and locked it. Behind her she heard Shep chuckle. She turned slowly. His gaze was electric. She felt a jolt move through her. No wonder Amanda had looked dumbstruck. The man was gorgeous.

"If you think I'm going to thank you for that—" Charlie began but lost the rest of what she was going to say as Shep took a step toward her.

Water droplets glistened in his dark hair. One broke free and coursed over the hard muscles of his chest to disappear into the hollow just above where the towel started.

"Shep." The sound that same out was more like a sigh. Or was it a plea?

"Charlie?" He was within inches of her now.

She felt as if the floor under her was no longer solid. If she even breathed, she'd lose her balance and fall into his arms. She was again that teenager, mesmerized. Desire spiked through her, making her knees weak.

It would have been so easy just to lean toward him and let gravity do the rest. Not that Shep would let her fall. Not this man. He'd sweep her up, carry her off to bed, lose that towel and—

Charlie swallowed and took a step back, dragging her eyes away from the spot where that water droplet had disappeared. She raised her gaze to look into that handsome face, those eyes filled with the kind of desire that now coursed red-hot through her veins. She felt something melt inside her.

Daniel had never looked at her like this. Shep was right. Daniel wasn't the one. He'd never been the one. She'd never felt like this with him. There was only one man who'd ever made her quiver inside like an autumn leaf in the breeze, and he was standing in front of her half naked.

But it was Shep's mouth and what that mouth had done to her all those years ago that had her pulse thumping. She wanted to kiss him like she'd never wanted to kiss another man.

"Say the word, Charlie," Shep said quietly.

The word was on the tip of her tongue when his cell phone rang.

Shep let out a curse but didn't move. His gaze held hers, daring her to tell him to let it ring.

Not tonight, she told herself silently. She wasn't going from one man's arms to another in the span of one night, no matter what Amanda thought.

"You'd better get that," she said, her voice breaking.

CHAPTER SEVENTEEN

BY THE TIME Shep was off the phone with Mulvane, Charlie had gone into her bedroom, tossed his discarded clothing out into the living room and closed the door. He sighed and, smiling to himself, picked up his clothes and headed for the couch.

He considered what the retired homicide cop had told him on the phone only moments before. A man named Jason Harper also had an interest in Lindy Parker's murder.

"I thought you might want to know," Mulvane said. "I'd forgotten about him until after you left and I was putting away some of my notes on the case. I saw one I made to myself more recently. The guy lives in Bozeman. I can give you his address."

Shep had been surprised by the familiar address. What a coincidence that he shared the same one as Daniel, Charlie's hopefully *former* boyfriend. So was Jason getting the information for himself—or for his roommate?

Dropping the towel and pulling on his boxers, Shep lay down on the couch and stared up at the ceiling.

As interesting as this lead was, his mind was on Charlie and what could have happened earlier. He still ached at the thought, even though he had to question what he'd been thinking. She'd just broken up with her boyfriend tonight. With everything else that was going on, she didn't need Shep trying to rekindle their teenage romance.

But the thought made him smile. He didn't think it would take much rekindling. That old chemistry was still there, just as he'd suspected. It was as if it had been banked for fifteen years and was now ready to burst into flame. This time, even stronger.

Not that he hadn't wanted to make love with her, even knowing that the timing was all wrong. The pull had been so strong. Daniel was all wrong for her, in Shep's humble opinion. And if he was being honest, okay, maybe he was jealous. Being here with her had brought back a lot of memories of what the two of them had shared.

He reminded himself that they weren't teenagers anymore and a lot of water had flowed under that bridge. They weren't the same people they'd been. But the way he felt about Charlie hadn't changed.

But it was more than that. He *liked* her. She was quirky and could drive him crazy without even trying. Ultimately, being around her made him feel capable of Herculean feats.

Shep felt a wave of guilt wash over him. Charlie was in trouble. Instead of lying here pining over her, he should be finding out who was behind the stalking, and putting an end to it. Sighing, he shook his head. He hadn't even been able to find out who was responsible for the Lindy sightings. Some hero he was.

He turned his thoughts to the problem at hand. The news about Jason Harper nagged at him. What was his interest in Lindy's murder? If Charlie really hadn't told anyone, how did Jason even know that Lindy had been her stepsister? Shep had to find out.

But then what? He knew he couldn't think that far ahead and yet, when Christmas vacation was over, he had to get back to school, back to his classroom, back to his students. He could feel the clock ticking.

Antsy, he looked around the room. There wasn't anything he could do this late at night but get some rest. Christmas was only days away—not that he could tell it by Charlie's apartment.

There was a tiny, sad, fake tree with questionable decorations in the corner of the kitchen counter and a few lights strung at the window, but other than that, little Christmas spirit. That just seemed…wrong. He would have to do something about that.

At least that was something he knew he could solve. The Lindy situation was a whole other matter. Not that there had been another sighting. But he'd die trying to put all this behind Charlie once and for all.

CHARLIE HAD TOSSED and turned all night. Just knowing that Shep was in the next room had driven her crazy. What had almost happened before his phone call? She had just broken up with Daniel and yet if Shep's phone hadn't rung when it did…

She told herself she wouldn't have succumbed that easily to Shep's charm. She wasn't a teenager anymore. But she had been more than tempted. She sighed. She could have fallen into his arms so easily…

This morning, she was still shaken. Worse, still tempted. She didn't feel in her right mind.

So much had been going on. Lindy, Amanda, Greg. She thought about Tara's baby daughter and the birth and smiled to herself. But now Tara was off for six weeks. Charlie would miss her desperately. But Tara had promised that she would be at Amanda and Greg's wedding after Christmas—if there was a wedding.

Getting ready for the day, Charlie braced herself for seeing Shep. But when she opened the door, he wasn't lying half naked on her couch. He was fully dressed in the kitchen. She caught a familiar scent.

"Pancakes?" she asked, her voice breaking with both relief not to find him half naked—and excitement at the prospect of pancakes.

"And bacon," he said, grinning. "Have a seat. I poured you some orange juice."

She sat and saw that he also had the newspaper beside her plate—opened to her horoscope. If Shep was trying to get on her good side, he was doing an amazing job of it. Or did this have something to do with what had almost happened last night? Was he trying to make her forget it? Or—

"It stopped snowing," he said, disrupting her thoughts. It appeared last night had shaken him as much as it had her. "Looks like there's another storm coming through."

Charlie found Capricorn and read, worried about what the weekend would bring.

Facing a time of uncertainty in your life?

You think? She read the rest.

Trust in yourself. Only you know what you need. Be ready to make a difficult decision regarding your future.

That sounded ominous.

Don't make the easy choice.

Was that Daniel? Or Shep, middle school math teacher and cowboy at heart? Not that either of those two choices were necessarily an option at this point.

She closed the Saturday newspaper as Shep put a plate of pancakes and bacon in front of her. It smelled delicious, making her stomach rumble. Had he read her horoscope? She thought of him in that towel last night and felt her pulse quicken.

He sat down with a plate of his own and nodded toward the newspaper. "So, good news today?"

She checked to make sure he wasn't making fun before she said, "I can only hope. I promised Tara I'd stop by the hospital."

"No problem. I'm waiting to hear from the judge."

She looked at him, studying him for a moment, suddenly worried that he wasn't telling her everything. "I thought that was the judge calling last night?"

"No, it was the homicide cop I talked to. Do you know someone named Jason Harper?"

She'd just taken a bite of pancake and almost choked on it. After washing it down with orange juice, she said, *"Daniel's roommate?"*

"He's been looking into your stepsister's murder."

She stared at him as if he were speaking a foreign language she'd never heard before. "I don't understand. Why would Jason do that?"

"I was hoping you would know. You said that you never told Daniel anything about your past. Is that true of Jason as well?"

Charlie nodded numbly. Until last night, she'd never mentioned anything to Daniel. "Jason and I have hardly said two words to each other in the past months since I started dating Daniel. Why would he care about Lindy's murder?"

Turning her gaze to her plate, she ate, barely tasting the food. Shep had been convinced that Daniel might be involved. She'd thought Shep was jealous. Now she wasn't so sure.

SHEP COULD FEEL her studying him. She'd known he wasn't telling her everything. She knew him too well.

"The cop who found her," she said quietly. "He's the one who told you this?"

He nodded.

"It doesn't make any sense. How could Jason even know that Lindy and I were related for that short period of time?"

It was something Shep planned to ask him when he caught up with him, but he didn't want to tell Charlie that. She'd already said that she wanted to help. She would want to come along when he talked to Jason since she wasn't working today.

Shep suspected the man would be more forthcoming without her there. He dug into his breakfast.

She took another bite, looking confused, and when she spoke, he knew she wasn't really talking to him. "Jason knew about my past? He never said anything. Why would he care? I can't believe that he was doing it on Daniel's behalf. Daniel didn't seem at all interested when I told him about Lindy last night. I don't get it."

They both fell silent for a few moments as they finished eating.

"Do you think Amanda will be visiting Tara as well?" he asked, changing the subject to a more pleasant one.

Charlie groaned. "I hadn't thought about that. By now, Amanda will have told everyone she knows about me and… you."

He grinned. "Hopefully, she's no longer thinking you're after her man. You aren't, are you?"

Charlie made a face at him and pushed away her plate. "I should get going."

He picked up both empty plates and rinsed them before

putting them in the dishwasher. Charlie went to brush her teeth and finish getting ready for the day.

When she returned to the living room, Shep was waiting by the door, already dressed for the Montana December weather outside. She didn't even bother putting up an argument as they went down the stairs together, but once outside, she declined his offer to drive her to the hospital.

"Tara's husband is picking me up. He just texted me, but thanks."

CHARLIE GLANCED AROUND as she waited for Joe, almost hoping to see Lindy. This time, she wouldn't hesitate. This time, she would go after the woman, chase her down, get answers one way or another. But even as she thought it, she realized that once the mystery was solved, Shep would be gone. Back to teaching middle school students math. Her hero.

Lost in thought, she didn't hear the voice calling her name on the street at first.

"Charlie?"

She turned, frowning as she saw a man hurrying up the sidewalk to her. He slowed, suddenly looking as hesitant as she felt and she recognized him.

"I thought that was you," he said and gave her a tentative smile. "I wasn't sure you heard me. You probably don't remember me, but I swear, you haven't changed a bit since high school."

"I think I'll take that as a compliment."

He laughed. "I forgot about your sense of humor. Smart as a whip, too. I'm sorry." He held out his hand. "Andy Walden."

She shook his gloved hand. Andy Walden. He was still

nice looking, but he no longer made her heart pound at the mere sight of him.

"Wow, it's been a while," she said, hoping he hadn't known about the unbearable crush she'd had on him. He couldn't have, right? Otherwise, he wouldn't have asked Lindy out or said those things about her. That would have made him cruel and she'd always thought he was nice.

"It's funny," he said, looking uncomfortable. "Seeing you brings back high school. I have to confess something." He let out a nervous laugh. "I always wanted to ask you out. I even talked to your sister about it. Asked her if she thought you'd go out with me." Color shot to his cheeks and it wasn't from the cold. "I can confess it now, but I had the worst crush on you."

She stared at him. "You told Lindy this?"

He nodded.

"Let me guess. She told you not to ask me out."

"She said you had a crush on someone else." He shrugged. "I know all this is ancient history, but seeing you just now... I should let you go."

"Do you live here now?"

"No, just passing through on my way to Seattle. My mother still lives here and my wife's family."

Tara's husband, Joe, pulled up to the curb.

Charlie hesitated only a moment. "I had a crush on you, too, Andy... Good to see you," she said and stepped toward the waiting vehicle.

Joe chatted on about the baby and Tara as he drove them to the hospital. Charlie hated that she could only half listen.

Lindy. That old anger had surfaced in a flash when Andy told her about his crush. What a manipulative, hateful liar her stepsister had been. And now she was back.

SHEP WATCHED THE exchange between Charlie and the man who'd stopped her on the sidewalk. It seemed friendly enough. Shep pulled out his cell phone and snapped several photos of the man—just in case he had to identify him. The man could have been asking questions for all he knew. Or he could be a friend. Either way, Charlie hadn't looked like she needed Shep's help.

Once she was safely inside Tara's husband's car, Shep got into his pickup and headed for the gaming company where Jason Harper worked.

He'd called the number Mulvane had given him. It went straight to voice mail. Even though it was Saturday, Shep had tried his work number. A receptionist told him that Jason was working but not in his office. Did he want to leave a message? He'd declined.

Shep found the video games office in a brightly painted old industrial building near the tracks—not all that far from where Lindy had been murdered. The place looked trendy. Most of the vehicles parked in the lot were equipped with racks on top for skis, snowboards, kayaks or canoes. Bozeman was an outdoorsy kind of town and the people who lived here reflected it. Nor was he surprised to see posted on the front door that employees were allowed to bring their dogs to work with them.

After speaking with the same receptionist he'd spoken to on the phone, he was told to take a seat. Moments later, Jason came out, followed by a large yellow Lab. He wore shorts with long underwear under them and a long-sleeved T-shirt advertising a local business that sold drug paraphernalia.

"Is there somewhere we can talk?" Shep asked as he took in the young man. Jason's hair was long and in blond dreads that he'd pulled back into a low ponytail. He looked fit and tan even though it was December. His brown eyes had narrowed at the sight of Shep, but he looked more interested than suspicious.

"Sure, we can go in the conference room. It's kind of crazy here today. We're having a holiday party later." He led the way down the hall, the dog following. "Can I get you something to drink?"

Shep declined. Jason got himself an energy drink out of a refrigerator at one end of the room and then ushered them into comfortable lounge chairs. There was no conference table. Instead the area looked like a nice living room.

It wasn't until they were seated, that Shep asked, "Why are you looking into Lindy Parker's murder?"

FORTUNATELY, CHARLIE didn't see Amanda at the hospital, but the woman had been there. A huge white teddy bear sat in one corner of Tara's room. Joe left the two of them alone to go get some things for Tara.

"Amanda?" Charlie said, blinking at the giant bear staring back at her.

"Who else?" Tara laughed. "She had to outdo everyone else. She even asked me what everyone had gotten the baby so far. The woman's nuts."

"You don't have to tell me. She stopped by my apartment after I left here."

"You have to be kidding."

Charlie shook her head. "She accused me of being after Greg."

Tara rolled her eyes.

"You should have seen her face when she met my...old friend."

Tara grinned. "I heard. She said he's gorgeous, especially wearing nothing but a towel and water droplets running down his incredible rock-hard six-pack. It sounds like Amanda couldn't take her eyes off him."

Charlie felt her cheeks flush. "Of course, she would have told you."

"Is it true? He came out of the bedroom from the shower wearing nothing but a towel?"

"He was trying to make a point."

Tara laughed. "Oh yeah? Is he really as hot as she said he was?"

Charlie sighed. "Hotter."

"Girl, I can't wait to hear this story, but what happened with Daniel?"

Charlie moved to the bassinet to look down at her namesake. "I think I broke up with him. I don't know. It's all so confusing."

"What a terrible problem you have."

Charlie admired the sleeping baby for a moment, before she turned back to Tara. "Joke all you want, but it is confusing. Daniel's here and now. Shep is...going away after the holiday and yet there are old feelings."

"Does he realize Shep sounds like a dog's name?"

Charlie grinned. "That's what Greg said."

"Greg knows about him?"

Charlie looked to the heavens. "By now everyone in the county knows."

JASON'S EYES WIDENED at the question. He took a sip of his drink and for a moment, Shep wondered if the man was going to respond. So he asked it again.

"Why are you looking into Lindy Parker's murder?"

Jason nodded as if to say he'd heard the question the first time. "And you are who exactly?"

"I'm a friend of Charlie's. Your roommate's former girl-friend."

His brow shot up at the word *former*. Apparently he hadn't heard about the breakup last night. Or maybe Daniel thought it was temporary.

"What is your interest?" Shep continued. "Or did Daniel put you up to it?"

Jason chuckled and leaned back as if to get comfortable. "Daniel? Not likely. He had no interest in Charlie's past. Or really all that much in her. I, on the other hand, was curious about her."

"It would have taken some digging to find out about her stepsister's murder since they didn't share the same last name."

The young man looked nonplussed. "I'm not sure how much you know about me, but I'm a researcher here. I like digging up information about all kinds of things. I get curious so I check them out."

"Did you tell Daniel you were 'checking out' his girl-friend? Did you tell him what you learned?"

"Why bother? Like I said, he had no interest. To him, Charlie was just a cute girl to date for a while."

"For a while?"

"I've been his roommate for almost a year. Everything with Daniel is temporary, especially women. I'm sorry, but your friend was no different."

Shep wanted to finally meet Daniel and punch him in the face. "What did you plan to do with the information you got on Charlie's stepsister?"

Jason seemed surprised. "Nothing. Like I said, I was just curious."

"Are you curious about all of Daniel's girlfriends?"

This time Jason looked a little embarrassed. "Charlie was

different. There is something about her..." He shrugged. "I wished I'd met her first. But then I don't think I have to tell you that Charlie is one of a kind, do I?"

WHEN CHARLIE RETURNED to her apartment, she found it empty. She had no idea where Shep had gone. After taking off her coat and boots, she checked out what she could find in the refrigerator since it was past lunchtime.

On the way from visiting Tara, her thoughts had been all over the place. Running into Andy and finding out another ugly thing Lindy had done to her had set her nerves on end. She realized that Shep had probably gone to see Jason. If she hadn't already planned to go see Tara this morning with Joe...

Pulling out her cell phone, she called Daniel since she didn't have Jason's number.

"Charlie! I'm so glad you called," Daniel said quickly. "Look, I don't know what happened last night except I know I was to blame. I'm sorry."

It was nice at least to hear him apologize. "I wasn't calling about that. I just found out that Jason did some research on me and my stepsister's murder."

"What?"

"He didn't tell you he dug into my background?"

Daniel swore. "I can't believe this. I've known Jason since high school. He's a hell of a researcher but I had no idea he was researching my girlfriend." She could hear the anger in his voice. "I swear ever since I criticized this ditzy girl he's been dating... I'm so sorry. I'm sure he did it to get back at me. Your life is none of his business. I'll talk to him."

"Thank you. I should go."

"Charlie, I hope we get to talk in the next few days. I mean, it's almost Christmas."

She thought of the present he'd said he had for her and felt guilty. She hadn't bought him anything—even before they broke up. "We'll talk soon."

Disconnecting, she looked around the apartment. Jason knew about Lindy. And Lindy was back, bringing with her all the horrible memories. Charlie thought of her mother's death, her father's hurried marriage, Lindy's cruelty and finally her stepsister's supposed murder.

For so long, she'd tried to put it all behind her. But standing in her small apartment alone and even more angry with Lindy, she knew it was time she faced the past head-on.

She found the stack of papers Shep had gotten from the homicide detective and made herself comfortable on the couch. Her heart hammered at the thought of finally knowing exactly what happened that night—and come to grips with the part she played in it.

AN HOUR LATER, she put down the last piece of research Shep had collected and wiped her eyes. The murder had been brutal. It was beyond her comprehension how anyone could have done such a thing.

She didn't believe it had been some stranger passing by. All her instincts told her that whoever had killed Lindy had hated her with a passion.

That alone shocked her. For years, she'd wanted to believe Lindy's death had been random. Some stranger who'd come out of one of the abandoned buildings in the industrial area nearby. Now, she realized with a shudder that the killer had to have been someone who knew Lindy and hated her as much as Charlie did herself.

WT COULDN'T REMEMBER the last time he'd gone ice-skating. When Meg suggested it, he'd thought she was joking. "Aren't we a little old for ice-skating?"

She'd grinned at him. "We weren't too old for what we did after our dinner date. What's ice-skating compared to that?"

Her grin made his cheeks flush. He'd never met anyone so outspoken. She made him feel alive and young again. She was full of surprises, up for anything, and she seemed to like him. All of it felt surreal. Being with her had awakened something in him he hadn't even known had dozed off.

He smiled and shook his head. "Ice-skating it is."

Now as he cruised around the rink with Meg beside him, he couldn't imagine why he had stopped ice-skating. It was exhilarating. Just like being here with her. What was it about this woman that made him want to discard all rational thoughts regarding his age, his social position, his stodgy lifestyle?

After going dancing and then going back to her place and making love in her king-size bed, he'd said, "You make me want to buy a VW bus and hit the road with no plan at all."

She'd laughed as she cuddled next to him. "So why don't we?"

He'd held her, getting glimpses of a future he'd never considered. "You'd be bored within a week."

"Try me," she said and turned to look at him. "What about you?"

"I don't know, but I have to admit, you have me looking at my future differently than I did just days ago."

She smiled at him. "That's a good thing, Billy."

That was when she suggested ice-skating and then he'd fallen asleep, smiling to himself. It was one of the best night's sleeps he could remember.

But that little voice in the back of his head warned him that this was moving way too fast. He needed to watch his step. Mostly, he needed to watch himself because this woman was dangerous when it came to a man's heart.

SHEP RETURNED TO the apartment to find Charlie curled up on the couch, his stack of paperwork next to her. He could see she'd been crying.

"Did you talk to Jason?" she asked. Her look told him she knew exactly where he'd gone.

He nodded as he shrugged out of coat and boots and tossed his Stetson on a hook by the door. The temperature outside had dropped. Snow drifted down from a white blanket of sky. There was little chance that Bozeman wouldn't be getting a white Christmas.

"Well?" she asked, pushing the paperwork aside and patting the couch next to her.

"He said he was just curious about you," Shep said. Instead of going to the couch, he went into the kitchen. "Want some wine? I'm going to have a beer."

She appeared next to his elbow as he bent to look in the refrigerator.

"What aren't you telling me? What haven't you been telling me all along?" she demanded. "I went through everything you've collected. What is it you're so afraid of me finding out?"

He pulled out a beer and turned to face her. "I don't know what you're talking about. Jason has a crush on you." He shrugged. "Who doesn't?" He tried to step past her, but she caught his arm.

"Lindy knew her killer and her killer knew her," Charlie said. "It was a crime of passion, isn't that what they call it? Which means it was someone who hated her with such intensity…" Her voice broke.

"I'm not sure where you're going with this—"

"Who could have hated her more than I did that night?" Charlie demanded.

"Hold on. Remember? You heard someone come into the house that night."

She was shaking her head. "Maybe I was wrong. Maybe I made it up to hide what I did."

"How can you say that when you don't even believe she's really dead?"

Charlie glared at him. "Whoever killed the young woman behind my house thought she was Lindy. It was so brutal… Maybe they did make a mistake. I know I saw Lindy recently. I had her scarf in my hand." She closed her eyes. "Maybe I'm losing my mind. Maybe I lost it that night."

He could see how confused and scared she was. He set down the beer and firmly took her shoulders in his hands. "You didn't kill her."

Tears streamed down her face as she opened her eyes. "How can you be so sure?"

"Because I know you." He pulled her into his arms and held her tightly against him. "I know you, Charlie." He let her cry, smoothing her hair as he kissed the top of her head. "I know you."

CHAPTER EIGHTEEN

SHEP KEPT her busy the rest of the weekend with several shopping trips to get food for meals he wanted to make her and more home improvement shows to watch and card games to play. Charlie knew what he was trying to do. He was trying to keep her mind off Lindy.

While she hadn't seen her stepsister again, Lindy was never far from her thoughts—just like the worry about what had really happened that night. Charlie had never thought she could feel so much hatred. But that night, something dark and depraved had taken over her. It had felt primal and putrid. She still shuddered with shame when she remembered that cold-blooded feeling.

Shep thought he knew her. He thought she wasn't capable of murder. But she feared he was wrong.

Monday, she dragged herself out of bed. Only a couple more days before Christmas and a week off. She couldn't wait, for so many reasons. Over break, she planned to do some investigating on her own. She had to know the truth.

She thought it was a good sign when she managed to get to her desk without seeing either Amanda or Greg. Her horoscope had made her laugh.

In the middle of a romantic triangle? Maybe it's time to free yourself from this dilemma you've been in. You know which choice you want to make.

She wondered if Shep had read her horoscope because he had seemed distant this morning. He said he was hungover from all the home shows they'd watched. She tried not to worry about it. She had enough on her mind.

Her cubicle felt empty without Tara. Charlie couldn't wait until Christmas break. Greg was giving everyone a paid vacation from Christmas Eve through January first. All she had to do was get through a couple more days.

The only drawback was the wedding. Amanda had insisted on a post-Christmas wedding at Big Sky Resort in the Gallatin Canyon outside of town. Greg had sprung for rooms at a hotel on the mountain with lift passes and rentals for anyone interested in skiing. The wedding was scheduled for Friday right after Christmas, and guests were welcome to stay two nights at the resort for free.

Charlie had no choice but to attend the wedding—she'd even asked Daniel to go with her back when they were a couple. Now she planned to come back home right after the wedding. She thought most of the other employees would take advantage of Greg's generosity and stay the whole two days.

"Charlie?"

She jumped at the sound of her name directly behind her and spun around to find Amanda hovering over her. "Amanda. You scared me."

The woman smiled, clearly enjoying her discomfort. "You seemed to be a million miles away. A penny for your thoughts."

"Actually, I was thinking about your wedding."

"Really? How interesting since I just stopped by to give you the information you'll need including directions to the hotel at Big Sky." She handed Charlie a pale lavender envelope. "You are planning to stay both days, I'm sure. Greg would be so disappointed if his favorite employee left right after the wedding."

"I bet you say that to all the staff," Charlie said and laughed as if it had been a joke.

"And you must bring Shep," Amanda said, lifting a brow. "How do you do it? Men just seem to flock to you."

"Hardly." Daniel had been her first boyfriend in months and now that was over. Shep... Well, it wasn't what Amanda thought it was. And he'd be gone soon no matter what happened. His students would be anxiously waiting to learn new math.

"I'm telling Greg you're bringing your latest beau," Amanda said. "Don't make me a liar."

"I wouldn't want to do that," Charlie said, wishing she hadn't been so heavy on the sarcasm. But Amanda either didn't notice or ignored it as she took off to deliver the rest of her lavender envelopes.

MAC CALLED JUST as Shep was heading back to the apartment after making sure that Charlie had arrived at her office without incident. The high school English teacher asked how they'd liked the cookies.

"They were delicious," Shep said, feeling guilty as he glanced over to see the package sitting on his pickup seat. He'd forgotten about them. But he knew Mac wasn't really calling about the cookies.

"I thought of someone else you might want to talk to. Lindy's math teacher. His name is Fred Jones. He's retired but I can give you his address."

Shep took down the address and phone number and thanked Mac.

"Give Charlie my regards," Mac said and disconnected.

Fred Jones lived south of town on Sourdough Road.

The house appeared to have been built in the late sixties: flat roof, white stucco, large windows, everything all on one level.

Shep's knock was answered by an older, physically fit man with short gray hair and a closely trimmed beard. After Shep introduced himself, Jones led him into the living room. Even the furniture was from the sixties. Shep sat on the long couch in front of a travertine fireplace.

"I'm here about Lindy Parker. I'm looking into her murder for a friend. I understand she was in several of your classes. I'm hoping you remember her and can tell me anything you remember about her."

Jones nodded and ran his fingers thoughtfully over his beard for a moment. "Lindy. Oh yes, I remember her well. She stands out not just because of her murder. The girl was such an enigma. One day she'd be all bright-eyed and excited to participate in class. The next, she'd be sullen and said she didn't know the answer to a problem she'd gotten right the day before." He shook his head. "Looking back, I suspect she was bipolar. How else could you explain it? I spoke to her mother about it, but my concern wasn't well received."

"What did her mother say?"

"That there was nothing wrong with her daughter. I was told to stay out of it. Very frustrating for a teacher who sees such potential going to waste."

"Did you also have Charlie Farmington in your classes?" Shep asked.

"The stepsister." Jones nodded. "She was smart enough but clearly not interested in math." Shep knew only too well how that was with his own students. "Always drawing in class."

"Did you ever see any trouble between the two sisters?"

Jones looked away for a moment toward the empty fireplace before he answered. "If you're asking if I saw Lindy bullying her stepsister...yes. I also tried to talk to the mother about that with even worse results. The mother didn't want to hear it, refused to believe that her daughter would do anything like that. You get the picture."

He did. But now there was no doubt that Kat had known how Lindy was treating Charlie. He felt his anger at her building again.

"She was very protective of Lindy," Fred said. "I saw that often with parents who knew there was something not quite right about their child. Denial is a difficult bridge to cross—until it is too late."

"I'm sure you followed the murder case at the time," Shep said. "Who did you think killed her?"

Jones raised a brow. "If you're asking who might have hated her enough to murder her, I think you know the answer to that. Do I think Charlie was capable? Aren't we all, if pushed far enough? You have to remember...only a child herself, Charlie was dealing with a teenager whose personality changed with the flip of a switch. She couldn't depend on her stepmother's help or apparently her own father's. How terrifying to live in that house with her stepsister being as cruel and manipulative as she was. That young girl had no idea what Lindy was going to do to her next. I can't even imagine that kind of mental torture over days, let alone months."

Shep could see that Lindy had scared Fred Jones when he'd witnessed her cruelty toward Charlie. He couldn't imagine either what Charlie had gone through.

But the teacher was wrong. Shep knew Charlie. She wasn't capable of murder. He'd stake his life on it.

CHAPTER NINETEEN

CHARLIE STEPPED OUT of her office building to find Shep waiting for her with a recently harvested full-size Christmas tree and a bulging shopping bag. "What are you doing?"

"Your apartment needs some holiday spirit," he said, handing her the shopping bag.

She glanced inside and saw decorations and a tree stand. "My apartment needs it? Or you do?" she asked as they began to walk the few blocks to her apartment with him dragging the huge tree.

"I thought it would brighten up the place," he said, grinning at her. "How was your day?"

"I got my official directions to the hotel for Amanda and Greg's wedding. It's at Big Sky right after Christmas. I assume you want to go?"

"You assume correctly."

She thought he would say that and smiled to herself, glad she wasn't going to have to do this alone. "Amanda is counting on it."

Tara had said she would try to make the wedding but with the new baby... In other words, she had an excuse. Charlie didn't.

"The invite comes with free lift tickets along with rooms in a hotel on the mountain. Hopefully it's large enough that we won't see either Amanda or Greg."

"Sounds cozy," he said as they reached her apartment.

Once inside, he leaned the tree against a wall and handed her what appeared to be Christmas cookies.

"If you tell me you baked these—"

He laughed. "Sorry. They're compliments of your teacher Mac. Larry McCormick. Remember him?"

"He was my favorite teacher."

"How did I know that?" He grinned. "Was it his dimples?"

"He *was* adorable." She laughed as she put down the bag of decorations and tore into the cookies. She took a bite before offering him the other one.

"They're all yours," he said. He dug out the stand and went to grab the tree. "I might need some help with this."

She put down the cookies and steadied the tree as he slipped it into the stand.

"I thought it could go in this corner," Shep said. "What do you think?"

"You've given this some thought, have you?" She couldn't help grinning at him as she picked up her cookie and took another bite. "Pretty tree."

"I got a deal on it since it's so close to Christmas. Lodgepole pine. Smells good, huh?"

She nodded. "Thanks."

"Don't thank me yet. You have to help me decorate," he said. "I'm thinking we should put on some Christmas music. Maybe have a little spiked hot chocolate."

Charlie felt rather than saw that Shep was trying too hard. "You talked to Mac about Lindy? What did he say?"

"Just that Lindy didn't apply herself. That he was worried about your relationship with her." He stepped away from the tree to face her, his expression suddenly solemn. "I also spoke to your math teacher, Fred Jones."

She felt a jolt, something in his expression warning her.

"He said he saw things about Lindy that bothered him and he tried to talk to Kat about them. She wasn't open to him telling her that Lindy was bullying you and not living up to her potential in his class. He thought Lindy might have had some kind of mental condition, but Kat was determined that she was fine."

"So other people saw what Lindy was doing to me," Charlie said. "That's…embarrassing."

Shep stepped to her, taking both of her shoulders in his large warm hands. "You have no reason to feel that way. Lindy was the problem, not you."

"Then why…" She met his gaze as her voice broke. "What did Mr. Jones say to you that upset you? Shep, tell me the truth."

"Wasn't that enough?" He let go of her and started to turn away, but she grabbed a fistful of his shirt and forced him back around to face her. His shirt felt soft and warm in her fist. She could smell his male scent mixed with her bath gel.

She breathed him in, suddenly wanting his arms around her—afraid she would need them when he told her what else he'd found out. "Tell me."

He met her gaze and she felt tears fill her eyes even before he spoke. "He was worried about you living with someone he suspected was so unpredictable and dangerous. He worried what that kind of situation might have done to you."

Charlie let go of his shirt. "He thinks I killed her."

"He doesn't know you like I do," Shep said quickly.

She started to turn away, but he pulled her into his arms. "You didn't do it."

She fought the embrace, but only for a moment, before

she settled into his protective hold. She'd been here a lot lately. She was getting used to it. Definitely a mistake.

But still she pressed her face against the warm softness of his shirt and breathed him in again, filling her lungs with his scent. His body felt so strong—like his arms around her.

They stayed like that for a long while. Charlie never wanted to move. She felt safe, sheltered, loved. Shep believed in her, always had. She was the one who'd had her doubts. Just like that day on the boot camp obstacle course.

She slowly lifted her face to look up at him.

The kiss was the most natural thing in the world at that moment. He lowered his mouth to hers. Her lips parted in response, her arms going around his neck, pulling him down as the kiss deepened.

She felt her heart soar as his arms tightened around her and he lifted her off her feet. Need was in every muscle of his body just as she felt her own need for this man she'd once loved with all her heart.

Shep slowly broke off the kiss and lowered her to the floor. His gaze locked with hers. There was that question again in his eyes. She felt it in her core. It would take only a matter of seconds to discard their clothing... The thought of their naked bodies melded together in her big bed...

He let go of her and stepped back, breaking eye contact. "This tree is not going to decorate itself." He turned away, saying over his shoulder, "Think you can find us some Christmas music?" Then he opened the shopping bag and began taking out lights and ornaments.

Charlie stared at his back, knowing that if she took only a few steps, if she placed her palm on his warm, strong back...

But her feet refused to move. She couldn't hurt this man

again. She wouldn't. Until she knew the truth about what had happened that night and what she might have done…

"Christmas music and wine," she said. She headed first for her phone to play Christmas music, then for the refrigerator and then the cupboard for glasses. Her fingers trembled as she took down the flutes for the wine. Why had he stopped kissing her? Why had he backed off? She knew he wanted her as much as she wanted him. What had he seen in her eyes that made him pull away?

Fear. Fear that he was wrong about her. It was why she hadn't gone to him, touched him, told him that she was falling for him all over again. She had to know the truth about who killed Lindy. Why someone was determined to make her think her stepsister and nemesis was alive.

Someone knew the truth about the murder. The same person who'd "brought Lindy back" to remind Charlie of what she'd done all those years ago?

CHAPTER TWENTY

SHEP THOUGHT HE'D blown it with that kiss. Not that he was sorry. He'd wanted to kiss her from the moment he looked up and saw her walking through the falling snow toward him days ago. But then he'd found out about Daniel.

Well, Daniel was gone. Hopefully. Still, Shep had to tread carefully with Charlie. And watch out for his own heart as well. Not that he took horoscopes seriously. He didn't need the stars to tell him he was in dangerous territory when it came to her. She'd left him once, broken his heart without looking back. He wasn't sure he could take her doing that to him again.

With Christmas music playing, they began to decorate the tree. He'd gotten the corniest ornaments he could find, knowing Charlie would appreciate them. Just hearing her laughter as she dug in the bag made him smile. For a little while, Lindy was forgotten.

When they finished, he had her plug in the tree and they clinked wineglasses, surveying their work, both pleased with the job they'd done. "Here's wishing you the best Christmas ever," he said in the glow of the twinkling multicolored lights.

"You, too." She watched him over the rim of her glass. "Don't you think we should talk about it?"

He didn't have to guess. "I thought the kiss kind of said it all."

"Really? I kind of thought it lacked clarity."

Shep took a step closer. "Maybe if I tried again…"

"Seriously, Shep, what's going on?" she asked, putting down her empty wineglass.

"Okay, let's talk. I suppose you want me to go first. Let's see… Here it is, Charlie. I thought I got over you all those years ago." His gaze met hers and held it. "Seeing you again, I realized I was only kidding myself."

She shook her head. "We were just teenagers."

He couldn't help the hurt and pain in his voice when he answered. "Is that why you left me the way you did?"

CHARLIE FELT AS if a cold wind had blown though the apartment. "We were too young. The timing was wrong."

"All things you've obviously told yourself over the years. What were you really thinking when you left that day?"

She didn't have to try to recall, but still she hesitated. "That I'd never meet anyone like you ever again."

His eyes filled with such sadness that she felt a knot form in her chest. "Why didn't you come back then? Or at least tell me how you felt?"

"I couldn't. I wouldn't have been able to leave you and what good would it have done? We couldn't have stayed together."

Shep sighed. "You had so little faith in me? I would have taken care of you."

"We were both headed for college, jobs and the volunteer work assigned by the courts. There wasn't time for us back then."

"You think we wouldn't have made time for us?" he asked, sounding disbelieving.

Charlie turned away, unable to see the disappointment

in his handsome face. "I did what I thought was best back then."

"And now?" He was so close, she felt his breath on her neck even before she felt his hand on her shoulder. He slowly turned her to face him. "What about now, Charlie?"

"How can you even ask that, given what you now know about me?"

He frowned. "What are you talking about?"

"Shep, anyone who knew about the bullying believes that I killed Lindy. I can't be sure what happened that night. Maybe I did this. At first I thought it was guilt bringing Lindy back—a figment of my imagination. But what if someone knows the truth about what I did and now they just want me to admit it?"

"You didn't kill her."

"How can you be so sure of that?" she cried.

"Because I know what's in your heart."

She shook her head, remembering how her heart had filled to overflowing with that terrifying, malevolent, dark hatred as she stood at the locked door, listening to her step-sister's screams. "And if you're wrong?" She pulled away. "Until I know—"

"All right," Shep said, turning her again to face him. "I'm going to prove it to you and then..." His gaze softened.

"And then..." she whispered as he pulled her into his arms. She leaned into him, wanting to believe he could see into her heart. Wanting to believe that guilt wasn't the reason her past had come back to haunt her.

CHRISTMAS EVE, CHARLIE announced she was going into work. "I want to get everything in order before the new year. The office should be empty, so it'll be quiet."

Shep understood. He liked to get into his classroom early

before any of the students began arriving and prepare himself for the day.

But after walking her to work, he found himself at loose ends. He felt stuck. The murder had been too long ago. He'd talked to everyone he could think of. Now he just felt confused. He couldn't understand what the Lindy sightings were about any more than he could understand the destroyed doll. What did whoever was doing this hope to accomplish? The Lindy look-alike could be acting alone, but who was behind it all and why? It made no sense.

As he walked back to the apartment along the busy snowy Main Street, he stuffed his hands into his coat pocket and felt a crumpled-up piece of paper.

Pulling it out, he stared at the scribbled writing. It took him a moment to recognize what it was. The list Wagner had given him with phone numbers for his stepsons. He could barely make out the names: Patrick, Frank and Allen.

Back at the apartment, Shep tried the phone number for Patrick. He got voice mail. He left his name and number and asked Patrick to give him a call, saying it was about Lindy Parker. Disconnecting, he wondered if any of three stepsons would even remember the name.

He called Frank next. A woman answered and told him Frank was at work. He left a message for the man to call him, saying it was about a family who lived near Frank's stepfather and a tragedy fifteen years ago.

Allen answered on the fourth ring. "Lindy Parker? Sure, I remember the murder. It's all the old man talked about for months. You'd have thought he knew her."

"Did *you* know her?" Shep asked.

The man scoffed. "Those girls were kids. I was almost thirty."

"So you didn't have any contact with them?"

"I saw them a couple of times coming out of the house headed wherever."

"Did you ever wave at them?"

"Seriously? In the first place, I was happily married. In the second, like I said, they were kids. No, I didn't wave at them. Is that all?"

"What about your brothers. They're younger, right?"

"You'd have to ask them but to my knowledge they didn't have any more contact with that family than I did."

Shep disconnected. Another dead end. He called the judge to ask if they had DNA back on the scarf. He was anxious since it was going to take a strange woman's DNA on the scarf to prove to Charlie that she hadn't seen the long-dead Lindy Parker.

"Not yet. Tell me what you have so far," Landusky said in his no-nonsense voice. But the judge sounded less gruff than usual.

Shep ran through all of it, which didn't seem like much, and waited for the judge's reaction. When he said nothing, Shep added, "I was thinking I would try to track down Lindy's father."

"I'm afraid that could be a problem. Apparently Kathryn never married him so there is no record of a husband. Nor is his name on the birth certificate. Lindy's birth certificate says it was a home birth in Brazil."

"Another dead end," Shep mumbled.

"I take it there haven't been any more Lindy sightings?"

"Not since Charlie literally ran into the woman and ended up with her scarf. But the apartment was broken into. We suspect the Lindy look-alike was searching for her scarf."

"Interesting. She doesn't want us having her DNA."

Shep knew he had to voice Charlie's concerns. "Charlie is worried that she might have killed her stepsister." He thought the judge would be shocked.

Instead Landusky asked, "What do you think?"

"No way. I know Charlie."

"For a short while years ago," Landusky pointed out but kindly.

"I *know* her," Shep said adamantly. "She didn't do it."

He heard a soft chuckle. "So I *was* right to ask you to see to this."

Shep didn't know what to say. He thought the judge disconnected, and so was surprised when he spoke again.

"I just got a text that the DNA report from the blond hair on the scarf has come back."

AMANDA WAS IN great spirits when she showed up unexpectedly—and unwelcome—at Charlie's cubicle. "What do you think?" she asked, turning in a circle so Charlie could assess her ski outfit.

"I think you shouldn't be here," Charlie said. "I mean, I thought you were taking the day off like everyone else."

"I am. I just picked up this outfit and I wanted to show it off but you're the only one here. What do you think?" Amanda did another turn in the cubicle. "It's Greg's favorite color. I'm going to wear it on the ski hill at Big Sky."

"It's *purple*," Charlie said before she could catch herself.

"Is it too much?" Amanda asked, sounding suddenly worried.

The outfit consisted of a purple sweater, purple bibs with a lavender scarf and purple mittens and hat with a lavender pom-pom on top. The only thing that would make it more purple would be if Amanda was chewing grape gum.

"I think it's perfect. It's…you."

Amanda gave her a side-eye for a moment before she

laughed and broke into a huge smile. "It *is* me. I'm so excited. About the wedding. About marrying Greg. About everything."

"As you should be," Charlie said and started to turn back to her desk. She really wanted to take care of some things before the holiday. But Amanda didn't take the hint.

"You know, since you're here… There is something I have to ask you," Amanda said, dragging her attention back. Charlie thought of her morning horoscope warning her to use good judgment in all things, especially those involving her job and the people she worked with. "I wouldn't ask, but I'm desperate. I need you to be my maid of honor."

Charlie felt her eyes go wide. All breath locked in her chest. For a moment she couldn't move, couldn't breathe, couldn't even blink. "Amanda, the wedding is in two days."

"I know. I just found out that my friend from Colorado broke her leg and is in traction."

"You must have another friend—"

"Pat is pregnant and due any day. She can't fly. I already told Greg that I asked you a long time ago to be my backup maid of honor and you said yes."

"*What?* Amanda! Why would you do that?"

"He thought it was a wonderful idea," Amanda rushed on, making Charlie doubt that had been the case. "So you really can't say no at this late date."

"I'm the last person you should ask. I mean I'm sure you have a close friend in town that you—"

"Actually, I don't," Amanda said, dropping her voice to a whisper. "I don't make female friends easily."

Big surprise, Charlie thought.

"Please. Greg and I both want you to stand up with us."

Groaning inwardly, Charlie tried to think of anything she might say to make this go away. Her cell phone rang.

She snatched it up. "I have to take this," she said to Amanda and hit Accept.

"I need to see you," Shep said. "I'm at the apartment. Can you take a break? I could meet you at the coffee shop next door to your office if—"

"That's quite all right. No, this isn't a bad time. I'll be right there." Disconnecting, she reached for her coat. "I'm sorry, Amanda, a client needs me right now."

"On Christmas Eve?" Amanda demanded. "Well, I can see why Greg is always speaking so highly of you. But what about—"

"Later. We can talk about this later," Charlie said, shrugging on her coat and sidestepping past the woman as she headed for the door.

Behind her, Amanda said brightly, "I'll call you with the details. You won't regret this."

The cold morning air was a welcome relief after the office. The last thing she wanted to do was stand up with Amanda knowing what she did about the woman's deceit— not to mention Greg's recent strange behavior. But for the life of her she couldn't think of a way out of it. She'd already said she would attend the wedding. Unless she came down with a contagious disease right after Christmas Day...

She walked the few blocks to the apartment and hurried up the three flights of stairs. She was reaching for the door when it was flung open. Shep's expression made her realize the wedding and Amanda were the least of her problems.

"What's happened?"

CHAPTER TWENTY-ONE

CHARLIE LOOKED FLUSHED from the cold and so beautiful that it took Shep's breath away for a moment. He knew he should have waited until she got off work to tell her the news. But he also knew that she would want to hear this—and right away.

Now that he had her back at the apartment though, he hesitated. He had wanted to tell her here, not sure how she was going to take the news.

"Maybe you should sit—"

"Just tell me," she snapped.

So he did, repeating everything the judge had told him about the DNA report on the scarf.

"What?" Charlie demanded, looking stricken. *"Lindy's alive? She's alive, just like I said."*

"No. All I'm saying is that the DNA on the scarf matches Lindy's. You recognized the scarf. Somehow her DNA survived on the fabric."

"Just as her fingerprints survived on my doll?" Charlie shook her head and began to pace. "I looked the woman in the eye. It was *Lindy*. The scarf proves what I've been saying all along. *She's alive.*"

He argued the facts, and the facts were that Lindy's body had been found behind their house. A positive ID had been made.

"I know all of that," Charlie said. "But I also know what

I saw. I looked into her eyes. She was startled to see me. She was upset enough that I had her scarf to apparently break into this apartment. If Lindy is alive, then there is only one person who knows the truth," Charlie said and headed for the door.

"Wait, where are you going?"

She turned to face him. "Shep, don't try to stop me. It is high time I faced my stepmother. I've spent years hiding from the past. Well, now it's come back to haunt me. I'm not hiding anymore. I'm no longer pretending it will go away if I ignore it. Someone wants me to remember all of it and if anyone knows what is going on, you can bet it's Kat."

"Charlie, I already talked to her. She threatened to call the police if she ever saw me on her doorstep again, let alone you. This could be one of your worst ideas."

Charlie made a dismissive sound. "I guess we'll find out soon enough, won't we?"

Kat opened the door, her eyes widening to see Shep on her doorstep again. Her jaw dropped when she saw Charlie. She tried to slam the door in their faces but Shep got a boot between the door and the jamb before she could.

"Get off my property. I told you not to come back. I'm calling the police," Kat yelled as they entered the house, driving her back into the living room.

"Call the police," Shep said as she fumbled her phone from her pants pocket. "I think they'll be interested in hearing how you're involved in stalking Charlie."

Kat hesitated in the midst of tapping out 911 on her phone to look at them. "I haven't been stalking anyone, especially her. I told you that."

"We have proof you're involved," Charlie said. "You

gave Lindy's winter scarf to the woman you have torment-ing me."

Kat froze, her finger hovering over the send button. "What are you talking about?"

"Lindy. I didn't just see her this time," Charlie said. "I literally ran into her. When we collided, I came away with her blue scarf, her favorite blue scarf that *you* bought her."

"That's not possible," Kat said feebly. "I haven't seen that scarf in years."

"We had the DNA on the scarf run," Shep said. "Charlie remembered it belonged to Lindy—and the DNA on it confirmed it. The blond hair was a perfect match. The DNA is Lindy's."

Charlie had known Kat would deny everything. But she hadn't expected to see her this shaken or so much in denial.

"I *saw* her," Charlie said, her voice breaking with her growing anger. "*It was her.* I don't know how but it was Lindy. So if that wasn't her body they found behind the house—"

"You're mistaken," Kat said, her voice barely audible. All the color had drained from her face and Charlie could see she was trembling.

"If anyone knows why she's stalking me in her favorite scarf that she knows I would recognize, it's you. You're her *mother.*"

"I can't believe this is happening," Kat said as she stumbled back and slumped into a chair. "I need you to leave." Her voice came out in a hoarse whisper.

Charlie wasn't leaving. Let her call the police. The woman owed her answers and damned if she wasn't finally going to get them. "Not until you tell me the truth."

Kat shook her head, her lips trembling as her eyes filled with tears. "You don't understand." Her gaze slowly rose to meet Charlie's. "My daughter…" The woman's voice cracked.

"You can no longer deny she's alive," Charlie said. "We have DNA proof. And I knew even before that. I had looked into her eyes. I knew her and she knew me. Lindy isn't dead, is she? It's the only explanation. But how is that possible?"

"You're wrong. It's not Lindy. Not my precious Lindy," Kat said and began to sob like a woman still grieving the loss.

Charlie felt a chill race across her flesh, leaving a trail of goose bumps. "Lindy is either alive or…" Her heart began to pound as she thought of what Shep had learned about Lindy from her teachers.

She turned to him. "You said the DNA from the blond hair on the scarf was a perfect match? That can only mean that Lindy is alive or…" She looked over at Kat who had slumped into the chair, head down. "Or there are two of them."

"Charlie?" Shep said.

"Either Lindy is alive or she has an identical twin," Charlie said as she frowned down at Kat. "But if she'd had a sister…"

She looked to Shep. He was staring at her as if she'd lost her mind. "I never heard any mention of a sister, let alone an identical one. Kat," he said when no one spoke over the woman's sobbing. "Is there another daughter besides Lindy and Cara?"

The woman's head came up with a jerk at a sound outside the house. Her sobbing stopped abruptly and she hastily began to wipe her eyes as she stumbled to her feet.

"Please, I can't talk about this now," she said, her voice hoarse as she rose and looked toward the front of the house. She wiped her tear-streaked face. "That will be my daughter

Cara. She doesn't know. She *can't* know. Please, you have to leave. I'll tell you everything, but you have to go *now*."

The front door opened. "Mom?" Cara stepped in loaded down with shopping bags and stopped at the sight of Shep and Charlie—and her mother's face. "Why is he here again? I'm going to call the police."

"No," Kat said, stepping toward her unsteadily. "They were just leaving." She looked imploringly at Charlie. "I'll walk you out."

Once outside, she asked Charlie for her cell phone number. Charlie watched while Kat put it into her own phone with trembling fingers.

"If we don't hear from you, we're calling the police," Charlie warned her.

"I'll call you later. I promise." Kat turned to see that Cara was watching them from the front step. "I'll explain everything." With that, she quickly climbed the steps and ushered her daughter back inside.

"How could Lindy have had an identical twin without you knowing about it," Shep said the moment they were alone in his pickup. "There has to be another explanation."

"It's the only thing that makes any sense. I don't know why I didn't realize it sooner. It explains the DNA match. If Lindy really was murdered that night, then this woman I've seen has to be her identical twin."

"But you would have known. Your father would have known. Did Lindy ever mention a sister?"

Charlie shook her head.

"If true, why keep it a secret? And where did this twin live?"

"I don't know," she said, looking over at him. He made good points. "I just know it's got to be true. For whatever reason, it was a secret. Kat didn't want anyone to know.

But Lindy knew, something that Kat apparently is just now realizing."

He shot her a look of disbelief. "Are you sure you aren't jumping to conclusions? Kat didn't admit that Lindy had a twin."

She gave him a pitying look. "But she also didn't deny it, did she? Shep, I looked into the young woman's eyes. Eyes I had looked in before. In that moment, she knew I recognized her. That's why she needed that scarf back. It was one thing to pretend to be Lindy to scare me, torture me, whatever her motive. It was another for me to know the truth. That she and Lindy shared the same DNA.

"So maybe Lindy isn't dead—but her sister is."

SHEP WATCHED AS Charlie hung up her coat and kicked off her boots before heading for the couch. His head swam. If Charlie was right…

On the way back the two of them had tried to make sense of all this. He knew he wouldn't be able to come to an adequate conclusion without more facts. But that didn't stop Charlie.

"Don't you see? It all makes sense," she argued. "You told me that when you talked to Lindy's teachers about her senior year in high school, they said they noticed she was different from day to day. Mr. Jones thought it was a mental imbalance, but what if the reason Lindy was different was because the girl in the classroom wasn't Lindy at all? It was her identical twin pretending to be her?"

Shep rubbed his temples. "Let's say it's true and that Kat had some reason to keep her second daughter a secret. Where did this twin live? And eat? How is it that someone wouldn't have noticed? And if they both were around those couple of months you lived in that house, Kat had to have known and yet you saw her reaction to our questions."

"Maybe Kat did notice. Maybe she knew," Charlie said with a shrug. "But what could she do? Expose the truth? Not if she was hell-bent on keeping the other daughter a secret. Anyway, we lived in that huge old Victorian house with all these floors and rooms we didn't use, including a really spooky basement none of us ever went down into. The twin could have lived right under our noses."

He couldn't help being skeptical. "So if they did switch at school, where did the other one go all day then?"

She shook her head. "Dad was at work. Kat was always out shopping or having lunch with friends. And remember what the man down the street told you? Someone had hidden a key under a flowerpot in the back. It had to be Lindy so her sister could come and go at will."

He shook his head, amazed at the way Charlie's mind worked.

"The question though, is where has the twin been since Lindy's murder? And why show up now?" she said.

"I believe the question is why Kat would lie about this daughter—if said daughter even exists."

"I have no idea," Charlie admitted. "Sometimes Lindy wasn't as awful as other times. If I'm right, then I was dealing with two different teenage girls with their own motives for what they did."

Shep had to admit the identical twin angle was making sense—if true. But just how dangerous was this other sister? More dangerous than even Charlie thought?

"Do you really think Kat is going to tell us the truth after all these years?" he asked.

Charlie checked her phone. Still nothing from Kat, he

thought. "You don't think she'll try to skip the country, do you?"

It had crossed his mind. "I don't think she'd do that to Cara, but I guess it will come down to how desperate she is to keep all of this a secret. If you're right about an identical twin, then Kat is first class at keeping secrets. She's also not above lying to us," he pointed out. He wouldn't put anything past her—and, he hated to point out, Kat hadn't actually admitted there was a twin.

"We'll see when she calls."

When her phone rang, they both jumped. She checked the screen. "It's Amanda." He could see she didn't want to take it.

"What's up?"

She told him what had happened at work. The ringing stopped—and started again.

"Amanda," Charlie barked into the phone. Earlier, she'd put her phone on speaker anticipating Kat's call.

"I have to know. Greg will be so upset if you aren't my maid of honor."

Shep saw her roll her eyes. "Fine."

"Tara will be so glad."

"Wait, why will Tara be so glad?" Charlie asked.

"Because she is going to be one of my bridesmaids."

"I thought this was a small wedding."

"It is, but the best man has a friend who's coming so I thought why not?"

"So Tara agreed to this?"

"Of course. It's a wedding! Who doesn't want to be in a wedding?" Amanda hung up.

"You're going to be her maid of honor," Shep said as he watched Charlie pocket her phone again.

"I had no choice," she said with a groan.

He couldn't help being worried. That couple was involving Charlie way too much in their romantic intrigue. Now the wedding?

Nervously, she pulled out her phone again. Like her, he was getting anxious. If Kat didn't call soon... He got up from the couch and plugged in the Christmas tree.

"Is that a present under the tree?" Charlie asked and shot him a look. "You bought me a present?" She sounded both surprised and excited.

"The tree just needed something under it."

She shook her head, but he could tell that it pleased her. He was betting she would shake that poor box half to death before Christmas, if he knew this woman, which he did.

Her cell phone rang, making them both jump again.

"Tell me it's not Amanda," he said.

"It's Kat," she said before she accepted the call. "You're in town? Why don't you come to my apartment?" He listened to her give the woman the address before disconnecting. "She's on her way."

CHAPTER TWENTY-TWO

"I DON'T HAVE much time," Kat said as Charlie let her into the apartment ten minutes later. "Cara has a Christmas Eve band performance tonight that I can't miss."

"Then let's not waste time with anything but the truth," Shep suggested.

Charlie took Kat's coat and offered her a seat. Kat perched on the edge of the couch, her purse gripped in her lap, her knuckles white.

"Does Lindy have an identical twin sister?" Shep asked.

Kat nodded and looked away.

"Did you know she's been stalking me?" Charlie asked.

Kat quickly denied it. "I didn't want to believe she was back. I had so hoped you were mistaken. But I can't deny any longer even to myself. It's true. She's here in Montana." Her voice wavered. "Lacey is…Lindy's identical twin."

"Why didn't anyone here know about her?" Shep demanded.

"She was raised by her father in Brazil."

Charlie shot Shep a look. "I don't understand."

Kat opened her mouth, and after a moment, the words just seemed to pour out of her as if they'd been trapped inside for too long.

"I met Matt Garcia when I was on spring break in Brazil. He worked down there for a construction company. He was handsome, came from as a wealthy family in Spain and made great money so we were able to do a lot of traveling and eating at fancy restaurants. I loved the lifestyle, but Matt and I had a tumultuous relationship at best. He wanted to get married and raise a family and I didn't. When I realized I was pregnant, he was delighted. He wanted a child. I…" She looked away. "I didn't."

Charlie could see how hard the confession was for her. But that, too, explained a lot, given how lenient she was with Lindy and her lack of mothering skills. Kat had often seemed as if she didn't want to be bothered by Lindy—or especially by Charlie.

"When I gave birth to twins, Matt knew how I felt. He told me that he was taking custody of them both. He had plenty of money to fight me in the courts if I tried to take them back to the States. I had no money nor did I speak the language as well as Matt. I knew I would lose. I didn't feel I had a choice. I couldn't raise the two of them alone. I told him he could have them. I'd given birth to them at home. He'd immediately gotten them passports because he planned to take them back to Spain to show his family.

"He named them Lindy and Lacey. He was really the only one who could tell them apart." She took a breath and let it out slowly. "I can't explain why I did it. I knew it was over between us. I packed up to return to the States and at the last minute, I grabbed one of the babies from the crib and Lindy's passport and flew home to the States."

"You didn't know which one you took?" Charlie asked.

"She was wearing a onesie with the name Lindy on it."

"And he didn't come after you?" Shep asked.

"I met someone right away, married and changed my name. I thought I'd put the past behind me."

Charlie knew that feeling.

"You never contacted Matt?" Shep asked.

Kat shook her head. "Not until after Lindy was killed."

Charlie wondered if Kat hadn't taken the baby out of spite. But if she was incapable of love, why have another child? "So you didn't hear from Matt or Lacey over the years?"

"No. I assumed that Matt had no idea what had happened to me. He had one of the babies, so I figured he was satisfied enough since I was unaware of him hiring anyone to come after me. My husband adopted Lindy and we changed her last name."

"So there is no chance Lindy's senior year that her sister tracked her down?" Shep asked.

Kat paled visibly.

"Several of her teachers mentioned that Lindy was different from day to day," he added.

Charlie saw the truth in the woman's face. "Lacey found her sister, didn't she?"

Kat lowered her head for a moment before she nodded. "I knew something was wrong with Lindy. She'd always been willful, but that year… I thought that somehow she'd found out about her twin and that's why she treated me the way she did."

"You really didn't know they were both living in the house?" Charlie asked.

Kat let out a sharp hard laugh. "I should have known sooner. Sometimes Lindy was so…hateful. It was as if I didn't know her. At some point, I realized she was Lacey."

"But you never let on?" Shep demanded.

Kat shook her head, her eyes filling with tears. "I didn't dare. I'd never told anyone." Her gaze shifted to Charlie. "Your father didn't know. No one did. One day I ventured down to the basement. I found a small room where someone had been living and some of Lindy's clothing and a dirty plate. I realized what had been going on right under my nose."

"I'm assuming Lacey disappeared from Brazil during the times she was in Montana with us," Charlie said. "How was it her father didn't notice?"

Shep added, "Shouldn't Lacey have been in school?"

"Lindy had been held back a year. Lacey had already graduated," Kat said. "She wasn't living with Matt at the time and she was able to come and go at will." She met Charlie's gaze. "I knew they were mistreating you, but I also knew that if I tried to stop them—"

"You were being *blackmailed* by your own daughters and you still did nothing?" Shep said.

Kat swung an angry glare to him. "You don't have to remind me how weak I was. How weak I still am when it comes to Lindy and Lacey. I thought that if I could just make it until Lindy graduated..." Her voice broke.

"Why continue to keep this awful secret?" Charlie asked, wishing she could find some sympathy for the woman. "You had to know how hurtful it was to both of your daughters."

"How could I ever explain why I grabbed only one of them? Why Lindy? I couldn't even be sure which one I took. Matt might have put the wrong onesie on her during a night feeding..." Her voice trailed off and Charlie felt a jolt so strong that she almost cried out.

"Oh my God, when Lindy was killed, you couldn't have known which daughter died." Charlie's eyes widened. *"You still don't."*

Kat shot to her feet. "It was Lindy, my precious Lindy. I know because Lacey returned to Brazil. Of that, her father was certain." She broke down. "Do you have any idea how all of this has weighed on me? I should have stayed in

Brazil and fought for my children. Or…" She looked away.
"There were so many times I wished I'd left them both in
Brazil with their father." She wiped angrily at her tears. "I
told Matt I wasn't cut out for motherhood. Why I impul-
sively took one…"

Charlie got up and handed her a box of tissues. She tried
to feel something for the woman but only felt for Lindy and
Lacey and their father.

"Who killed your daughter, Kat?" Shep asked when the
woman finally pulled herself together again.

Kat shook her head and sat back down. "At first I
thought…" Her gaze drifted to her stepdaughter.

Charlie felt as if Kat had plunged a knife into her heart.

"You know Charlie didn't do it," Shep snapped. "You're
afraid Lacey killed her sister, aren't you?"

"I don't know who killed my Lindy. I refuse to believe
that Lacey would hurt her twin," Kat cried, shaking her
head adamantly. "No. Why would she?" But even as the
woman denied it, Charlie could see that it had always been
Kat's greatest fear.

"Maybe out of jealousy?" Shep said. "Don't you think
that's why she was so cruel to Charlie? Lacey knew that
she should have been the other sister living in that house."

Charlie heard his words, felt them register. The evil sister. The one who was so horrible to her. Had it been Lacey
and not Lindy?

"Or maybe Lacey killed her to get back at you," he said.
"After all, you chose her sister over her. That made Lindy
your favorite. Not to mention the fact that you knew Lacey
was living in that house and yet you let her remain in the
basement, a secret."

Kat's eyes filled with fresh tears. "No, I don't want to
believe that."

"You said you contacted Matt after the murder," Charlie said. She needed to know the whole story and feared that Kat could make an escape at any moment.

Kat swallowed and nodded, swiping at her tears. "Matt told me that..." She hesitated as if not wanting to say it. "Lacey had a complete breakdown on her return. He said she'd had other problems before that. He hadn't been able to control her. She would take off and be gone for weeks on end without any explanation."

"Matt didn't tell her she had a twin?" Charlie asked.

Kat shook her head. "He was afraid of what she might do. When he found out that she'd been living in our basement for a short while, he was shocked that she had somehow found out about us. Once I told him what I thought had been going on before the murder, he realized it explained the change he'd seen in his daughter. Before that, he thought she was just being a typical teenager."

"You said she had a breakdown when she returned to Brazil after the murder?" Shep asked.

"Lacey was so hysterical after Lindy's murder that... he had to have her institutionalized for her own safety. He blamed me of course for all of it. If I'd left Lindy with him..."

"That shouldn't have come as surprise, given what you did," Charlie said.

"When did you speak to him?" Shep asked.

"I was still in the hospital after the accident. Don't you see? I'd lost everything, both daughters, my husband, everything." She looked up, meeting Charlie's gaze. "I couldn't help myself, let alone you."

Charlie knew that wasn't the reason Kat hadn't reached out to her, but she let it go. Kat looked as if she might break down again.

"You said he institutionalized Lacey?" Shep said. "Like in a mental hospital?"

Kat nodded.

"But now she's out? She has to be out if she's the one who is terrorizing Charlie again."

It took Kat a moment to answer. "I heard a few weeks ago that Matt had been killed in an accident on a construction job. Apparently Lacey had been doing better so she was allowed to attend her father's funeral with an attendant. The attendant was found unconscious with a head injury and Lacey was gone."

"And we know where she turned up, don't we?" Charlie shuddered at what the young woman was capable of doing. "Why me? Why wouldn't she haunt you and your new daughter?"

But she didn't wait for an answer because it came to her like a bolt of lightning. Her eyes filled with tears as she swung her gaze to Shep. "Because she blames me for her sister's death. Which means she was there that night."

"Clearly, all this hatred has little to do with you, Charlie," Shep said quickly. "It's misdirected."

Kat clutched her purse. "I know what you both think of me. But I can't change the past. If I could…" She rose again. "I have to go."

"Not yet. What happened to Charlie's doll? The one her father bought her?" Shep asked.

The woman blinked. "The doll? Oh, that doll. I forgot all about it. It was such a beautiful, valuable doll, I couldn't leave it in that old house since I knew you wouldn't be back for it, Charlie."

"You couldn't have gotten it to Charlie anytime over the years," Shep asked.

"If it makes you feel any better," Kat said, clearly ignoring him, "you aren't the only one who's been terrorized by my daughter. When you told me about the doll, I knew Lacey had been in my house. I'd noticed other things that had gone missing. Mostly money, jewelry, favorite things of mine. I thought I'd imagined it at first—just like that lingering scent of Lindy's favorite perfume." Kat bit her lip as if to hold back more tears. "It was Lindy's favorite so of course Lacey would wear it."

"She destroyed the doll and left it on my doorstep."

Kat's expression crumpled for a moment. "I'm sorry, I didn't know the doll was missing from my room. But you're not the only one she wants to hurt. It's why after the band concert tonight I'm taking Cara and leaving town." She looked pointedly at Charlie. "I would suggest you do the same."

"I'm not running," Charlie said as she rose to her feet. "I've been running for too long."

Shep joined her and put his arm around her.

"You do realize, Kat, that the police will now be involved," Shep said. "They're going to want to talk to you."

"I have to think of Cara. I'd hoped to keep all of this from her until she was older. She is so sweet and innocent. I don't know what effect this will have on her, so I'm not waiting around to see what Lacey will do next. I can't for Cara's sake."

"I think it's too late for that," Charlie said. "I'm betting Cara already knows about Lacey. Otherwise, how has Lacey been getting in and out of your house without you noticing?"

"Also there was a second set of fingerprints on Charlie's doll," Shep said. "Not Lacey's which would be so similar to Lindy's. I'd wager they're Cara's."

Kat's face froze for a moment. She seemed to stagger and

looked down at the floor as if it had opened and she'd gotten a glimpse of hell. She appeared to shrink before their eyes.

As she turned to leave, her face taut with fear, Charlie saw the woman's world crumbling around her.

CHAPTER TWENTY-THREE

CHARLIE WAS STILL in shock after Kat's visit. Shep had gotten on the phone to the judge, filling him in. It was clear that WT agreed. It was time to call in the law. The judge must have asked if she was up to being questioned by the police.

She saw Shep look over at her and smile before he said, "She can handle it. She's a lot stronger than she looks."

"You really think Lacey killed her twin?" Charlie asked after he finished his call.

"Mulvane said it was a crime of passion. I'm betting Lacey was there that night and knows what happened. If she was involved, it would explain her breakdown."

"Then she also knows that I locked Lindy out of the house. That could explain why she wanted to make me think I was losing my mind."

"Kat said Lacey had had problems before," he said. "If she was mentally unstable, who knows what could have gone down between the twins. You heard what Kat said. I got the impression she's afraid of her daughter." He sat down next to her. "The judge is contacting someone he knows in the police department. They are going to want to talk to us, especially you, about all of this."

She nodded. "Why didn't I see it? I thought Lindy's strange mood swings were just her being an unhappy teenager. Now looking back, she was often like two completely different people. If Lacey was the one who was so cruel to me, why didn't she confront Kat?"

"Maybe Lindy wouldn't let her," Shep suggested. "Lindy wasn't happy with her mother's marriage, but she was smart enough to know that if Lacey blew the whistle on Kat, things could get a whole lot worse."

That made sense, Charlie thought. So Lindy would have allowed her sister into her life, letting her play a role to keep her quiet until... Until Lacey got sick of it and wanted more? She worried that they might never know.

But Lacey was still out there. What would she do next?

The person she really couldn't get her head around was their mother. "How could Kat have done what she did?" she said, curling up in her spot on the couch to face Shep. "How could any mother do that?"

He shook his head. "Not everyone is cut out to be a parent." His cell phone rang. He answered it. "Yes. No, that would be fine." He disconnected. "You ready to go down to the police station? This is not the way I imagined us spending Christmas Eve but..."

Charlie nodded. "I just want this over."

"It won't be over until they catch Lacey," he said, as if he had to remind her.

HOURS LATER, CHARLIE climbed into bed completely exhausted. She'd been asked a million questions. In the end, she knew that the chance of Lacey being caught was slim. Even if she was, the woman hadn't done anything really threatening, just as the officer had said. Lacey was wanted in Brazil so she would be extradited if found. But even a stalking charge would be hard to make stick in this country since Charlie had only seen Lacey a few times even with the destroyed doll as evidence. If Charlie saw her again, she was to call.

She felt deflated and was sure Shep felt the same. He'd been angry, hoping the police could do more. As it was, they couldn't even confirm her and Shep's stories because they hadn't been able to reach Kat. Her husband had no idea where she'd gone, but she'd taken their daughter, Cara. History repeating itself, Charlie thought.

She hoped for sleep, but as she lay in bed, all she could think about was Lacey and how she must have felt when she learned about her twin and what her mother had done. She had to be the one who had tormented Charlie in high school. The one who'd played those awful tricks on her. Had Lindy been innocent all along? And yet she was the one to end up murdered behind the house.

She could hear Shep tossing and turning on the couch in the living room. Like her, he was having trouble getting to sleep. She thought about the present under the tree from him.

Tears filled her eyes. What if he was he right? What if she had trusted him after boot camp? Could they have been together all these years? The thought made her chest ache. She would never know what she might have cost them. Was it too late? Could Shep ever trust her again? Why did that mean so much to her?

Finally, too exhausted to keep her eyes open, she drifted off into a troubled sleep filled with monsters all wearing Lindy's and Lacey's faces.

CHRISTMAS MORNING, Shep got up and turned on the Christmas tree lights before seeing to the coffee. It all felt so normal, being here with Charlie, he thought as he went to get her newspaper outside her apartment door.

He could feel the holiday slipping away. It wasn't that many days before he would have to return to Stevensville and his classroom. The thought made him hurt. How could he leave if Lacey hadn't been found yet? He couldn't.

At the sound of Charlie's bedroom door opening, he put the paper on the table and poured her a cup of coffee. Glancing at her as she came into the kitchen wrapped in a thick white robe, he wondered if she felt anything like he did. The way she reached for the mug of coffee, he suspected she hadn't slept well either. He'd had a terrible time getting to sleep last night only to have nightmares, something he hadn't had since he was a kid.

He watched her flip to the horoscopes and read. He'd already looked.

Problems? Put your personal life on hold for a few days to deal with them. The good news is that you are finally getting the recognition you deserve. Enjoy it.

She groaned as she tossed the paper aside, then took a gulp of her coffee and glanced toward the window. "It looks freezing outside. Everything is frosted."

"It's December in Montana," he pointed out as he joined her at the table. "Of course it's freezing. It's what everyone hopes for, right? A white Christmas. By the way, Merry Christmas." He smiled at her from across the table.

Charlie met his gaze and gave him a slow smile. "Oh my gosh, it is Christmas Day." Her smiled broadened. "Merry Christmas, Shep."

He felt that pull at his heart as he looked at her and had to swallow the lump that rose in his throat. He'd never dreamed they would ever be sharing this holiday together and yet here they were. Destiny? Not something he believed in and yet as he looked at her, he could only hope.

"Do you want your present now or after breakfast?" he asked. "I know how you are about presents."

"Shep—"

"It's not a big deal," he said quickly. "Just something I saw and I thought of you."

CHARLIE USUALLY DID little on Christmas other than go to a midnight service on Christmas Eve. She had no family, and friends were with their families the night before Christmas. Tara had given her the small tree in her kitchen, which she kept out all year long.

There was nothing more lonely than a Christmas tree with no presents under it. And she wasn't about to buy presents for herself to put under a tree. That was too pathetic.

In truth, she'd been excited about the present Daniel had said he'd gotten her for Christmas. But at the same time, she hadn't had a clue what to get him. The other day, when she was shopping for a present for Tara's new baby, she'd thought about what she could get Shep, since he'd gotten her something. What would mean something to him?

Now, looking into his blue eyes filled with excitement because of the gift he wanted to give her, she knew she couldn't deny him this.

"Okay, presents before breakfast."

He grinned and jumped up. "Stay right there."

She watched him rush into the other room to retrieve the package he'd left under the tree.

When he carried it into the kitchen, he seemed to hesitate before he handed it to her. "I hope you like it."

Charlie took her time unwrapping the rather large box, making him sigh and shake his head. He'd only given her one other present and she'd been so surprised that she'd torn into it, paper flying. But she'd been sixteen and madly in love.

Now at almost thirty, she was still in love, she realized. Still madly. But also afraid that she was about to get her heart broken. It had been hard enough to heal at sixteen. She feared she never would at thirty.

"Charlie, come on. Open it. I promise it won't bite you," Shep said from across the table.

She smiled at him and, shoving away the paper, opened the box and then froze.

"It's not exactly like the one from your mom and dad, but it's as close as I could find."

She couldn't speak, could barely breathe. Tears filled her eyes as she looked at the soft, new, leather-bound photo album. He'd remembered. The album had been the only thing she'd grabbed that day before the policeman had turned her over to social services. It was all she had left— photos growing up with her mother and father.

"I saw that your old album was full," Shep said tentatively, as if not sure how to gauge her reaction. "I hope it's okay. I thought you could start collecting new memories… Charlie, say something."

She looked up him, still so choked up, she wasn't sure what would come out if she dared tried to speak. Tears coursed down her cheeks. She quickly wiped them away before they fell on the new leather. He looked so worried, so handsome, his eyes so filled with…love. She swallowed the lump in her throat and said the first words that came to her lips.

"I love it. I love…you for remembering."

Relief washed over his face for a moment before he broke into a smile. "I was so afraid…" He didn't need to finish.

"It's beautiful," she said, touching the warm leather. "It's perfect."

She pushed to her feet and stood on shaky legs for a moment. "I did go shopping for you but—"

"No, it's fine," he said quickly. "I don't need anything. I hope you didn't think you had to get me something. Really, I just wanted—"

"I do have something for you." She left the kitchen and went to her bedroom. She'd put the envelope in the top drawer of her nightstand. It seemed too small now, too insubstantial, too little, maybe too late above all else.

But she took it out, holding it in her hand, noticing how the paper had yellowed, the edges of the envelope dogeared from years of carrying it around with her. She took a breath and let it out, her heart so full that she still had trouble breathing, before she returned to the kitchen.

Shep was busy starting their breakfast. She could tell he was embarrassed. He thought he'd put her on the spot with the present. She smiled to herself, seeing that he didn't want her upset about not buying him anything. That was so like him.

"This is for you," she said, feeling her own embarrassment at her unsightly gift.

He looked from her to the envelope in her hand and back again. "Charlie?"

She could understand his confusion as he took the battered envelope from her. His name was printed on the outside, the ink faded.

There was a question in his gaze, but he slowly lowered himself into a kitchen chair. She felt her heart rise to her throat as he carefully opened the envelope and took out the single sheet of paper inside.

Dear Shep,

He had been holding his breath but now had to let it out as he breathed and continued reading.

This is the hardest thing I have ever done. It makes the judge's boot camp seem easy. I love you. With all my heart, which is breaking as I write this. But we are too young. All this happened too soon. I know that but it doesn't make this any easier.

He had to stop to swallow before he could go on. All these years, he believed that she'd left because she hadn't loved him. Not enough.

I'm going to leave later tonight, because if I see you tomorrow as we planned, I won't be able to go, and I have to for both of our sakes. I know you said we would find a way. But I love you too much. I don't want to keep you from whatever life promises are ahead of you.

Blinking back his own tears, he saw where the paper was wrinkled and the writing smeared from her tears so long ago.

Don't hate me for taking this way out. If it hadn't been for you that day on the obstacle course... I owe you whatever good things happen in my life.
   I'll never forget you. I'll never stop loving you,
Charlie

At the bottom of the sheet of paper was a drawing, re-minding him again of how Charlie was always doodling that summer they were together. He studied the doodle and felt his heart stutter in his chest. His throat went dry. "It's us."

She had drawn them holding hands as the sun rose behind them.

For a moment, he couldn't look at her. His eyes burned with unshed tears as he carefully folded the letter and put it back in the envelope with great care.

She had loved him. She hadn't just walked away as if what they had wasn't something special. Why hadn't she gotten this to him? Didn't she know that he would have moved heaven and earth to find her?

He nodded to himself. She knew. She knew that once he saw this letter, there would be nothing stopping him from finding her, from keeping her. His heart cried out that they could have made it even as young as they were. But his common sense knew what a struggle it would have been. Their love could have overcome the obstacles. He was sure of that. But at what cost?

Setting the envelope carefully on the table, he looked up at her, this woman he'd loved for so long and thought he'd lost forever. They couldn't rewrite the past. The future stretched out in front of them. If he was smart, if he was lucky, if he was reading the look in her eyes correctly...

"Charlie."

And then he was on his feet and she was in his arms and he was kissing her and holding her and saying all the things he never got to say to her all those years ago.

CHAPTER TWENTY-FOUR

CHARLIE HAD TOLD herself all the rational reasons she couldn't, wouldn't. But once she was in Shep's arms again, all those arguments flew out the window. It was Christmas. He'd just given her the best present she could ever ask for. And yet neither of those was the reasons she said yes.

For the first time in a very long time, she didn't feel the hand of doom hanging over her. There was no dark cloud dogging her. She was stepping into sunshine without an umbrella. It seemed inconceivable, but she wasn't afraid of what tomorrow would bring. She could embrace the moment without fear.

The look he'd given her had required only one word. Yes. Yes, she wanted him. Yes, she had never stopped loving him. Yes, she could no longer fight it.

The realization had made her laugh with glee. She loved this man. This middle school math teacher who'd come to Bozeman to try to save her because he still loved her even after the way she'd left him all those years ago.

"Yes?" he asked as his gaze locked with hers.

"Yes." It came out on an excited breath. *"Yes."*

Shep laughed and swung her up into his arms. Kissing her, he shoved open her bedroom door and carried her to the edge of her unmade bed before slowly lowering her to her feet.

Their gazes locked. She could feel her own heart thundering in her chest as he kissed her again. Deepening the kiss, her body pressed tight against his. She could feel every hard inch of him. He pulled back only enough to untie the sash on her robe. She felt it fall open, heard his surprise as he looked down at what she was wearing.

"That's my T-shirt," he said.

"What's left of it," she admitted. "It went from soft to so thin now that…" She didn't have to tell him that the T-shirt was almost transparent. As his gaze moved over her, she felt her hard nipples pressing against the sheer fabric.

"You kept it."

She nodded, emotion threatening to choke her. "It smelled like you. And then it didn't, but it was still yours."

He shook his head as if he couldn't believe it. Couldn't believe her. Desire burned in his eyes. His gaze locked with hers as he slipped her robe from her shoulders. It dropped to the floor at her feet, the T-shirt following it. His gaze moved over her body like a caress. Heat rippled over her right behind it, then goose bumps.

"Charlie, you're so beautiful." His voice broke.

She reached for his Western shirt, making the snaps sing as she jerked it open. Her palms pressed against the warm skin of his chest, feeling the hard muscles beneath. As he stood there in nothing but jeans, she was reminded of him in only a towel. Could this man be any sexier?

He pulled her to him, kissing her deeply before trailing warm kisses down her throat. She shivered with longing as he pressed his lips to the hollow between her breasts, then took one hard nipple in his mouth and sucked gently. A moan escaped her. She arched against his mouth as he took the other nipple. His fingers caressed a path across her stomach and found her center.

She felt the wet warmth as he touched her in a way that

made her insides go liquid. He took her higher and higher until she cried out with joy and sweet release. Her legs threatened to give out under her just before he swept her up into his arms again and lay her down on the bed.

She didn't remember taking off his jeans, but her one desire had been to feel his naked body against her own.

For years, she'd thought of the boy she'd known. Now she found herself wrapped in the arms of the man he'd become. She felt the old memories fade as the two of them made love with an even stronger, more sustainable passion.

LATER, SATED AND drifting in a cloud of contentment, she looked over at Shep. She could feel his hand on her bare thigh. There was a smile on his face, his eyes shining as he glanced over at her.

"Does that answer any questions you might have?" he whispered.

She shook her head. "It requires no explanation." She grinned. "But can I at least say, *wow*."

He laughed. "My sentiments exactly." He rolled on his side to face her. "Charlie." He grazed his knuckles down her cheek, his gaze locking with hers. "I love you."

"I love you, Shep. I always have. I always will."

He smiled and leaned forward to kiss her. "Merry Christmas, Charlie."

"Merry Christmas."

CHAPTER TWENTY-FIVE

CHRISTMAS DAY PASSED in a blur. There was cooking together in the kitchen listening to holiday music and laughing. There was more lovemaking. There were card games and board games. And later there were glasses of wine while sitting on the couch with only the lights of the Christmas tree twinkling in the room.

It had been one of the best days of his life, Shep thought the next morning when he awoke in Charlie's bed with her in his arms. For a while, he'd been able to forget about Lindy and Lacey and the fact that Charlie was still in danger. He was actually looking forward to leaving town and going up to the ski resort at Big Sky for Amanda and Greg's wedding.

"I thought we'd get some breakfast when we arrive at the resort," he said after they'd showered and dressed and were having coffee in the kitchen.

She glanced at him over the rim of her mug. They'd made love again this morning before heading for the shower together. They couldn't seem to get enough of each other.

"Your horoscope says that you've come through some confusing times, but that you have chosen the right path. Have confidence you have a bright future ahead." He actually got her to smile. "Maybe it won't be as bad as you think, maid of honor."

Charlie groaned. "My phone blew up this morning with

the details. Amanda bought me a dress to wear. She said she can't trust me to have bought something appropriate or worse, that I didn't buy something special at all." She shook her head. "She is right about that anyway. She said she guessed at my size—with Greg's help." She groaned as Shep raised a brow.

"I'll be glad when these two are married. Greg has definitely taken a special interest in you that I find disturbing."

She nodded. "You aren't the only one."

"But once he sees us together…" He reached across the table to take her hand. "I can't find the words for how I feel this morning."

Charlie grinned. "Maybe you feel the same way I do. Spectacularly amazing? Are you really going to ski?"

"Snowboard. I took it up a couple of years ago. I could give you a lesson."

She laughed.

"Did I ever tell you that I love your laugh?"

She laughed again.

"Or I could keep you warm inside the lodge."

"I HAVE BEEN dreading this trip," Charlie admitted. "But the idea of curling up with you in the lodge definitely has its appeal." That wasn't all. It would be good to get away from town for a while. Away from the Lindy/Lacey problem.

"They got another ten inches of snow last night," Shep said. "I'm actually glad that we're going. I'll just be glad when the wedding part is over."

She was having trouble keeping her mind on the wedding. Kat had apparently skipped town with her youngest daughter, just as she said she was going to. And Lacey? No one knew.

"The police aren't going to do anything, are they?" she said to Shep.

He didn't seem surprised at the trail her thoughts had taken. "There isn't a lot they can do. You gave them a photo of Lindy so they'll be on the lookout for her twin. That's about all they can do at this point unless she tries to get on a plane."

"Or until she breaks the law by killing me."

"Exactly," Shep said, squeezing her hand. "But she has to kill me first to get to you."

Charlie grimaced. "Thanks, that makes me feel so much better." She glanced at her phone. "I should get dressed. According to Amanda's schedule, we have rehearsal this afternoon, followed by a dinner." He let go of her hand as she rose and finished her coffee. "But I'm warning you right now. I will need breakfast sooner than Big Sky. I don't remember having dinner last night, which means I didn't, and after…" As she met those bottomless blue eyes, she grinned. "I need sustenance."

SHEP SEEMED IN a great mood as they drove out of Bozeman toward Big Sky and Charlie found it contagious. She thought about how angry he'd been with Kat, with the police, with the situation. But today, with the sky a brilliant blue, the sun turning the fallen snow to sparkling crystals, he seemed…free. At least for a while.

Lacey was not completely forgotten though. But this two-day wedding retreat had come along at the perfect time. Charlie was sure Shep was feeling it as well. A sense of freedom. Not to mention the exhilaration and buoyancy of being in love. She'd forgotten what that felt like and realized with a start that she hadn't felt it with Daniel. She'd been happy to have a boyfriend, but they'd never shared this kind of intimacy—let alone love.

She was going to enjoy it. As long as it lasted. *Where did that come from?*

They stopped at a small café in the Gallatin Canyon and had a late breakfast with a view of the river flowing under a thick sheet of ice. As they drove toward Big Sky, the snow grew deeper. It was clumped on the pines, piled in the parking lot, drifting beside the road. The temperature seemed to drop the closer they got to the ski hill. Ice crystals hung in the air, glittering in the sunlight.

"Beautiful," she said determined to embrace winter and this weekend.

"Yes, isn't she," Shep said and grinned when she turned to mug a face at him. "You are beautiful, Charlie. Inside and out."

"You're embarrassing me."

He laughed. "I know for a fact that it takes more than that to embarrass you."

She narrowed her eyes at him. "You're enjoying this."

"Being here with you? You'd better believe it."

"No, I mean this wedding weekend. When I told you about it, I thought you wouldn't want to go."

"You knew I was sticking to you until all of this Lindy/Lacey trouble is over. No way I wasn't coming with you. Anyway, I like weddings."

She gave him a side-eye. "I've never met a man who liked weddings except for the open bar."

"You have now." He drove for a moment without looking at her. "I've thought about the kind of wedding I'd like to have."

Charlie raised a brow as her heart took off at a gallop. "Seriously? I can't wait to hear."

He relaxed behind the wheel as if in thought. "Well, you're going to have to wait because I only share that kind of information with the woman I'm going to marry."

She felt herself flush. "I'm never sure what to believe with you."

"Believe that this time," he said, looking over at her, "I'm not letting you go."

Charlie's gaze locked with his for a moment. She felt such love that it brought tears to her eyes. Her heart drummed in her chest as a pleasurable warmth rushed along her veins. He had no idea how badly she wanted to believe that they were going to get a second chance.

AMANDA CAME RUNNING out of the hotel as they drove up— beating even the valet to Shep's pickup, almost before he'd come to a stop. "Come on. You're late. We have so much to go over."

Charlie turned as if to say something to Shep but Amanda cut her off. "She'll see you later. We have a lot of do and the day is more than half over." She shoved a sheet of paper at him. "There are all the times and places where you need to be." She practically dragged Charlie out of the truck.

"Your keys, sir?" the valet said and Shep handed them over. Getting out, he retrieved Charlie's bag and his own and let the valet drive away before he walked through the hotel entrance.

Inside, he took a moment to look around...and realized he was looking for Lacey. He'd told himself that she couldn't know about the wedding, that this weekend he didn't have to worry, but he still did. Until she was caught, he would keep worrying.

His cell phone rang as he reached the reception desk.

He saw it was Paul Wagner and stepped away to take the call. "Mr. Wagner."

"Call me Paul," the elderly man said. "After you left, I got to thinking. I was so sure my boys didn't know those girls. Did you have a chance to talk to my stepsons?" Before Shep could answer, Wagner went on, "I found something. It's a photograph from a box the boys left behind when they moved out. Figured I could store it better than them, I guess." He grumbled under his breath for a moment. "Anyway, I'm sure it doesn't mean anything. But it appears my boys knew one of them well enough to have their pictures taken with her. If you'd like to swing by."

"I'm out of town. But are you telling me your stepsons knew Charlie or Lindy?"

"Not Charlie. At least she's not in the photo. But I'm holding a picture of two of my stepsons posed in a photo with the blonde between them. They're both grinning like they just scored a six-pack of Bud. I would imagine a friend took the photo. I can't imagine the oldest, Allen, being involved in any tomfoolery. Like I said, I don't think it means anything. But it might jar their memories, not that they probably can help much."

Shep felt a small jolt. He hadn't tried to call two of the stepsons back and they hadn't returned his calls. He'd been thinking that once they found Lacey, they would have their killer. Now here was Paul Wagner giving him more suspects. Possibly. Just because the stepsons were photographed with Lindy, that didn't mean one of them had anything to do with her death. The photo could have been a one-off.

Still… "Is there any way you could text me the photo?"

Wagner's laugh was high and shrill. "*Text?* I might be able to take a photo of the snapshot and email it. I'll give that a try. If I fail, maybe I could get my neighbor to help. She's much more techie than I am."

"Thanks. I appreciate it." He gave Wagner his email address, disconnected and walked back over to the registration desk to check in. As he got his key, leaving Charlie's for her at the desk in case he missed catching up to her, he wondered where she was right now. Heading for the elevator, he thought he'd drop off the bags and find her.

He couldn't shake the bad feeling he'd had since Wagner's call. What if Lindy's killer wasn't Lacey? What if it was someone that Shep wouldn't even recognize if he passed him in the hotel hallway—and neither would Charlie?

More than ever he wanted to see the photograph of the man's stepsons and Lindy.

CHAPTER TWENTY-SIX

"I'M SURE it's just cold feet," Charlie said not for the first time as she poured them each a glass of wine. She'd spent several hours trying on the dresses Amanda had brought for her to wear as maid of honor. Finally, Amanda had approved of a little navy one that Charlie actually liked. It was Amanda's gift to her.

Charlie really didn't want to take any gifts from her, but she wasn't up to arguing. Amanda seemed high-strung and nervous enough as Charlie watched her pace the anteroom outside where the rehearsal and wedding would take place.

"That's all it is," Amanda agreed. "Cold feet. I mean, I *want* to spend my life with Greg. He's a good man. He wants to help me start my own business. He's solid, you know?"

"Right, solid," Charlie said, handing her a glass of wine. "Today's just the rehearsal. Easy peasy."

Amanda took the wineglass and stopped pacing for a moment. "Have you ever been married?"

"No," Charlie had to admit. She'd never even come close. She thought of Daniel. Even if he had bought her a ring for Christmas, she wouldn't have married him. She realized after being with Shep that she'd subconsciously measured every man she met by him and they'd all fallen short. Not that there had been that many.

"Greg's a great guy," Amanda was saying. "He takes

good care of me. He wants me to be happy." Her voice broke. "I know you think I'm awful but I do love him and he loves me. Did I tell you where we're going on our honeymoon? Bora-Bora. We're going to stay in one of those little huts on the water. We'll even have our own private pool where we can skinny-dip. Naked."

She was familiar with skinny-dipping, Charlie thought. A sudden memory of a teenage Shep, his tanned, lean young body glistening with water droplets, filled her mind. She'd seen that improved body in the shower again this morning.

Amanda cleared her throat. "Not that I haven't skinny-dipped before."

Charlie definitely didn't want to hear about that. "So it's all good," she said and poured herself another glass of wine. It was way too early to start drinking, but she needed fortification. Amanda had insisted she try on a half dozen dresses earlier.

"I let Greg hire the photographer. I hope he's good. There will be photos of you and me. That's why I wanted your dress to complement mine. I don't care what Tara wears. There probably won't be many photos of her anyway. But I definitely want good ones of Greg and the best man."

"Who is the best man?" Charlie asked, not that it really mattered. She felt guilty for not having more interest as the maid of honor—just as she did for mentally counting down the hours until Greg and Amanda were married and on their honeymoon.

"Royce Braden," Amanda said, watching Charlie for a reaction.

It didn't take but an instant. Charlie choked on her wine. "Amanda, tell me Royce isn't…" She saw the answer in the woman's face and swore under her breath.

"You said you didn't hear my conversation," Amanda cried, going on the attack.

Holding up a hand to stop her, Charlie lowered her voice. "You have been having an affair with the *best man*?"

"He isn't the best man yet."

"What is his relationship to Greg?" Charlie demanded.

Amanda had the good grace to look uncomfortable. "His best friend."

Charlie swore again, wishing she'd said a flat no to this. She could have even just not given a reason when Amanda had asked her to be maid of honor. Just said no, hell no.

Speaking slowly and clearly, Charlie said, "You expect me to stand up there with you and Greg and your lover while you say your vows?"

"I made a mistake, all right?"

"Yes, asking me to be your maid of honor was definitely a mistake."

"No!" Amanda cried. "Getting involved with Royce was a huge mistake. I'm sorry. I broke it off. I swear. It will never happen again." She grabbed Charlie's free arm. "Don't abandon me. What would I tell Greg? He thinks so much of you."

Charlie groaned inwardly. She thought she might throw up.

"Please," Amanda begged. "Haven't you ever made a mistake, one you regretted your whole life?"

Charlie felt herself weaken as she thought of a locked door and a screaming stepsister on the other side. As she freed her arm from Amanda's talon-like grip, she also thought about walking away from Shep all those years ago. Then she thought of agreeing to be this woman's maid of honor.

"Yes, I've made my share of mistakes," she admitted reluctantly. "But Amanda—"

"I promise that I'm going to make Greg a good wife," Amanda said, all smiles.

"You sent me a dead mouse."

She flinched. "I shouldn't have done that either. I was upset."

"Were you also upset when you put eye drops in Greg's and my chocolate mousse that made us deathly sick?"

"I regret doing that as well. I borrowed Greg's eye drops from his suit pocket when he went to talk to those other people. I was upset and jealous at lunch that day and I'd had too much to drink."

"Not an excuse," Charlie snapped. It was all she could do not to walk out of here and not look back. But she remembered Tara was involved in this wedding now. She couldn't abandon her. She'd go through with the wedding but then that was it.

"Please don't back out on me. I'll beg. Is that what you want?"

"No." Charlie didn't want begging. Still the words were hard to say. "I won't back out." Only because she was trapped.

"Thank you so much." Amanda threw her arms around her, hugging her so tightly Charlie couldn't breathe.

She wiggled free and gulped down the rest of her wine. "But after this…"

"I won't give you any more trouble. Did you forget? I'm quitting as office manager and starting my own business at home. Maybe the next office manager will like you better."

Charlie shook her head as she put down her empty wineglass and excused herself, saying over her shoulder, "I'll see you at the rehearsal."

SHEP DROPPED THEIR bags off in their room. He had no idea what would happen next with him and Charlie. They couldn't move forward until Lacey was found and stopped from whatever she had planned. The odds that Lacey had killed her sister in a fit of jealousy were still good. He couldn't bear the thought that they might never know for certain who the killer was. He wasn't sure Charlie could live with that uncertainty.

He was trying to find her when he walked by the lounge. A breaking news alert on the television behind the bar caught his attention. He stopped cold as he recognized the face even before he saw the name on the screen.

Jason Harper?

Hurriedly stepping into the bar, he pointed at the television and asked, "Can you turn that up?" The anchor was talking about a hit-and-run accident in Bozeman that took the life of an employee at a local gaming company.

"You know the guy?" the bartender asked.

Shep nodded. According to the story, the police were looking into the accident. Area surveillance cameras had caught a dark SUV plowing into Harper when he came out of a local business and was crossing the street to his vehicle. The SUV was later found abandoned. Police say it had been stolen earlier that day from a south side residence. The news program cut to another story.

"Bummer," the bartender said, shaking his head. "What are the chances someone stole a car and accidently ran this guy over? Probably some kids out for a joyride."

Shep wasn't buying that the driver of that car had been some kid on a joyride. Especially considering that the dead man was Daniel's roommate and had been privately investigating Lindy Parker's murder.

He pulled out his phone as he stepped away from the

bar. It took a few minutes before Daniel came on the line. Shep introduced himself quickly as a friend of Jason's from Billings. He wasn't sure the ruse would work, but he didn't think Jason and Daniel had been so close that they knew all of each others friends. "I just heard the news."

"Everyone here is in shock. It's his day off. He said he had some things to do... I still can't believe it."

"This is way off in left field, but Jason told me he was looking into some old murder case involving a girl in Bozeman fifteen years ago. You don't think..."

"Whoa," Daniel said. "I hadn't even thought of that. I just heard he'd done that. Have you met his girlfriend? I think she's the one who put him up to it."

"His girlfriend? He did mention a blonde."

"Yeah, that's her. Jason told me she was freaky, freaky scary. She was obsessed with death."

Lacey? "What was her name?"

"I never met her so I don't know her name and he never mentioned it. I saw her once waiting for him outside of work. A nice-looking blonde."

"I might mention her to the cops," Shep said. "Or maybe you already have?"

"You're right. I should."

Shep quickly got off the line, more determined than ever to find Charlie. He'd thought they were safe here in Big Sky. But he recalled how Lacey had found Charlie at the baby shower. It could have been even easier for her to find out about the wedding and already be on the mountain—after killing Jason Harper.

CHAPTER TWENTY-SEVEN

ESCAPING AMANDA, Charlie hurried down to the reception desk to get her key. Back upstairs, she'd barely walked into her room when there was a knock at the door. Shep? She was already smiling as she opened the door. She needed a friendly face and someone who could commiserate.

Her smile dissolved as she was startled to see who was standing there. "Greg, what are you doing here?" In her surprise, the words were out before she could call them back.

"I need to talk to you."

"Now is not a good time," she said quickly but he was already coming into the room. She stood, still holding the door open, as she watched him walk to the window and look out, his back to her. "I'm meeting a friend downstairs. I'm already late."

"This won't take long," Greg said as he turned to look at her. "Can you please close the door? I'd prefer this not be overheard. It won't take long, I promise."

She didn't want to close the door, but more than that, she didn't think she wanted to hear what he had to tell her. He looked so serious. Just like at the bar the other day. But it was clear that he wasn't leaving until he had his say.

Slowly she closed the door, but didn't move away from it. "What is this about, Greg?" she asked, her throat tight. She worried that she already knew. But if the wedding was canceled, that meant they would get to leave, so maybe it was better to just rip off the bandage and end this quick, right?

"I tried to tell you the other day in the bar." He looked nervous, his gaze flicking around the room as he took a few steps toward her. "There was this other woman—"

"Shouldn't you be telling this to Amanda?" Charlie interrupted. Why was he determined to tell her any of this?

He shook his head. "This doesn't have anything to do with her."

"But you're getting married tomorrow. I was with her earlier. She's so excited. She can't wait to be your wife. She was telling me that she's going to be a really good wife to you." She knew she was babbling but he was making her so nervous, she couldn't help herself. She didn't want to hear that he wasn't going to marry Amanda, she realized.

"I met this other woman years ago," he continued as if she hadn't interrupted him. "Do you remember your first love?"

She nodded, thinking of Shep, wishing for him right now.

"You never get over it—if it's the real thing. For me, it *was* the real thing." He let out a self-deprecating chuckle. "Unfortunately, it wasn't for her. Maybe that's why I keep making the same mistake, falling for the wrong women."

Oh boy, here it comes, she thought.

He was standing directly in front of her now, having slowly crossed the room until he had her nearly pinned against the door. "I know about Amanda."

Charlie had nothing to say to that.

"I know about her and Royce. Don't look so surprised. I'm no fool. But that doesn't change anything." He shrugged. "She had to get it out of her system. I understand that."

She groaned inwardly, unsure where this was heading.

"I also know that she's the one who sent you the mouse. If she was still bothering you, you'd tell me, wouldn't you?"

"Of course."

He looked at her as if to say she was a terrible liar, which she was.

"I don't know what her problem is with you," he said with a shake of his head. "I guess she senses that I have a connection to you."

Oh no, this isn't going there.

"I'm so sorry," Greg was saying.

"There isn't a problem," Charlie said quickly, her heart pounding as she reached for the door handle behind her. "I'm going to be her maid of honor. In fact, I really need to get downstairs to meet—"

"You asked me at the bar if I'd hired a headhunter to get you." He chuckled again, smiling as he looked at her in a way that made her even more nervous. "I lied about using a headhunter for the rest of my staff. I should have told you the truth. I wanted you and I was determined to get you."

She felt light-headed. This was *not* happening. Not with the wedding rehearsal this afternoon. Not with her alone in this room with him. She felt a sliver of fear work its way up her spine. Could she get out the door without him stopping her? How far did he plan to take this? "Greg—"

"It's all right." He reached for her just as she heard a card being inserted in the locked door behind her.

She let out a silent thank-you as the door opened only a few inches before it collided with her body.

"Charlie?" Shep's voice was the most wonderful sound she thought she'd ever heard.

"Shep!" She quickly slipped past Greg and moved away from the door to allow Shep to enter.

One look at her face and he said, "What's wrong?" and took a step into the room, stopping short of her boss. "I didn't realize you had company."

"Greg was just leaving," she said. For a moment it was as if they were all frozen in place.

"I'm sure we'll get another chance to talk," Greg said, nodding at her as he moved toward the open doorway.

It wasn't until he'd left, closing the door behind him, that Charlie threw herself into Shep's arms.

"YOU'RE SHAKING LIKE A LEAF," Shep said, holding her tightly against him. "What the hell was that about?"

Charlie pulled back. She still looked pale and shaken. "I have no idea but from the way he was talking… I'm not sure there is going to be a wedding. I think he might have hired me for more than my design skills."

Shep held her by her shoulders so he could see her face. "What are you talking about?"

"I don't even know. For a moment, I thought he was going to profess his undying love." She shook her head. "He was talking crazy… I didn't know where he was headed, but it was the same stuff he was talking about when he followed me into the bar the other day."

Shep didn't like it. He wanted to go after the guy and set him straight. Charlie was scared. Greg had unnerved her. "He sounded like he plans to try to talk to you again— before the wedding."

She looked as if she was having trouble believing this was happening.

"Do you think he's going to cancel the wedding?"

"I have no idea. You heard him. He's bound and determined to tell me something." She shivered.

He pulled her close again for a moment. "I'm glad we're

staying in the same room. I'll try to stay at your side until this is over."

"You'll get no argument from me."

"That might just be a first," he joked as she stepped from his arms. "Are you sure you're all right?"

"Thanks to you showing up when you did." She took a ragged breath and let it out. "I just know I don't want to be alone with him."

"I'll do my best to make sure that doesn't happen." He watched her take her bag over to the bed and set it down. He could tell that she was still scared, still worried.

"He was such a good boss," she said. "I'm afraid this will mean the end of my job."

"I'm sorry."

"I can find another one." She tried to smile. "I just don't understand any of it. He's never acted like this before. Maybe it's the wedding."

Shep hated to add to any of that but he wanted to be the one to tell her. "I have some rather shocking news." She looked up expectantly. He quickly told her about what he'd seen on the news downstairs in the bar about Daniel's roommate.

"You don't think it was an accident?" she asked as she sat down on the edge of the bed, looking even more shaken.

"He was looking into Lindy's murder and now he's dead? No, I don't think it was an accident."

Charlie hugged herself, looking chilled in the warm room.

"I called Daniel at work," he said.

Her gaze shot up. "Why?"

"I wanted to talk to him about why his roommate had been investigating your stepsister's murder. You have to admit, it's strange."

"And?"

"He thought it had something to do with some girl Jason was dating. He said Jason described her as 'freaky, freaky scary.' Daniel said he never met her or knew her name, but that he saw her once waiting for Jason outside of work. A blonde."

"You think it was Lacey?" she demanded, eyes wide.

"I think it's more than possible given Jason's hit-and-run. All I can imagine is that he was getting too close to the truth."

Her cell phone rang, startling them both. Charlie groaned as she checked the screen. "It's Amanda." She let it ring again. "I guess if we find out it's over, we can leave." She crossed her fingers of her left hand and picked up the phone with her right. "Hello?"

"I need you down here. The rehearsal's been moved up an hour. Greg is so anxious to make this happen he's making everyone crazy. He says he wants us down here right now. He's waiting and said to make sure you got word." Amanda's laugh indicated that she'd been through a few glasses of wine and that if anything, she was more nervous than before.

Charlie shot a look at Shep. "I'll be right down."

"*We'll* be right down," he said as she disconnected. "I'm no longer sure of who I have to keep you safe from."

She flashed him a smile an instant before tears filled her eyes. "Have I told you how glad I am that you're here?"

He nodded and pulled her into his arms. "There's nowhere I'd rather be on this earth than with you," he said against her hair. He felt a rush of emotion as he drew back to look at her. This love he felt was so strong, it made how he'd felt about her years ago pale in comparison.

With it came fear for Charlie. Lacey was still out there

and if he was right, she'd killed Jason. So far, Lacey had just been taunting Charlie. But it felt as if she was no longer fooling around. All his instincts told him she would be coming after Charlie next.

CHAPTER TWENTY-EIGHT

CHARLIE DIDN'T KNOW what to expect as she and Shep went to meet Greg and Amanda. Tears and hysteria were definitely high on the possible list though. Greg had wanted both Amanda and her downstairs. Charlie really doubted it was because he'd moved up the rehearsal. She was hoping that by the time she and Shep reached the lower room, the fireworks would be over.

But as she pushed open the door, Shep right behind her, she was shocked to find that Amanda had been right. Greg had moved up the rehearsal by an hour. The preacher was standing at one end of the room holding a large Bible. In front of him were Greg and Amanda. Greg had his arm around her. They were both smiling.

"There you are!" Amanda said, a reprimand tinging her words. She disconnected herself from Greg to rush toward them. "Oh, you brought your…friend. He looks just as good in clothes. Are you ready?"

"Ready as I will ever be," Charlie said under her breath as she noticed how many chairs had been brought in on both sides of the aisle. Were that many guests really coming?

She must have asked the question aloud.

Mugging a face at her, Amanda grabbed her arm forcefully and said, "Greg has a lot of friends and associates and I have a few friends."

"Just not one you wanted to ask to be your maid of

honor," Charlie said under her breath as Amanda squeezed her too hard.

They both turned toward where Greg was standing, waiting with the preacher. Charlie did her best not to meet Greg's eyes as she let Amanda lead her toward the preacher. "Where's the best man?" she whispered.

"Late. As usual," Amanda replied just as quietly. They reached Greg, and Amanda let go of her.

"As soon as the best man arrives..." Greg said. "I don't believe we've met," he said as Shep started to take a seat in the front row. "Not formally, anyway."

"Shep, this is my boss, Greg Shafer," Charlie said. "And this is Westly Shepherd, my—"

"I'm the man who's going to marry Charlie," Shep said and smiled at her. "That is if she'll have me."

She felt a little light-headed.

"Really?" Greg said. "I didn't realize it was that...serious."

"Oh, I'm very serious," he said, not taking his eyes off her. Charlie felt her cheeks flare.

"Of course she'll have you!" Amanda cried. "Look at her, she's practically glowing. I wish I'd known," she said, hurrying to hug Charlie. "If I'd known, we could have had a double wedding."

Charlie couldn't speak. Shep had practically asked her to marry him. And just the thought of a double wedding with Amanda... She mentally slapped herself. Shep was just doing this to keep Greg away from her. It wasn't like he'd just asked her to marry him. Yet when she met his gaze again...

She flushed as her heart hammered in her chest.

"Well, it's nice to meet you," Greg said, shaking Shep's hand. "You're a very lucky man. I can't tell you how much

I admire Charlie. We love having her on our team. Don't we, Amanda?"

"Absolutely," Amanda said, sounding bored.

Charlie was relieved when the door swung open and a man hurried in.

"Who the hell moved up the rehearsal?" Royce Braden demanded before laughing and grabbing Greg in a bear hug.

The man was bigger than life, tall, broad-shouldered, jovial and handsome. He also looked younger than Greg and much more athletic. If Charlie had wondered what had possessed Amanda, she no longer did. She was still shocked at Greg's attitude about the…affair.

But then that brought up the question of why Royce would sleep with his best friend's fiancée when he could probably have his pick of women.

"You really are anxious to tie the knot, aren't you?" Royce said as he looked past Greg's shoulder. His expression sobered as he took in Charlie. "This must be Charlie Farmington, the amazing designer I've heard so much about."

Greg made the introductions while she wondered if it had been Amanda or Greg who'd been singing her praises. That ridiculous stray thought made her laugh to herself.

"Glad I finally got to meet you," Royce said as he looked past her to Amanda who hadn't moved, who didn't even seem to be breathing.

The preacher cleared his throat and asked. "Wasn't there more in the wedding party?"

"Yes, a bridesmaid and another attendant," Greg said. "But they couldn't make the rehearsal. Don't worry. They'll be here tomorrow."

"I guess we'd better get to it then," the preacher said.

"I'm sorry to have moved up the rehearsal. I appreciate you all for being such good sports."

So it hadn't been Greg who'd moved up the rehearsal, Charlie thought, and kept her eyes on the floor as the pastor began.

Things went quickly until the end.

"And," the pastor said, joking, "we might as well see if anyone wants to object before the real thing tomorrow."

A tense few moments seemed to steal all the oxygen out of the air before the man continued to the part where he would pronounce Greg and Amanda husband and wife.

SHEP WAS RELIEVED. In the end, the wedding rehearsal was quick and relatively painless. He did notice one thing though, when the preacher asked if there was anyone who objected to this marriage…

Greg had looked at Charlie and so did Amanda, then Amanda turned slightly and looked at Royce. A thick fog of tension seemed to fill the room before the pastor moved on and it was over.

Greg suggested they all go to the bar where he'd ordered some champagne. Shep started to say that he and Charlie had other plans, but the man insisted.

"You're coming to the rehearsal dinner as Charlie's plus-one, aren't you?" Amanda asked him. "Or is there someone else she's invited?" She looked around as if she thought another man might materialize. "With Charlie, I just never know."

Shep held his tongue as they all headed to the bar for one glass of champagne. Amanda scuttled off to make sure the staff had heard about dinner being early to accommodate night skiing. At least that was the excuse.

Mostly, he worried about why Greg had come to Charlie's room. What had he been about to tell her and why did all of this feel like it was being rushed? What was the hurry?

Shep just hoped that Greg had gotten the message that Charlie wasn't available. Had he really thought she might be interested in him? Why else would he want to tell her about his past love life? Maybe he'd planned to ask her advice about marrying Amanda.

Whatever it had been, Shep planned to keep an eye on Greg and do his best to keep him away from Charlie—at least while he could. But what about after she returned to work at Greg's company? Somehow he didn't think that a marriage license was going to keep the man from pursuing Charlie.

Shep's cell phone rang. He slowed to let the others get a little ahead, but still in sight. Royce was walking beside Charlie, trying to engage her in conversation. From this distance, he appeared to be flirting with her. Shep knew he could be reading more into it than there was—until he saw Amanda's expression when she rejoined them. She was livid and not doing a very good job of hiding it.

"Hello?" Shep said into the phone.

Paul Wagner's thin, craggy voice came on. "I sent that photo. Let me know if you don't get it and I'll try again."

"Thanks," Shep told him and checked. "It hasn't come through yet."

"Well, I just sent it. Could take a little longer. I might try to send it again. You know, the more I think about, I'm sure it won't be of any help. But you can call if you don't see it."

Shep promised to do just that and caught up with the others.

"Here's my plus-one," Royce announced as a young, shapely brunette came rushing down the hall toward them.

"Meet Ruby Jo," he said and looped an arm around the woman.

"I just love weddings," Ruby Jo announced, voice high and sweet as if she were talking to a baby. "They always make me cry."

"Me, too," Amanda said, her gaze deadly and aimed at Royce.

If Greg noticed, he didn't show it. He seemed lost in his own thoughts. But as he poured the champagne, Shep saw him stealing glances in Charlie's direction.

It was clear he was still determined to talk to her.

Two GLASSES OF champagne later, Charlie collapsed on their hotel bed laughing. When she saw Shep's expression, she laughed even harder. Wiping her eyes, she sat up and faced him. "Why do you look so upset? That has to be the weirdest wedding rehearsal you've ever been to."

"There did seem to be a lot going on behind the scenes."

She laughed again. "Amanda was trying so hard not to look at Royce. And Royce! Clearly he was trying to make Amanda jealous. I mean feeding his date one nut at a time from the dish on the bar. I swear Amanda flinched every time Royce bent over to whisper in his date's ear. I caught her rolling her eyes every time Ruby Jo laughed, which was often."

"That was the highest pitch laugh I think I've ever heard," Shep agreed with a grin as he sat down on the end of the bed. "I think you enjoyed the intrigue more than I did though. I was busy watching Greg."

"Oh, I think he got the message. Didn't you see how attentive he was to Amanda? I don't think he'll bother me again." The few times Charlie had stolen looks at Greg, she'd seen him being sweet and loving to Amanda. "He probably just had a case of cold feet and was hoping I would tell him it was going to be fine."

"You know it was more than that or you wouldn't have been scared."

She couldn't deny it. "He was just so intense. But getting married is a big deal. Did I tell you that he knows about his best friend and Amanda? He doesn't seem to be bothered by it. He said she was just getting it out of her system."

Shep shook his head. "How could he not be jealous?"

She shrugged.

"Charlie, you know what he wants to tell you. He doesn't want to marry Amanda because he's fallen for you."

"No," she said, shaking her head.

"What else could it be? Why share his past relationships? Why talk to you about any of it? You're his *employee*."

"Right. I hope I have a job after the holidays." She kept telling herself that once Greg and Amanda were married, he'd go back to being professional again.

"You really think you can continue working for him?"

Charlie felt her heart thump. "This is the best job I've ever had. The thought of losing it—"

"You can get another job. You know that. You already said you could."

She nodded. It was true. She knew she could find another job. Eventually. But she'd liked this one just fine before all this. "You really think—"

"That he's getting up the nerve to tell you how he feels about you before he walks down the aisle? Yes, I do. Frankly, I wouldn't trust him around you *after* the wedding."

She stared at him. "You're jealous."

"Damn right I am."

"You do know that I've never given him any reason."

"I know that."

She swallowed. "But he admitted that he hadn't sent a headhunter after anyone but me. He said he—" she made an embarrassed face at him "—had to have me."

"Well, I know that feeling." Shep brushed a lock of hair back from her face, his fingers skimming over her cheek and sending tiny electrical pulses through her. "Isn't he always telling you how much he likes you, how much he respects your work?"

"That doesn't mean he's fallen for me."

"How could he not? You're beautiful, smart, talented, amazing. But even if I'm wrong, he has to know he's about to make a major mistake marrying Amanda. I think he's looking for a way out and he thinks it's you."

She hoped Shep was wrong. "I don't see this turning out well," she said, hoping he would disagree. He didn't.

"Unless he goes back to just being your boss, which I don't think he'll do, and add to that Amanda's insane jealousy of you…" He shook his head. "I'm sorry, it doesn't look good."

She groaned, knowing he was right.

"Hopefully Greg won't get another chance to talk to you alone before the wedding. I'll have to keep you busy." He grinned and she felt her blood heat as he kissed her.

When he broke off the kiss, Charlie looked into all his eyes and wanted to take him up on every promise she saw there. She wanted to feel that heat, that passion, that pleasure and give it back in spades. She wanted him and knew she always would.

"If you had any idea what I want to do to you right now…" He slowly began to undress her as she grinned at him, daring him to show her.

AFTER THEY made love, they showered and reluctantly got ready for the rehearsal dinner. Shep would have much preferred staying cuddled in bed with her.

"Did I tell you that I confronted Amanda earlier today about the dead mouse?" Charlie asked. She slid a dark green velvet dress over her head and let it slither over her body. "She admitted it—and admitted putting the eye drops in my dessert and Greg's. She said she got them out of his suit jacket pocket."

"Did she say why?" He couldn't help being worried.

"She blamed it on the drinks she had."

"Are you sure we shouldn't just get out of here?" he asked.

She smiled. "I wish we could, but Tara is coming tomorrow. She's going to be in the wedding. I can't do that to her. And in truth, I can't do it to Amanda, as awful as she is. I feel sorry for her. I don't think her other maid of honor broke her leg and is in traction. I think everyone turned her down."

"With good reason," he said and kissed her. "I'm glad that you feel you can't leave. You're a nice person, Charlie."

She worried at her lower lip with her teeth for a moment. "I hope I don't regret it."

He felt the same way. "Well, after tomorrow, they will be married," he said. "With luck."

They found everyone waiting for them at the bar and were quickly shown into a private dining room.

Shep kept Charlie close, right where he wanted her. Fortunately Greg stayed in his own lane, behaving like a man who was marrying the love of his life the next day. Even Amanda did her best not to pay any attention to Royce and Ruby Jo.

Still Shep was glad when the meal was over.

"Night skiing!" Greg announced. "Get whatever you need from the shop and I'll see you all up on the mountain."

"Are you going snowboarding tonight?" Charlie asked when they returned to their room.

"Not without you."

"Then you leave me no choice." She tilted her head to one side, grinning at him. "Guess we're going night snowboarding."

He eyed her suspiciously. "You're going to kick my butt up on that hill, aren't you?"

She grinned. "I guess we'll see but I'm going to try."

He laughed. "It's one of the reasons I love you so much."

His heart fluttered and he felt warm clear to his toes as she kissed him. "Glad to hear it," she said. "Let's do this."

CHAPTER TWENTY-NINE

THEY RODE UP the ski lift together with stars and a sliver of moon hanging in a midnight blue sky. Charlie breathed in the cold night air, feeling more alive than she had in years. Shep put his arm around her, pulling her closer. Below them in the glow of the lights, skiers and snowboards looked small and dark against the snow as they made their way down the mountainside.

As the chairlift slowed, they both slid off and down the hill partway to finish buckling up their snowboards. "Ready?" she asked, grinning at Shep from under her helmet.

And then she took off down the slope. The hill had been groomed, but there was a good foot of snow along the edge and even more in the trees. She headed for it, boarding into the shadowy semidarkness. She looked back once and saw that Shep was right behind her.

They cruised down the mountain, in and out of the trees and the deep featherlike snow. Charlie had forgotten how much she loved this. She ducked to avoid a pine branch. It brushed over her helmet, sending down a cascade of new snow. Behind her, she heard Shep swear and knew he must have caught the swinging branch.

When she looked back, he was getting up from the deep snow. Laughing, she found herself at the edge of the ski hill. Other skiers and boarders were now carving their way across the hill. She dove back into the trees to avoid them and hadn't gone far when she sensed someone behind her again. She assumed it was Shep, but he was following her awfully close. A lot closer than he had been before.

She turned her head to look back into the darkness of the pines an instant before she was hit hard just below her shoulder blades. The blow knocked her off balance and sent her crashing downhill. She saw a tree coming and threw herself to the side, striking a smaller tree before burrowing deep in the snow.

The impact with even the small tree knocked the air out of her and for a moment, she didn't know which way was up. She was under the snow, unable to breathe. Fighting her way to the surface, she gasped for breath and sucked in icy snow crystals that burned her lungs.

Furiously she wiped the freezing cold snow from her face with her glove and looked around in confusion. She didn't see anyone close, but there were two ski tracks nearby that had cut through the trees before returning to the groomed ski slope.

Who had hit her from behind? She was barely able to process the thought before Shep came boarding up to her.

"Charlie? Are you all right?"

She wasn't sure. She lay in the snow, still gasping. Her side hurt where she had struck the tree, but she didn't think anything was broken. "Someone hit me."

He stared at her as he helped her up. "Someone out of control?"

"Maybe, but it felt like I was hit with a fist."

SHEP HAD SEEN another skier in the trees just before he'd lost sight of Charlie. But all he'd seen was a bundled-up shape. It had been too dark to make out much more.

"Are you sure you're all right?" he asked, not for the first time since they had left the ski hill and returned to their room. They'd both changed, Charlie into yoga pants and a sweater, Shep into jeans and a T-shirt.

"It probably was just a skier out of control who hit me," she said as if trying to convince them both.

"Did you get a look at the person?" he asked.

"It was dark. All I saw was a blurry figure as I was falling. But it was definitely someone on skis."

"That leaves the suspects wide open since most everyone was on skis tonight," he said, looking at her with concern. "Did Lindy ski?"

She nodded. "I remember she was looking forward to winter. She said she'd learned to ski at age three. But Lacey had grown up in Brazil. I guess it's possible she'd learned to snow ski. Kat said Matt had money. He could have taken her to the Alps skiing for all we know."

If Lacey had found out about the wedding and followed them up here... "Or it could have just been someone skiing out of control. An accident."

He shook his head. "The person didn't even stop to see if you were all right?"

She shrugged and he saw her flinch. "I'm just sore," she said quickly, seeing his worried reaction.

They both startled at the sudden loud knocking at their door. Charlie looked at him with an expression that told him she was thinking the same thing he was. Amanda or Greg. Or both.

"Don't answer it," she whispered.

The pounding grew louder. Then a male voice called, "Charlie?"

Shep exchanged another look with her, this one more than surprised. *"Daniel?"* he mouthed.

She nodded.

"What is he—"

She held up her hands, eyes wide.

Shep stormed to the door and threw it open to find Daniel getting ready to knock again. He was dressed in ski pants and a jacket. He held his stocking cap and gloves in his free hand.

Daniel blinked at the sight of Shep and shifted his gaze to look past him into the room where Charlie was sitting on the bed. "I need to talk to Charlie," he said.

"Daniel? What are you doing here?"

Shep realized that Charlie had gotten off the bed and was now right beside him.

CHARLIE WAS HAVING trouble believing this. Was this Amanda's doing? She stepped past Shep to face Daniel. "We broke up, so I ask again what are you doing here?"

"I was invited. Remember? You invited me." Daniel's tone was peevish.

With a groan, she remembered that she had. It seemed like eons ago.

"But we broke up. Why would you come after—"

"I tried to reach you first," he said. At her raised brow, he added, "Well, I *thought* about calling you but then decided maybe it would be better just to see you here." He looked past her back into the room. "Wow, didn't take you long."

"You and I broke up."

"I thought once you calmed down… Still…" He looked again into the room at Shep.

She stepped out into the hall, forcing Daniel to move back from the door. She wanted to close the door for this discussion but didn't want Shep to think she had anything to hide. She didn't.

"It isn't what you think," she said quietly.

Daniel smirked.

"Shep is an old boyfriend who came back to…" She realized that maybe that's what it had been at first. But it was now exactly what he thought. "It isn't any of your business."

"Still," Daniel repeated and glanced down the empty hallway for a moment. "You heard about Jason."

She nodded. "I'm sorry."

He shrugged and looked at her again. "So I guess you don't want me here."

"It's a bit awkward since we broke up and I've moved on."

"I can see that but you're cool me with staying, right? I thought I'd ski since I'm here."

She rolled her eyes.

"Hey, I didn't even know we were broken up, so cut me some slack."

"Look, Daniel, I don't care what you do, but you and I are done."

He looked down at his ski boots for a moment. "So I suppose you don't want your Christmas present."

"No, I don't." She crossed her arms over her chest. "Out of curiosity, what did you get me?" *Please don't let it be an engagement ring.* She didn't need more guilt.

He brightened. "Three of my favorite video games. I thought we could play them at your place and it would give us something more in common."

Her friends thought he was going to ask him to marry her. She tried to keep her face straight as she said, "That was a thoughtful gift."

"I was trying, Charlie."

He probably thought he had been. "You aren't coming to the wedding though, right?" she asked.

"It's in the morning?"

She nodded.

"No, I think I'll ski instead. There's supposed to be fresh powder."

"Good choice." She turned to go back into the room.

"No hard feelings," Daniel said. "Maybe I can return the video games and get my money back."

She watched him walk away for a moment, then turned back to her open door—and caught movement at the other end of the hallway. It was only a glimpse of a figure—with long blond hair.

This time she didn't hesitate. She took off running down the hallway, shoving open the door to the stairs before bounding down them. This time Lacey wasn't going to get away.

SHEP HAD TRIED not to listen to Charlie's conversation with her former boyfriend. He knew she'd left the door open on purpose. He smiled to himself, thinking of what she would say when she came back into the room after allowing him to overhear everything.

Daniel had gotten her three of his favorite video games? What a romantic. Shep knew he shouldn't make fun of the guy, but it just proved how wrong he'd been for her.

And you're so right for her?

Yeah, he was, he told himself. Even though he'd just heard her refer to him as "an old boyfriend." And then she'd added that it wasn't any of Daniel's business. All Shep knew was that he'd move heaven and earth to make her happy. Isn't that why the judge had asked him to come see what was going on with her?

As the conversation died down outside the room, he suddenly saw Charlie take off at a run down the hall.

What the hell? He jumped up and rushed out of the room

in time to see her take the stairs. Where was she going in such a hurry?

He didn't know, but his pounding heart told him that given the way she'd taken off, it couldn't be good. He ran down the hallway and shoved open the exit door. He could hear the clamor of footfalls echoing up through the stairwell.

Taking the stairs as fast as he could, he went after her. What would make her do something like this?

A thought struck him so hard he almost missed a step.

Lacey. Had Charlie seen Lacey and was now chasing her? Had Charlie lost her mind? What would she do if she caught her? The idea sent him barreling downward until, two floors below theirs, a stairwell door swung open, catching him by surprise.

CHARLIE HEARD A door open and close one floor below her. She was so close now she knew she would catch Lacey. She raced down the last set of steps, grabbing the ground floor door and bursting out of it into the lobby.

Her heart was hammering, pulse a thunder in her ears, her breath coming out in hard gasps. She slid to a stop and hurriedly scanned the lobby, knowing the woman couldn't have gotten away. Not this time. Charlie had been right behind her.

The lobby was full of people moving about through furniture and plants and plastered columns. Charlie couldn't have lost her. She couldn't have.

The blonde came into view as she passed a group of people gathered talking in the middle of the lobby. She wasn't moving fast, just walking, as if not the least bit worried about Charlie.

A stab of anger sent Charlie's blood pressure skyrocketing. Lacey thought there was nothing Charlie could do about her. No way she could stop her.

Charlie darted between the tall pots of plants and the large furniture and cut her off before she could reach the door. She came shooting out from the side, grabbed Lacey's arm and spun her around to face her. In all honesty, she didn't know what she was going to do with her other than demand answers.

The woman let out a startled cry and tried to pull free.

Charlie looked into the blonde's face—a face she'd expected to be so familiar. It all took only a few seconds for her to realize that the woman she'd just chased down numerous flights of stairs wasn't Lacey at all.

"What?" the woman demanded, pulling her arm free.

Charlie was so shaken for a moment that she couldn't speak. "I'm sorry. I thought you were someone else."

Looking indignant, the blonde continued out the door. Charlie realized that other people in the lobby were staring at her. She started to stumble back when a pair of hands grabbed her and steadied her.

"This way."

She recognized Greg's voice. He was the last person she wanted leading her out of the lobby. He quickly drew her into what appeared to be a small atrium. But she was still so shocked, horrified actually, that she didn't want to add to the scene by shaking his hold from her arm. It was a wonder she hadn't tackled the woman to the floor.

"Are you all right?" Greg asked as he let go of her.

Charlie blinked. Her horror began to fade as she realized this was the last place she wanted to be with the last person on earth.

She took a step back.

"Charlie?"

She took another step back, then realized that all she was doing was moving deeper into the shadowy atrium. "Please let me leave."

He looked surprised. "Why are you acting like this?"

The shock of earlier was wearing off quickly as anger and fear took over. "Why are you determined to get me alone? You're getting married tomorrow. I don't want to hear about your old loves or your new ones and I certainly don't want to hear how you feel about me. I don't want to hear about any of it. Don't you realize that you're making it impossible for me to work for you?"

Greg took a step back, holding up both hands, a shocked look on his face. "Oh no, that wasn't my intent at all. I'm so sorry. I... Yes, I had been wanting to tell you something—not apparently what you were thinking though. I'm in love with Amanda. But I can see now what you must have thought. I certainly didn't mean to scare you."

He took another step back. "I...I don't know what I was thinking. I'm so sorry. I don't want to lose you at the company. I'm such a fool. Please forgive me. I promise nothing like this will ever happen again. You have my word."

ALL SHEP CAUGHT was the last part of Greg's speech. He'd found them in the atrium after asking in the lobby if anyone had seen the woman he'd described. Apparently a lot of people had. Another guest pointed toward the atrium, saying, "A man took her in there after..." The woman had smiled rather than go on. "She seemed upset."

In the atrium, two figures were silhouetted against the lights coming from outside the hotel. "Charlie?" Shep said.

By the time he'd caught his breath and limped down the rest of the steps after almost colliding with a door, he'd lost

Charlie and feared she'd caught up with Lacey. Instead, it seemed Greg had caught up with Charlie.

At the sound of her name, she glanced over at him, then quickly moved toward him. Greg stepped out of the way to let her pass without turning around. As Charlie rushed into Shep's arms, he saw Greg hang his head.

"Are you all right?" he asked quietly as he led her out of the atrium. People in the lobby were watching them with interest.

"I've been better," she said as they headed for the elevator.

Back in their room, she told him everything that had happened. "It wasn't Lacey. If you could have seen the look on that woman's face." She began to laugh, then cry.

He pulled her close. "Hey, it was an honest mistake. That woman had no idea what you've been going through."

"I definitely acted as imbalanced as I have been," she said between sobs.

"You're fine. I would have done the same thing. What am I saying? I ran after you."

She met his gaze. "You did the same thing and you got hurt because of me."

"It's just a twisted ankle as I tried to avoid nailing the edge of the door face-first. It wasn't one of my most graceful moments. But we both survived."

She nodded. "You heard what Greg said?"

"He sounded sincere. You getting angry at him must have done the trick. Once he realized he'd lose you as an employee…"

"I still don't know if I'll be able to continue working for him," she said.

"Well, you don't have to make any decisions tonight, maid of honor."

Charlie groaned. "Oh, the wedding. We still have that to look forward to."

"Once it's over, I say we go back to your apartment in Bozeman."

Curling against him, she nodded.

"What a night, huh?" he said.

"What a week," she said, sounding as if she would be asleep before her head hit the pillow. "I don't know what I would have done without you."

"Hopefully, you'll never have to find out," he whispered into her hair and realized that she'd already dozed off.

CHAPTER THIRTY

"PINCH ME," AMANDA said when a still half asleep Charlie opened the hotel room door to her. "Pinch me. I can't believe this is really happening. I'm getting married today!"

Charlie wanted to do more than pinch her. "What time is it?"

"Get dressed. We have so much to do. You do remember that it's a morning wedding, right?"

Charlie groaned, telling herself all she had to do was get through the wedding.

"I've had coffee and breakfast sent up," Amanda went on. "Enjoy. But I expect to see you in an hour downstairs in the anteroom."

"You got it," Charlie said and closed the door on her. Before she could reach the bed though, there was another knock at the door. She grimaced at Shep, who had sat up in bed and was grinning. Why was he so cheerful in the mornings? She turned back to the door, anticipating not being so nice to Amanda this time, only to find it was a young man from the hotel with a cart full of food.

She had him leave it in the center of the room, found a tip for him and closed the door behind him.

"Come back to bed," Shep said and patted the space next to him.

"You heard what Amanda said. You want her coming back here?"

He only grinned as she climbed back into bed.

Later, her skin glowing, she showered, grabbed some coffee and breakfast, and made her way down to the anteroom.

"Well, look at you," Amanda said. "Breakfast definitely woke you up it seems. How was it?"

"Wonderful. Thank you."

Amanda looked past her. "Is he planning to hang around?"

Charlie glanced over her shoulder to see Shep nearby. "He is. He worries about me."

Amanda lifted a brow, but must have thought better of what she was clearly fighting against saying. "I saw Daniel," she said as they moved deeper into the anteroom. "He didn't seem to think you'd broken up with him."

"He was confused. He isn't anymore."

She frowned. "I just don't want him barging into the wedding."

"He won't. So let me see your dress."

Amanda beamed. "It's so beautiful. It's like something a princess would wear. I won't tell you how much it cost. It would floor you. Greg is so good to me." They stepped into the dressing room and closed the door.

Hanging on the door to the closet was a dress with a massive skirt that crinkled as Amanda touched it. "Isn't it amazing?"

"Amazing," Charlie said, hoping Amanda didn't see her surprised look at its volume. She wondered if it would even fit between the chairs as the woman came down the aisle.

Amanda suddenly teared up. "I'm so happy. Greg has been so wonderful. Last night we drank champagne down in the hotel bar until it closed." That explained what he'd been doing in the lobby last night. He must have seen Charlie rush in—everyone in the lobby had.

"He loves me," Amanda was saying. "He loves me so much." All Charlie could do was nod. "He would do anything to make me happy."

She wondered if Amanda had seen Greg leave the bar to come after her. "So did the two of you have champagne with Royce and his date?" she asked casually. If Royce had been there, then Amanda wouldn't have even noticed Greg leaving the bar.

"Greg insisted they join us. It was the polite thing to do. I mean, Royce *is* the best man. He isn't serious about that woman though. He's just trying to make me jealous. Whatever."

Charlie quickly changed the subject as they began to get ready for the wedding. She was counting down the minutes, afraid it still might not happen.

SHEP HUNG around in the anteroom. From where he stood, he was able to watch the lobby as people came and went. He didn't see Lacey, but that didn't mean she wasn't here, he told himself.

Wedding guests began to arrive and were led into the main room where the ceremony would take place. As the time got closer, Shep tapped on the dressing room door. "Everything okay in there?" he asked.

"We're fine," Amanda called.

Closer to the door, Charlie said, "We're ready and waiting."

Only then did Shep enter the main room, find a seat and try to relax. He felt as if there was a bomb ticking in the room. He just wanted the happy couple married. Not that he thought Greg wouldn't bother Charlie again. Still, he wanted this to be over. He wanted the Lacey problem over as well. He and Charlie couldn't move on with their lives until then. It was all he'd been able to think about today as he watched for Lacey and waited for this wedding to be over.

The pastor came in and took his place, followed by Greg and Royce, both in tuxes. Shep tried to discern if Greg was having second thoughts. The man looked a little nervous, but it could have been excitement. Royce, on the other hand, looked bored.

A movement from Greg caught Shep's eye. He reached into his suit pocket and pulled out a tiny bottle. Shep watched Greg put eye drops into both eyes before returning the vial to his pocket.

Amanda might have been telling the truth about putting the eyedrops into the desserts that had made both Charlie and Greg sick. Or was it possible it had been Greg who'd made Charlie sick so she would think it had been Amanda? Why would he do that? Had he put the eye drops in his own mousse, too? Or had he only pretended to be sick that afternoon?

Shep heard his cell ping and realized he should have already turned it off. He eased it out and saw that he had an attachment from Paul Wagner with a note that read Patrick, right and Frank, left. He opened the attachment and felt shock ricochet through him as he stared at the photograph.

In the shot was Lindy or Lacey, who knew which? She stood between two men, both considerably older than the seventeen-year-old. She was grinning at the person taking the photo. The men had their arms around her, one looking at the photographer, the other looking at Lindy/Lacey.

Even in profile, Shep recognized the man who was staring at the teenage girl instead of the camera. His mind argued that it couldn't be. Wagner had said the man's name as Patrick.

Shep looked up in confusion. But there was no doubt. Greg Shafer had changed from that love-struck twenty-something-year-old staring longingly at Lindy/Lacey. But he hadn't changed so much that Shep didn't recognize him, no matter what name he went by now.

He stared at the photo, trying to make sense of the cold wave of fear that moved through him.

Not that it mattered. What did was that Greg Shafer had been in the same neighborhood as Charlie and Lindy/Lacey whenever he visited his father. Beyond that, Greg had known one of the twins.

A coincidence that Charlie was working for a man who'd been that close by at the worst time of her life? Not a chance. Was that what he'd been trying to tell her?

He wanted to stop the wedding, find Charlie, put an end to whatever this was. But as he pocketed his phone, the organist struck up the first chord of the wedding march. As everyone stood, a million thoughts raced through his head. He looked at all the people who had gathered for this wedding, and he tried to breathe.

What would stopping the wedding buy him? The best thing he could do would be to let Greg and Amanda get married and then find out the truth about Greg Shafer later. Could this possibly be what Greg had to tell Charlie? Hadn't he told her something about them having a *connection*?

Did it have something to do with the murder? Did Greg know something he wanted to tell her? Charlie had heard the killer come into the house. Mulvane had found blood on the stairs the killer had left behind after he'd brutally killed Lindy.

Shep's heart pounded. Perspiration popped out on his

forehead even though it was cool in the room. The music was a dull roar in his ears. He stared at the groom, terrified of his thoughts. Greg's gaze was on the door that had just opened at the end of the room.

Shep turned to see Charlie as she made her walk down the aisle. She took his breath away, making him forget all about Greg for a moment. All he could think about was what a beautiful bride she would make. The navy blue dress Amanda had chosen for her was tasteful and fit her perfectly. Her long curly hair was pulled up, loose dark tendrils framing her face.

She met his gaze and smiled, her brown eyes warming to liquid honey. He felt his heart lift and soar. He wanted this woman—for life. He wanted to marry her, have children with her, grow old with her. He found it hard to breathe and felt as if he would die if he lost her.

He had to swallow the lump that formed in his throat as she passed. As Shep turned to watch her approach the pastor, he caught Greg looking at her, his expression unreadable.

Was it longing? Or was it fear? Had Greg been there the night Lindy died? Was he afraid that Charlie had seen something? That she knew more than she'd told the police about that night? His hands fisted at his sides before he saw Greg's attention shift to the young woman coming down the aisle. Tara, Charlie's friend who'd had the baby just days ago.

Greg was looking past Tara to his bride.

Shep turned to see Amanda swishing toward the altar. She'd chosen a very voluminous dress that brushed both sides of the aisle. Static seemed to crackle and pop as she moved. But it was her expression that surprised him. There was something almost fragile-looking about her. Definitely vulnerable. Shep wondered if she had any idea what she was getting herself into.

He was only thankful that this wedding would soon be over. That earlier sense of foreboding he'd felt was now a thunder in his chest.

The preacher cleared his voice and everyone sat. Shep lowered himself into his chair. He realized he was holding his breath, terrified that something horrible was about to happen and he wouldn't be able to stop it.

CHARLIE FELT IN a daze as she listened to Greg and Amanda share their vows. This was really happening. All the wild days since she'd first seen Lacey standing across the street from her apartment seemed to lead up to this moment. She felt as if she'd been caught in a whirlwind that had brought Shep back into her life.

Amanda had wanted her to pinch her because she couldn't believe it was finally her wedding day. Charlie felt the same way. She'd never dreamed she could feel this way at just the sight of Shep. She was beyond happy. Beyond content. Beyond her wildest dreams.

With a start, she realized that she hadn't checked her horoscope this morning. She never forgot, but this morning… She took a breath and let it out slowly. Maybe it was for the best. What if it had said something terrible was going to happen today?

She heard the pastor say, "If anyone has any reason why these two should not be wed in holy matrimony, speak now or forever hold your peace."

The room fell silent. Charlie held her breath.

SHEP REALIZED IT was almost over. Well, the wedding at least. He was anxious to talk to Greg. Why had the man kept it a secret from Charlie that he had lived just down the street? That he had known her stepsister? And why had

Greg wanted her on his team so badly? Maybe more important, what had Greg been so hell-bent to tell her?

His head ached, his pulse a roar in his ears, as he stared at Greg while the pastor pronounced the bride and groom husband and wife.

"You may kiss your bride," the pastor said and the room broke into cheers and clapping as the guests rose to their feet. The woman in front of Shep wore a large hat, blocking his view of the front of the room.

And then he heard the gunshot.

It echoed through the room, followed by a cacophony of shouts and screams. He heard someone yell, *"He's shot! Greg's shot!"*

Shep began to push his way toward the front of the room, fighting to get through the wedding guests who were panicking like cattle during a stampede.

A second gunshot boomed, adding to the pandemonium. Shep finally got a glimpse of the pastor, white-faced, holding his heart and leaning against the far wall. The room was a blur of movement and noise with raised panicked voices and screams.

In front of the pastor, Greg lay on the floor bleeding, Amanda in that huge wedding dress kneeling next to him. There was no sign of the best man—just as there was no sign of the maid of honor. But Tara was kneeling next to Amanda trying to stop Greg's bleeding.

Shep's gaze shot to a doorway off to his right in time to see a blond woman with a gun.

The gun was pointed at Charlie's head as the woman dragged her down a hallway, around a corner and disappeared.

CHAPTER THIRTY-ONE

LACEY'S FINGERS BIT into Charlie's arm as she steered her away from the wedding, a gun literally to her head. Charlie had been so shocked at first that she hadn't been able to move. No one had for those few seconds after Lacey came out of a side door and shot Greg.

Lacey had grabbed Charlie, fired a shot into the air and put the barrel of the gun to her temple. "Don't think I'll kill you?" Lacey had whispered as she backed Charlie out of the room. "Think again."

It was that second shot that had sent everyone scurrying in a panic.

Except Shep. Charlie had seen him fighting to get to her through the terrified guests.

Lacey had forced her down a hallway, her grip painful but not as worrisome as the gun to her head. Charlie had no doubt that Lacey would kill her. She'd had no choice but to come along with her. Lacey had already shot Greg. Charlie didn't want her shooting anyone else. Especially Shep.

"I don't understand," Charlie said as Lacey hurried her down yet another hallway. She had no idea what Lacey was planning to do with her. She assumed eventually she would kill her. All she could do was hope that before Lacey pulled the trigger again, there would be a chance to turn the tables. "Why would you shoot my boss?"

"Why do you think?" Lacey snapped. "Do you really not

know why he hired you?" Apparently not. "He lived down the street from you. You didn't recognize him?"

Recognize him? Lived down the street? A cold spike of ice rattled up her spine. "You mean when we were teenagers?"

"He went by Patrick then. Patrick Gregory Shafer. He was that old man's stepson. Did you really not know about him and Lindy?"

Charlie felt blindsided. She stumbled and Lacey's grip tightened. "Still, why did you shoot him?"

"Because he deserved it," she snapped. She pushed open door after door, a labyrinth of passages behind the scenes in this massive hotel, and hurried her along. Charlie thought she heard running footfalls somewhere in the maze behind them. Shep.

"What happened that night?" Charlie asked, thinking she had to no the truth.

"That night you locked Lindy out of the house," Lacey said, grinding the barrel of gun into her temple hard enough to make Charlie cry out. "You knew she was afraid of the dark."

"You both tormented me, but I suspect you were the real mean one."

Lacey laughed. "Oh, I wouldn't say that."

Charlie could feel time running out. "Did you kill your sister?"

Lacey slowed at the next doorway to meet Charlie's gaze. "I would never have hurt Lindy. *Never.*" Her voice broke. "It was *him*. Patrick Gregory Shafer. He had told her that he was in love with her. I tried to warn her. She didn't know anything about men. That night I met him out in the woods. He thought I was Lindy. I told him I didn't love him and that I never wanted to see him again. I did it for her own good." Tears filled Lacey's eyes. "How was I to know that he could come back that night when he heard Lindy screaming for you to let her back in?"

Charlie felt her heart drop. She remembered what Shep had told her. "But Lindy had to know about the key hidden at the back door."

As they passed through another doorway, she saw that they had entered the kitchen. It was empty with breakfast over and lunch still hours away except for several prep cooks who took off the moment they spotted the gun.

"I didn't have time to put the key back," Lacey said. "By the time I looked out the basement window and saw them arguing, it was too late. I couldn't get to her in time."

The words shocked her. "You saw Greg kill her?"

"He didn't know there were two of us. He didn't know." The words came out on a ragged breath. "I just wanted him to leave Lindy alone. She couldn't have a boyfriend. Why couldn't she see that?" Her voice broke. "I didn't know he was going to kill her. He thought she was the one who'd said all those awful words to him. He didn't know about me. Not until he saw me walk into his wedding and shoot him. He looked like he'd seen a ghost. But then he knew. That second when I pulled the trigger. He knew the mistake he'd made killing Lindy."

Charlie felt the grip on her arm loosen. She saw her chance as Lacey pulled her past hanging racks of pots and pans and large stoves…past where the two prep cooks had been working. Charlie spotted the knife lying next to a chopped pile of veggies. Pretending to stumble, she brushed the edge of the large metal table and surreptitiously grabbed the blade's handle. Just as quickly, she broke free of Lacey's grip, shoved her and the barrel of the pistol away from her head and drove the knife into Lacey's side.

A shot went wild, pinging off the wall behind Charlie's head.

Lacey looked down at the knife protruding from her side and aimed the gun this time.

Charlie had only a second to reach for one of the cast iron skillets hanging next to her. She swung it as hard and fast as she could. The heavy skillet struck Lacey's arm and the gun broke from her grasp, flying through the air to skitter across the floor away from them.

Before Charlie could swing the skillet again, Lacey struck her in the chest with her fist, knocking her back. The blow reminded her of the one that had struck her in the shoulder blades up on the ski hill.

Charlie crashed into one of the tables full of pots and pans and went down, the cookware clattering around her as everything hit the floor.

She watched breathless as Lacey pulled the knife blade from her side, dropped it and went after the gun.

SHEP HAD raced down the hallway where he'd last seen Charlie and Lacey. He followed the sound of hurrying footfalls through a maze of hallways. He tried to make sense of what he'd just seen.

Lacey had shot Greg. Or did she know him as Patrick? There was no doubt that she knew who he was. Otherwise why shoot him? But then again, why shoot him at all, especially on his wedding day? Shep could think of only one reason she would do that. It was all tied to whatever had happened the night Lindy was murdered all those years ago. Tied to why Lacey had come back.

But now Lacey had Charlie. He knew how she had felt about Charlie all those years ago, how she'd tormented her. More recently, Lacey had tried to scare her. Or was it warn her? Either way she had a gun and Charlie. He thought of the destroyed doll and didn't even want to contemplate on what malicious feelings Lacey still harbored against Charlie.

He'd gotten turned around a couple of times and for a few moments, he'd thought he'd lost them for good. He didn't hear the echo of footfalls ahead of him.

Then he heard a gunshot on the other side of a door.

Shep hit the door at a run and burst into a huge hotel kitchen. Lacey was raising the gun, aiming... He rushed forward, thinking only of stopping her at all costs. Before he could reach her, Charlie swung a large cast iron skillet, catching the wrist of Lacey's gun hand. The gun went flying as Lacey shoved Charlie into a table, and Charlie went down in a shower of pots and pans.

Lacey saw him and went scrambling toward something on the floor. The gun.

He ran at her full bore, slammed into her and took them both to the floor. She grabbed the gun, tried to raise it. He shoved her harder to the floor and twisted the weapon from her grip, putting all of his weight on her to hold her down.

Behind them, he heard Charlie getting to her feet.

"Why?" she asked as she came over to Lacey. "Why stalk *me* if you were really after Greg?"

"You worked with *him*. I thought you knew," Lacey said.

"I didn't know," Charlie said, sounding close to tears.

"You locked her out," Lacey spat.

"The back door was open," Shep said. "Greg came in after he killed your sister. He would have killed Charlie, too, if that policeman hadn't come to the front when he did. Where were you? Hiding somewhere?"

Lacey made a sound like wounded animal and began to cry.

"You were the one who cut my hair," Charlie said. "It was you. The doll—"

Lacey cut off her tears with a laugh as brittle as glass and just as sharp. "I cut your hair." She chuckled. "When I told Cara… It was her idea to cut the doll's hair. She always wondered about the doll her mother kept on the top shelf in her room and wouldn't let her touch." Lacey laughed. "My little sister."

Two security officers came running in, guns drawn. Shep handed Lacey over to them and turned to find Charlie still holding the huge cast iron skillet. He took it from her and set it on one of the metal tables.

They could hear Lacey's laughter echoing through the hotel. Charlie's eyes filled as she stepped into his arms.

EPILOGUE

THAT FOLLOWING SUMMER, the wedding was small and held in a meadow alive with wildflowers. Shep would have married Charlie sooner, but by the time everything with Lacey was sorted out, he had to get back to school, back to his students, back to teaching. Charlie had needed time to come to grips with the past and look for another job closer to Stevensville, where he was.

The winter had been long, the spring even longer. It had been a time of healing. Shep talked to Charlie every day as she began to stitch her past and present together. She knew now that she wasn't responsible for Lindy's death. So many people were involved in what happened that night—Lacey at the forefront. Shep and Charlie told the police everything that Lacey had confessed to them.

But it was a letter that Greg had slipped under Charlie's hotel room door just before he'd gone downstairs to get married that helped tie up loose ends. He'd been determined to tell her what he'd done. He'd been in love with Lindy. He'd been twenty-four to Lindy's seventeen. He'd wanted her to run away with him—just as Lacey had found out. What he hadn't known was that the young woman who came to him that night and broke things off wasn't Lindy but her identical twin.

Shep often wondered about Greg's last few minutes of life as he lay mortally wounded on the floor at his wedding.

His expression had been one of shock, according to Lacey. He really must have thought he was seeing a ghost—until he realized the mistake he'd made.

What Greg must have thought in those last few minutes as he stared at Lacey! Like Charlie had, he must have thought Lindy had returned from the grave for justice.

In the letter, he told Charlie that he'd wanted to make it up to her—what he'd done to her stepsister and that was why he'd gone to so much trouble to hire her—along with the fact that she was very talented. But the more he was around her, the more guilt he'd felt. He had wanted to confess.

All Shep could think about when he'd seen the transcript of the letter was the sound of footfalls Charlie had heard on the stairs that night. Had it been Greg and if so, what was he planning to do when he got to Charlie's room and found her there?

He'd come into the house, he'd started up those stairs… Had he planned to kill Charlie? Had he been worried that Charlie knew about him and Lindy? Had he worried that she might have seen what he'd done? Had he been worried right up until his death that Charlie knew the truth?

Kat had called one night after hearing the news about Lindy's killer having been found. Shep was still in Bozeman with Charlie so she'd put the call on speaker so he could hear.

"The man was twenty-four," Kat had said. "What had Lindy been thinking? What had *he* been thinking? I told Matt I didn't want children. I told him I would be a horrible mother. I thought when I had Cara that I would get another chance and do it right this time. We all deserve second chances, right?"

Charlie'd had no answers for her. Neither had Shep. "What will you do now?" Charlie had asked.

"My husband wants me to come back home with Cara, but I don't know. Cara wants to be there for her sister's trial. I don't think it's a good idea. Lacey's been writing her."

"You know Cara's the one who defaced the doll," Charlie had said.

Kat had been so quiet, they'd both thought maybe she'd hung up. "I think I'll take Cara to Europe. It will be good for us both. The farther away the better, don't you think? At least until the trial is over. Charlie? I'm so sorry."

Neither of them had known what else to say. Two months later, Charlie had seen the obituaries in the *Bozeman Daily Chronicle*. Kathryn Ramsey and her daughter Cara had died in a suspicious house fire in Spain. They had only been renting the house for a few days. Arson was suspected. The fire was under investigation.

Charlie had called him to tell him about the fire. "You don't think Kat would purposely start the fire, do you?" she'd asked.

"Because she feared that Cara might be like Lacey?" He hadn't wanted to believe that. "It could have been Cara and she accidentally got caught in it. Didn't Kat say that Cara and Lacey were writing to each other? Lacey must have some strong resentments toward her mother and maybe even her little sister."

Shep hadn't wanted to think about it. Kat and Cara were gone and Lacey would never see the outside of a prison cell. That part of Charlie's life was behind her, behind both of them.

Now, as Shep admired his amazing bride, he couldn't believe that fate had given them a second chance for happiness. Charlie was the most beautiful thing he'd ever laid eyes on. She'd wanted a wedding in sunshine and she'd gotten it. The day was crystal clear, Montana's big sky a deep blue over their heads.

"Do you take this woman to be your bride?" Judge WT Landusky asked in his gravelly voice. The judge had agreed to marry them, coming all the way from New Mexico in his and Meg's classic VW van, which was now parked at the edge of a meadow. The two of them had looked like old hippies when they arrived, but the judge had changed into a suit and tie for the ceremony.

"Well?" Landusky snapped.

"I do take this woman to be my bride," Shep said around the lump in his throat.

The judge smiled and looked over at Charlie. "And do you take this man to be your—"

"Yes!"

Landusky shook his head and muttered. "You haven't changed a bit, young lady. All right then," he said, raising his voice so those gathered could hear. "Then with the authority vested in me, I now pronounce you husband and wife. Son, you can kiss your bride!"

And Shep did. A cheer rose from the meadow, sending birds flying into the summer air. Shep took a mental snapshot as the kiss ended and he looked into Charlie's eyes. He never wanted to forget this moment. "Hello, Mrs. Shepherd."

CHARLIE GRINNED AT him, tears in her eyes as he took her hand and they turned toward the small crowd gathered.

The rest of the day was a blur of hugs and good wishes. The judge and Meg left after the reception in a nearby bar. They'd been traveling around the country in an old VW van the judge had apparently bought Meg for her birthday.

Charlie loved how happy they were. The judge swore that Meg had taken years off his life. They were headed for the West Coast, to watch some rock band they wanted to see before the members were too old to take the stage.

Shep's friends and her own had attended their wedding. Tara brought her husband and kids, including Charlie's namesake. Amanda was there with Royce. She'd wanted to be Charlie's matron of honor, but Tara had already gotten the honor. Amanda had inherited Greg's money and his company. She and Royce were running it. Tara had quit and gotten another job.

It was good to see everyone. Charlie was amazed how many of her friends had driven all the way to Stevensville for the wedding. People often forgot just how large Montana was until they tried to drive across it.

As the reception died down, Shep pulled her aside. "You ready for the honeymoon?"

She grinned at him. "You're not going to tell me anything, are you?"

"Nope. It's a surprise." He patted the breast pocket of his Western suit jacket where he'd put the tickets. He had the rest of the summer off from teaching and Charlie didn't start her new job until September 1.

"How long is this honeymoon going to be?"

"For the rest of our lives," Shep said as he pulled her into his arms and kissed her. "Buckle up."

* * * * *